THE
FORBIDDEN
PLACE

THE
FORBIDDEN PLACE

SUSANNE JANSSON

Translated By Rachel Willson-Broyles

GRAND CENTRAL
PUBLISHING

NEW YORK   BOSTON

Copyright © 2017 by Susanne Jansson
Translation copyright © 2018 by Rachel Willson-Broyles

Cover design by Elizabeth Connor
Photo of bog © Trevor Payne / Arcangel
Photo of stain © Kathy Collins / Getty Images
Cover copyright © 2018 by Hachette Book Group, Inc.

Grand Central Publishing
Hachette Book Group
1290 Avenue of the Americas, New York, NY 10104
grandcentralpublishing.com
twitter.com/grandcentralpub

Originally published in 2017 as *Offermossen*, in Swedish, by Wahlström & Widstrand
First U.S. Edition: September 2018

Grand Central Publishing is a division of Hachette Book Group, Inc. The Grand Central Publishing name and logo is a trademark of Hachette Book Group, Inc.

The publisher is not responsible for websites (or their content) that are not owned by the publisher.

The Hachette Speakers Bureau provides a wide range of authors for speaking events. To find out more, go to www.hachettespeakersbureau.com or call (866) 376-6591.

The quotes on p. vii are from *Att umgås med spöken* (*Walking with Ghosts*) by Göran Dahlberg, Ruin, 2014, and *djupa kärlek ingen* (*deep love no one*) by Ann Jäderlund, Albert Bonniers Förlag, 2016.

The quote on p. 88 is from *Wilful Disregard* by Lena Andersson.

The quote on p. 89 is from *Som en gång varit äng* by Ann Jäderlund, Albert Bonniers Förlag, 1988.

The quotes on p. 132 are from *Ways of Seeing* by John Berger, Penguin Modern Classics, 2008.

The quote on p. 223 is from *On Photography* by Susan Sontag, Farrar, Straus and Giroux, 1977.

Library of Congress Cataloging-in-Publication Data

Names: Jansson, Susanne author. | Willson-Broyles, Rachel translator.
Title: The forbidden place / Susanne Jansson ; translated By Rachel Willson-Broyles.
Other titles: Offermossen.
Description: First U.S. edition. | New York : Grand Central Publishing, 2018.
Identifiers: LCCN 2018003369| ISBN 9781538713051 (hardcover) | ISBN 9781538713013 (audio download) | ISBN 9781538713037 (ebook)
Subjects: LCSH: Women scientists—Fiction. | Murder—Investigation—Fiction. | GSAFD: Suspense fiction
Classification: LCC PT9877.2.A67 O4413 2018 | DDC 839.73/8—dc23
LC record available at https://lccn.loc.gov/2018003369

ISBN: 978-1-5387-1305-1 (hardcover), 978-1-5387-1303-7 (ebook)

Printed in the United States of America

LSC-C

10 9 8 7 6 5 4 3 2 1

To Alma and Edvard

It's said that every living person is carrying around ten dead souls. The weight gets on your nerves.

—From *Att umgås med spöken* (*Walking with Ghosts*) by Göran Dahlberg

What doesn't exist
Creeps in everywhere
And takes up space

—From *djupa kärlek ingen* (*deep love no one*) by Ann Jäderlund

It would be wrong to say that no one saw or heard any-thing. There were, naturally, many witnesses as the shots echoed out that night, and as a figure suddenly fled from the house and into the waiting car.

Perhaps the witnesses went on their way afterward, or maybe they also watched what happened when the police arrived and the bodies were carried out. But they didn't speak. They darted around in the bushes, rested in the trees, or soared over the ground. They were one with nature, often unseen by people. Perhaps all of them were animals—large or small, quick or slow, sharp-eyed or half-blind.

In any case, the true story of what really happened in that house soon scattered and disappeared.

Just as so many things so often do.

PROLOGUE

As evening approached, the wind started to pick up. It blew lightly across the treetops at first, but then it began to gust harder and harder until it was tearing at everything it could reach. Darkness would fall in just over half an hour.

In the car park outside the manor house, Johannes climbed off his bicycle and leaned it against a lamppost. He pulled a band around his dark hair and fastened it in a knot at the nape of his neck. This weather was truly awful. Not the sort of weather any normal person would go for a run in.

Fine then, he wasn't normal.

As he locked up his bike, he cast a glance over at Nathalie's cottage. The light of the kerosene lamp flickered in one of the windows, and he could see her moving around inside. Shadows danced across the walls, slow and evasive.

Like her.

She had slept over a few nights before. But when he woke up in the morning, she was gone. The bed was empty.

Sure, she'd said she had to get up early the next day, but that didn't stop him from feeling disappointed. They'd had a nice evening—and then she just left without a word, or even a note.

It could probably be chalked up to the usual reason: *fear of intimacy*, he thought as he stretched; she suddenly felt vulnerable and so she retreated. A plausible explanation if you wanted to play psychologist.

The rain was coming down harder now, and the urge to ditch his run was getting stronger. He wasn't dressed properly, he knew, but then again he hardly ever was. He'd never been the type to pay attention to weather reports—at most he would glance out the window—which was probably because his mother was the exact opposite. A different article of clothing for each degree on the thermometer; a special outfit for every occasion. His entire childhood had been full of fiddling and adjusting and changing clothes to make sure not a single drop of rain or chilly gust of wind could penetrate any of the layers.

Now, as an adult, he sometimes felt exhilarated if he accidentally got wet or cold.

He started running toward the path and took a right, away from Nathalie's cottage. The forest was on one side; the other side gave way to a peat bog, a view he had become quite attached to: that wide-open desolation; that squat, gray vegetation; it looked even more uncompromising and remarkable as the rain fell and the wind picked up.

He remembered the sight of the white frost on the peat

moss out there in the wintertime. There had been something unearthly about it, so fragile and seductive; he had never seen anything like it.

At one point a large moose showed up out of nowhere, swaying its way over the frozen pools, which rang out, crashing and tinkling like sorrowful chimes. Today the monotonous pounding of his own steps sounded like heavy blows, as if he were hammering his way forward, persistently, mechanically.

After the first section, the winding path turned into a long straight as it headed toward the old peat quarry. He could still glimpse the road here and there as it ran parallel, and soon he could see the car park for the bog. It was empty. He seldom saw anyone out here, but on this particular evening, with the rain whipping at his face, it felt extra deserted.

Here and there, narrow wooden walkways led into the bog. For a moment he thought about cutting across and taking a shorter route, but the boards looked slippery. It seemed too risky. You'd only have to lose your balance, and—

"Ouch!"

He had stepped awkwardly on a rock, even though he'd gone running here so many times that he knew every last root, every single rise like the back of his hand. The pain vibrated through his leg, then suddenly retreated in a flash, only to return in full force a minute later.

Damn it!

He hopped on one leg and tried to find something to steady himself against, but at last he collapsed on the path.

It really hurt. The wind and the rain tore and whipped at his clothes as he tried to stand, but he couldn't put any weight on his foot at all.

He waited a little longer to see if the pain would subside. Meanwhile, he cursed himself for leaving his phone at home. How would he manage to get back to the manor house on one leg?

There was plenty of brush along the path, and it occurred to him that he might be able to break off some of the sturdier branches and improvise a pair of crutches. It seemed like a good idea, but after a while he had to give up—the branches he found weren't strong enough.

Once he had made it some distance down the path by alternately hopping and dragging himself along, he looked out over the bog. That was when it struck him. It had stopped raining—and the wind had died down too, for that matter. It was perfectly still.

How strange.

The moon sailed out from behind the clouds in the dark sky. It illuminated tendrils of fog as they slowly swept across the damp ground.

He thought he heard a noise. Was it the wind? Or an animal? It almost sounded like a wail. Like faint cries.

Then he saw a glow coming down the path.

A flashlight. Someone was coming!

"Hello!" he called.

No response.

"I need help," he went on. "I hurt myself…"

The glow came closer. And closer. At last it blinded him and he had to shield his eyes with his hand.

"Hello?"

Then the flashlight pointed in a different direction and his vision cleared.

He had time to think, *What is happening?*

Then everything went black.

ONE

Three weeks earlier

*K*nock, knock, knock.

Nathalie woke up with a start. She pressed her fingers to her temples to make the knocking in her head go away.

Knock, knock, knock.

Knock, knock, knock.

A glance at her alarm clock told her that there were two hours left before it was time to get up. Pretty much the same as usual, in other words. No point in trying to go back to sleep.

There never was any point.

She sat up on the edge of the bed and wondered instead whether there was anything she had left to do. No. The apartment was clean and most of her belongings had been stored away. The suitcases that weren't already in the car were packed and in the hallway. Everything was ready.

She showered and ate breakfast standing up, trying to leave as few traces behind as possible. She wrote a note for the people who would be staying in the apartment while she was gone and placed it on the kitchen table.

I left a few things in the fridge; maybe you can use
them. The account number for the rent is in an email I sent
yesterday.
    Hope you enjoy your stay.

                       Best,
                       Nathalie

The street outside was empty and quiet, typical for a Sunday. She placed the last of her luggage in the trunk, got behind the wheel, and drove off.

She headed north out of Gothenburg on the E45 highway before the city could wake up. It felt like she was sneaking away after a one-night stand.

She stopped at a service station after a little while to get gas, buy a cup of coffee and pick up a few things to help her get through the first couple of days. Then she pressed on. And soon the landscape changed. Darkening, deepening.

Just imagine—it only took a few hours to travel so many years back in time. To this land of lakes and forest. To the place where she actually belonged.

She had always felt like a stranger in the big city by the sea. The rollicking, volatile, unreliable sea. She had never fitted in among the people who were always out sailing, who liked bare rock cliffs and the horizon, who worshipped the sun and wanted the weather to be as persistently warm as possible. It was as if they expected the same from her, some inner kind of get-up-and-go she'd never had access to but had, to some extent, learned to fake.

Each summer when she set her feet to the warm granite of Bohuslän and waded into the water for a swim, it felt like the sea wanted to spit her right back out again, out of sheer reflex. As if it knew she didn't belong to its natural domain.

A September rain had started to fall against the windscreen. Hesitant, quiet. As though autumn were tiptoeing in, as though it didn't want to disturb or upset.

Come, she thought. *Just come.*

Just fall.

We'll do it together.

She passed the Åmål exits and turned off at Fengerskog. She felt a wave of unreality wash over her, as sudden as it was overwhelming, and she asked herself what she was about to do. What she was about to set in motion. At the same time, she realized she was almost there, and that it was way too late to turn back.

She slowed down by the art school and the old factory; she knew that nowadays it was a space for studios, galleries and workshops. At the crossroads, where once there had been only a small grocer's, there were now also a bakery and a café, and she could see young people with canvas totes drinking their morning lattes or tea out of tall glasses. Then the buildings gave way to forest; after a while, the road turned into a birch-lined avenue that led up to the manor house.

A couple of cars were parked in the gravel drive. She stepped out, leaving her luggage in the car, and crossed the gravel to the front entrance.

It was a stately building with four towers, a white plaster façade, a tin roof the green shade of linden blossoms, and large windows looking out on its surroundings. It had been built on a small rise, as manor houses often were. Frequently they also look out over a beautiful landscape—a pretty lake or rolling hills.

This manor house was different. It gazed out over modest, quiet scenery. A vast landscape of fading colors, squatty pines and sinking ground. It was a landscape the sun seemed not to reach, a landscape that never dried out. The ground was always weeping, always wallowing.

And now she had returned of her own accord.

"Are you the one who's renting the little cottage?"

The woman, who introduced herself as Agneta, was the manager of the manor. She wore a kaftan-like beige dress with wide bands of embroidered edging, which made her imposing body look like a pillar. Her dark blonde hair was cut to hang straight down over her shoulders, with a blunt fringe at the front.

"Yes, that's right."

Her husband was right behind her, a head shorter and dressed in a dark suit, his eyes nervously sweeping the room.

Gustav, Nathalie thought. *Like a bodyguard. They're just as I remember them.*

"Then I'd like to welcome you to Mossmarken and Quagmire Manor. I hope you're aware that the building you're renting is a simple cottage. It is mostly used during the summer months."

"Yes, I'm sure it won't be a problem. It does have heat, doesn't it?"

"Two fireplaces and a gas fridge. But that's all. You can fetch water from the cellar here, and you can charge phones and computers and such in our office. There's a shower and toilet in the hall upstairs. And of course there's an outhouse behind the cottage too. What else..." she said, apparently thinking it over. "Oh right, the bike. There's an old bike you can borrow if you want to. Where are you from, by the way?"

"I live in Gothenburg."

She noticed the old portraits on the wall of the foyer—elegant ladies in voluminous dresses and proud gentlemen in military get-ups. She had been captivated by them as a child, and by one of the paintings in particular: the one of Sofia Hansdotter, wife of a landowner who lived at the manor in the late nineteenth century. She remembered Sofia's pea-green dress and melancholy gaze.

It was said that she had lost seven of her eight children. That she had been crazy. That she had smothered the children in secret and then begged her husband to let her bury them in the bog near the manor. Because she wanted to keep them close, she said. Her husband had complied to avoid causing even more damage to her broken heart. Until one day, when the eighth child had just been born, in a moment of sudden clarity, he realized how all the children had died and decided to take the newborn from its mother. It was said that Sofia then walked down to the place where she had buried her children, stepped right out into the mire, and vanished. No one had done anything to save her.

The eighth child grew up to be a strong, healthy man who later took over the manor. He was the great-grandfather of the current owner, Gustav.

"Gustav and I have run this place as a guest house for over thirty-five years; before that it was kept by his parents," Agneta went on, with a presence that suggested that this wasn't the first time she'd told the story of the manor. "The estate has been in Gustav's family since the 1600s. You can see all the old ancestors on the paintings around us." She made a sweeping gesture with her hand.

At that instant, a woman came down the stairs.

"Here comes our cook, Jelena, who makes the best smoked whitefish this side of Lake Vänern—if you'd like to eat up here some time."

Jelena was pale and thin, as far from the clichéd image of the plump matron as a person could get.

"And here we have Alex, our caretaker," Agneta said as a

tall, muscular man came through the door. "You can give him a shout if anything needs fixing."

Alex stopped, his eyes fixed somewhere up by the chandeliers, and gave a curt nod. Then he kept walking, heading for the back rooms.

"Gustav and I are available on weekdays from nine to four, in case you have any questions. Most of the time we're in the office in the next room along, unless we're up a ladder painting a barn door or fixing a broken tractor or the like. The rest of the time, you're likely to find us in the east wing, which is where we have our home. It's fine to contact us outside office hours as well." She paused, then went on. "That should be about it. This is what we call the off season; there's not much going on just now. Are you here for any particular reason, if I may ask?"

"Yes...I'm working on a doctoral dissertation. It's about how the greenhouse effect influences the process of decomposition in wetlands. I'm a biologist."

"I see." Agneta smiled, motioning toward the window. "You came here because of the bog. Interesting."

"Yes, I was planning to do a few last field experiments..."

"It is quite unique, this bog," Agneta continued. "They say it was once a so-called sacrificial bog."

"Right."

"Maybe you've heard of those? Apparently, back in the Iron Age, various offerings to the gods were buried here. Even people, actually. We have brochures about it in the office. Around the new millennium one of those bodies was found here, from 300 B.C. It's at the Karlstad Museum now..."

Nathalie nodded. "Yes, I think I did hear about that."

"The Lingonberry Girl," Agneta said.

"Okay," said Nathalie.

"Yes, that's what she's called, the girl they found...but speaking of the bog, I hope you'll be careful when you go out there. It's very marshy in some spots and the boardwalks are slippery this time of year. But I suppose you're used to it."

~

The cabin was below the manor house and had one room plus a kitchen. The kitchen consisted of a counter and washbasin with no tap, a large wood-burning stove, and a dining nook with a traditional kitchen sofa and two chairs. The room was furnished with a bedframe on legs, a wardrobe, a simple desk, and, in front of the tile stove, two old easy chairs and a tiny table.

The autumn chill had forced its way through the thick timber walls. It felt raw inside, but it smelled fresh and clean.

A large mirror was leaning against the wall in one corner. Nathalie sank to the floor, sitting cross-legged, and observed her face. She never ceased to be surprised that she always looked so much more energetic than she felt. Her sand-colored hair, which she trimmed once a year, was still cut the same way a star stylist had suggested eleven years earlier as Nathalie was preparing for a modeling session. Simple, medium-length, a soft bob—easy to maintain.

When she was eighteen she had been "discovered" outside a cinema and offered a modeling contract, even though she was really too short—apparently she was expected to be immensely grateful that they were willing to overlook this fault.

She had just finished secondary school and was hoping to earn a bit of easy cash, but she couldn't handle all the hustle and bustle. She couldn't tolerate the hairspray that stung her nose or the powder brushes moving over her face or the commands in front of the camera: rather brusque orders that were supposed to make her radiate something *exceptional*—she never understood what. After two weeks she'd had enough.

The hairstyle was her only significant legacy from that parenthetical aside in her life. It took very little effort but helped her keep up her advantageous appearance, which she chose to maintain for purely practical reasons: it kept those around her satisfied and preoccupied by what was happening on the surface.

There were two jugs of water and a large basket of wood in the entrance. She began by lighting both the kitchen stove and the tile stove, and then she unpacked her groceries and placed her clothing in the wardrobe. Last of all she unrolled a large map of the area, tacked it on to the wall next to the desk, and pulled on her slippers and a heavy sweater.

She walked around for a moment, looking at the room. The fire crackled and popped, and so much smoke leaked from the stove that she had to open a window.

After a while, everything seemed to be working. She warmed up a can of tortellini from the service station and ate a piece of bread with cheese spread from a tube.

Behind the house was a small garden, hemmed in by overgrown dog-rose bushes, and in front there were two wooden lawn chairs. A few meters past them was the path that wound its way around the bog.

She put on her jacket, cautiously sat down on one of the chairs, and gazed out at the scenery. It felt like nothing had changed, as if everything had remained as it always had been—and not just for the past fourteen years but for centuries, since time immemorial. The knotty, gray pines. The pools of water, like blinking eyes, between damp green tussocks. A homey sort of desolation in a muted palette; the shimmering heads of cotton grass on their slender, rust-colored autumn stalks.

The flute-like song of the curlew: she could hear it echo beneath the skies although the bird had long since migrated away for the winter. She could hear it even though she hadn't listened to its bubbling, cheerful song for so long; that aerial display and call—she had truly loved it before everything changed, before it transformed into scornful, mocking laughter in her memory, a threatening warning trill about what was to come.

When she considered what she was about to subject herself to, she felt bold, bordering on reckless. It was as though she had crossed a line out of some compulsion, even though she wasn't properly prepared.

If she gazed westward she could see the electrical poles rising above the foliage. Those were the same poles that had been outside her old bedroom window, the ones that had served as her landmark and salvation each time she got half lost out there. The thought was almost incomprehensible: if she just followed those poles, she would eventually arrive at the place where everything began and ended.

It was still dark out when she woke on her first morning in the cottage. The darkness was one of the few signs of autumn she didn't appreciate. The dark mornings, the dark evenings; more light lost with each passing day. Summer was preferable in that respect: at four in the morning, the usual time she was awakened by the knocking in her head, the day had already begun. The light made it easy to shake off the weight of surging into consciousness, that wordless feeling that something was wrong even as her brain was fumbling for an explanation. The autumn darkness, though, had the opposite effect. It seemed to want to brood on those difficult feelings.

She lit the kerosene lamp next to the bed and walked over to the tile stove. It was still warm. She hugged it gingerly like a large, long-lost friend, moving close to it with her eyes closed, letting her palms, thighs and one cheek rest against its warmth. The word *prayer* flitted through her mind. *Was this what it felt like?*

Then something scraped against the window, a sharp sound.

What was that?

She slowly walked over and tried to peer out.

Magpies?

She couldn't see anything. Nothing but the outdoor lights up at the manor house, a hundred meters away, two little blobs floating in the darkness.

When it was this dark out, the light of the kerosene lamp made her vulnerable. There were no curtains to draw. But there were nails at the upper corners of each window. She stood on a chair, tied two knitted sweaters together, and tried to hang them so that they would cover the window closest to the bed. It was clumsy work. She would have to remember to find a blanket. Or a sheet. For the other windows, too.

She took yesterday's paper from her suitcase and crawled back under the duvet. She tried to read an opinion piece about energy policy, but she couldn't concentrate. The windows were glaring at her. The darkness was staring in.

Shit. How was this going to work?

She hadn't counted on feeling so exposed. That wasn't part of the plan. No, forget all that. Now it was time to focus on two things: work and that vague, underlying task, the one she suspected had something to do with her personally. Something had pulled her in this direction, maybe for years. Something that she hadn't listened to on a conscious level, but still somehow had followed. Like a yearning from the underground. A call from within.

No one knew she was here at Quagmire. No one but her adviser, who was off traveling as well.

Nathalie liked the thought of just going away somewhere. Because there was something cleansing about vanishing from your usual surroundings, a kind of ultimate freedom.

Fourteen years ago, she had left this region without a word. Now that she had returned, it was like mirroring herself, plying the thread all the way back to work out the knots and start again.

Most of her friends would hardly notice she wasn't in Gothenburg; they were researchers just like she was, spread out all over the globe.

The only people who might start to wonder were her foster parents.

In the past few years, Nathalie hadn't had the energy for the effort it took to keep up her relationship with them, and as their contact grew more infrequent their reproach grew stronger, especially from her foster mother Harriet.

"Is this the thanks we get, after all we've done for you?" Harriet had said the last time they'd had something that could be likened to a conversation. They had dropped by with flowers for her birthday, and Harriet had been unable to hide her feelings. Her round face turned bright red and she had to fight to prevent herself from crying.

Nathalie's foster father Lars had sat there with his coat on for the entire visit. He had kept tugging at his mustache and staring at the floor.

"Let's leave now," he said at last. "It's time to give up on all this. She doesn't want it."

His cynical attitude made Nathalie feel a certain amount of affinity with him, but beyond that she hadn't felt a thing. Nothing. And that was what Harriet had realized.

Before she left, Harriet studied her, her eyes narrow, her sympathy gone, and said in a broken voice, "You are horrible, do you know that? I've always thought you act the way you do because of what happened to you, but now I don't know any more. Maybe you're just *like* that: superficial, cold and ungrateful."

With her dressing gown tied firmly around her waist, Nathalie sat down in the center of the room to take control of and defy the feeling of vulnerability. She spread a stack of documents out in front of her: the results of the measurements and experiments she had performed so far in Germany, Holland, Poland and Denmark.

The silence, she thought, looking around. It was so quiet in the cottage. So demanding. Maybe she just needed to get used to it.

She tried listening to all the sounds that surrounded her in spite of it: a lazy fly buzzing its last verse in the kitchen window, the crackle and draft from the stove, the muffled cawing of a raven close by. She switched to focusing on smells. That was more difficult: burning wood, soap, soot.

She spread out her diagram of nitrogen fractions and thought about the deviations. Why, for example, had there been higher amounts in Germany than in Poland? Did it have to do with the time of year, was it because of the nature of the surroundings, or was it linked to global climate change?

Those of her international colleagues who worked on similar questions had mostly conducted studies in the polar regions, enormous areas that were always frozen. Now that global warming was causing these areas to thaw, processes were beginning in the ground that released even more greenhouse gasses into the atmosphere. The question was how much was added and how it affected warming on the whole.

Nathalie had previously been part of a Nordic research team who studied the same phenomenon in the mountainous regions of Sweden. When an opportunity popped up with the chance to focus more specifically on Nordic and central European wetlands, she jumped at it right away—and got the job.

Her research would surely turn into a meaningful addition to the climate research that was so important when it was time for politicians to make decisions. But only once her visit to Mossmarken was booked and almost totally planned was she struck by the realization that it was more than just work-related interests that had brought her here. That there were personal motives, that her choices and decisions were grounded in something entirely different than she'd first thought.

However obvious it might seem in retrospect, those thoughts had overwhelmed her. They had shoved her up against the wall and made certain that she would listen this time, before they let go. And although she still hadn't dared to dig very deeply in her own mind, at least she hadn't backed away.

She had made her way here, to this desolate place in the wetlands between Dalsland and Värmland.

And maybe that was the most important thing.

~

She left the cottage only when she needed to shower, fetch water or charge her computer and mobile phone. She needed to anchor herself in the house, to find a stable starting position before she began to head out into the bog for real.

She drew preliminary sampling sites on her map. She would take samples in a total of twelve different parts of the bog, spread over two days, so as to make sure her test results were significant. Then she would do it all over again in November, once the ground was colder.

During the first few days, she didn't speak to a single person. But every afternoon, at approximately the same time, she noticed a man about her own age jogging by on the path outside. Each time, he glanced curiously up at the cottage.

One day as he approached, she was on her way back from

the outhouse. He stopped, resting his hands against his thighs to catch his breath. At first they pretended not to notice each other, but then he nodded at her in a quiet greeting.

"Hi," he said, still breathing hard. "Do you live here?"

She found herself feeling trapped. She hadn't expected to run into anyone out here; she had been looking forward to avoiding involuntary contact with the outside world.

"Yes, I guess so," she said. "Temporarily. I'm just renting."

She turned around to go inside.

"Nice place. My name's Johannes," the man said, raising his hand to say hello. "Could I...possibly trouble you for some water? I forgot to bring my bottle. I'm awfully thirsty."

"Of course." She went inside to fill a glass, then handed it to him.

"Thanks," he said, then drained it all at once and handed the glass back. He wiped the sweat from his face with the bottom of his shirt, then stretched his back and ran his hand over his shiny hair.

Raven hair. The words flew through her mind. *Handsome.*

"Is this a nice place to run?" she asked, mostly just to have something to say.

"It's fantastic. This place, I mean..." He shook his head as if he couldn't quite find the right words. "I'm a student at the art school over in Fengerskog, and no one else I've talked to seems to have been here. Which is ridiculous. It's so pretty here. But that's fine with me," he said with a smile. "It's nice to be alone out here."

He nodded at her.

"What about you? What are you doing here?"

She hesitated. The words inside her felt stubborn; they didn't want to come out; they wanted to hide, or just rest. They were tired of being dutiful, keeping up the eternal game. At the same time, there was something about him she found intriguing.

What's more, she couldn't deny that at close quarters he turned out to have rather hypnotically smooth skin, *olive*, as that shade would be called. She would have nothing against getting an opportunity to observe it in secret for a while, pondering what types of genes and fatty acids could lend such advantages to skin cells.

"I'm measuring the greenhouse gasses out in the bog," she said, pushing a lock of hair behind her ear. "Among other things. Or, I'm going to. I haven't actually started just yet."

"Greenhouse gasses?" he asked. "Is that for a company?"

"No . . . I'm working on my dissertation. In biology."

"Oh, that's interesting." His gaze seemed to sharpen somehow. "I would love to hear more," he said, pausing as if to feel out the situation before he went on. "But I don't want to bother you. I'm sure we'll see each other again; I run here almost every day."

He raised his hand once again, then went on his way, up toward the car park.

Nathalie observed the muscles in his thighs and calves as he went. *Long and supple*, she thought. *Full of stamina.*

During the next few days she stayed inside around the time of Johannes's runs. She kept away from the windows, yet was still close enough to sneak a peek without him noticing.

One afternoon, she acted on impulse and made a whole pot of tea. She was sitting in one of the chairs outside the cottage with a cup when he passed by.

"May I offer you some tea?" she called.

He stopped, ran one hand across his cheek, and raised his eyebrows in surprise. At first she couldn't tell if he was surprised or just thought it was a strange invitation, and she immediately regretted asking.

But then he said, "I'd love that," and approached her.

She felt both excited and a little nervous as she gathered milk, sugar and another cup and placed it all on the little table between the chairs.

He took a seat. His movements were slow, gentle; he didn't take up more space than he needed, but he didn't take less either. *An openness toward everything, nothing to hide* ran through her, and, at the same time, she felt a chill gust through her chest: *Like me, but the other way around.*

He put several scoops of sugar into his cup. When he noticed her skeptical smile, he laughed.

"I know. My dad was from Morocco, so the sugar craving is in my blood."

The afternoon sun sank quickly as they leaned back.

"So, what's it like to be a student here?" she asked.

"It's just fine. Good teachers. Nice classmates. There's lots of peace and quiet, so it's easy to get work done."

"But doesn't it get a bit lonely? If you get sick of just studying?"

"Maybe, a little. But it's not hard to find stuff to do if you feel like getting out. There are concerts and parties and things." He turned to her as if to shift the focus away from himself. "But tell me. How are you planning to go about your work? Measuring greenhouse gasses—how do you do that?"

She told him about the samples she would be collecting over the weekend. He listened with interest.

"I don't suppose you'd like company?" he said afterward. "It sounds exciting. I'd really like to see how it all happens. I could help you, and . . . carry stuff. Or something."

Silence.

Something twisted inside her; that sinuous desire entwined with a blunt, harsh sense of danger. And, on top of that, the thought of the advantages it would bring to have two more hands.

"You want to?" She looked straight ahead. "Sure, why not. It would definitely make things easier."

~

She would have to go out in the bog on her own first, she thought, without Johannes. She needed to subject herself to the bog all by herself, with no one else around. She also needed to prepare the sampling stations. She would insert sawn-off sections of drainpipe into the ground at twelve different locations. Next time she would attach lids with small rubber corks into which you could insert a syringe and withdraw gasses.

She had woken up unusually late this morning. The knocking in her head seemed milder than before. But the worry was pounding; it seemed to wander around her body, from her chest to her head and then down into her stomach. Now it was occupying her whole body. She felt like an abstinent junkie, but her drug of choice was repression and denial. *What good will this do?* asked the devil on her right shoulder. *What is there for you here? Go back home.* There was no angel on her left shoulder, only emptiness. A spot that had been erased. Her eyes burned behind their lids as she heard herself think: *Me.*

She lingered over breakfast, propping the door open to feel the lovely autumn weather, walking back and forth between the rooms, writing a list of things she must not forget once it was time to head out to take measurements.

*   *   *

Below her was the path that led into the bog. All she had to do was follow it, place one foot in front of the other. It was no more difficult than that. Shouldn't be.

And at last she did it, without thinking, like when you go for a swim even though the water is cold because somehow it's the right thing to do, and because it almost always feels good afterward.

Her feet on the path. Her flesh on this earth, again. The time between now and then, compressed into the fragile wing of a butterfly, obliterated in a few fleeting wing-beats.

She followed the path for a bit. Then she turned to head into the bog at the point where five well-worn boards, side by side, cut through the landscape in a long and angular line. They didn't seem to have done much to the walkways since she'd seen them last, but she assumed repairs of some sort must have taken place.

After all, it had been fourteen years.

The light was dim and the air chilly. The terrain was vast and yellowing, graying. The trees, which she had always thought to be hunched, squatting—now she felt as if they were bowing down in reverence. Curtsying and nodding. As if they were saying hello.

She greeted them in return, cautiously opening herself up, relaxing. Letting herself be carried forward. Time came loose from its framework and collapsed, bit by bit, until she felt like a part of everything around her. It was like she was moving within a mosaic and the pieces that made up her body were melting into the pieces that were the surroundings.

She walked slowly and for a long time before she gingerly stepped out onto a few sturdy tussocks and sat down to lean her back against a small pine.

Then she just sat there, enveloped in the rhythm of her own breathing. A light rain began to fall. The drops ticked as they landed on her raincoat, like drizzle against a canvas tent in the morning. It smelled like an evergreen forest. Her wet boots were full of half-yellowed bog-myrtle leaves; they were beginning to drop from the stems by now. She took a few leaves in her hand and rubbed them gently between her fingers, inhaling the sharp, spicy scent and closing her eyes.

A few minutes passed. A quarter of an hour, maybe. Then the mist crept toward her like a curious animal with unclear intentions. It licked its way across the wet ground, reached her feet and swept around her.

As though it were saying: *You. It's you. It's been a long time.*

She didn't move; hardly breathed. She just sat perfectly still with her eyes half closed and waited for the moment to pass.

She didn't notice it, but words came whispering out of her mouth. *I know. It took some time. But now I'm here.*

When the clock struck nine on Saturday morning, she was waiting for Johannes outside the cottage, dressed in work trousers, a windbreaker and sturdy boots. Her backpack was full of coffee, lunch and equipment for taking measurements. Johannes leaned his bike against the cottage and walked toward her in his jeans and sneakers, with a hoodie under his denim jacket. He threw up his hands as she eyed his clothing.

"Isn't this okay?" He laughed. "Sure," he answered himself. "It'll be fine. Let's go."

"It's pretty wet out there," she protested.

"Then it will feel even nicer to come in and warm up afterward."

They each carried some of the equipment and took the same path she had walked the day before. She oriented herself with her GPS and soon they came to the first station where she had sunk a sawn-off drainpipe. She took six black plastic lids from her backpack, each two decimeters in diameter with a rubber cork in the center.

"Watch this," she said, pointing at the cork. "I'll insert a needle in here to extract the gasses that rise from the ground. Then I transfer the gas from the syringe to these bottles."

She opened a case of small sampling bottles in neat rows.

"At each station we'll take four measurements—after five, ten, fifteen and twenty minutes. Are you with me?"

"I'm with you."

"We're measuring the amounts of nitrogen, nitrous oxide and methane the bog gives off. Nitrous oxide and methane are actually more potent greenhouse gasses than carbon dioxide. They have a greater effect on the climate."

"Evil stuff, then?" he said.

"Not really. Without greenhouse gasses, we wouldn't be able to survive on earth. It would be too cold. The problem is, as the average temperature rises, the processes in the ground increase as well, which means that more greenhouse gasses are released than is necessary, which in turn makes the planet get even hotter... which causes even more gasses to be released. And so on. It becomes a self-intensifying cycle." She began to walk toward the sample site. "I'll show you the first time, and then you can try it."

Johannes nodded and smiled in amusement. "Okay! Got it."

She attached the first lid, hurried to the next, ran back and stuck the needle into the cork on the first lid, and then did the same on the other. Then she started her stopwatch.

"In five minutes it will be time for another measurement," she said, squeezing the contents of the syringes into the small bottles in the case. "Then you can take the sample from the one over there while I do this one."

"I feel nervous," Johannes said, his jaw tense.

"Understandable," she said. "You could screw up my whole study."

"Stop it."

"Just kidding. It's fine. It's super-simple; you can handle it, no problem."

She gave him a syringe. "You'll have to keep control of your fingers. Things get pretty bloody sometimes, especially if it's cold and you get stiff."

When five minutes had passed, they stood ready at their respective lids.

"Let's go," she said, sticking the needle into the cork as she glanced over at Johannes. He performed the entire task with a smile of concentration on his lips.

"Brilliant," she said when he was done. "You're a natural."

He clasped his hands together and raised them in the air in a triumphant gesture. "I knew it."

"Five minutes until the next one. Shall we have some coffee?" she said.

She poured the coffee into two mugs and watched him shyly as he drank. His shoes were already dark with moisture.

"What is the actual definition of a bog?" he asked, gazing out at the scenery.

"Well, first and foremost, a bog is a type of wetland," she said as she handed Johannes the folding chair she'd brought. She sat down on a sit pad. "A wetland is an area where water is present for most of the year, at or just above ground level. We usually say that half the vegetation has to be hydrophytic."

"Hydrophytic?" Johannes said with a laugh.

"Water-loving."

He raised his eyebrows. "I've learned a new word. Sounds a little...dirty."

"Right? And there are lots of types of wetlands—one type is a mire, which we can divide further into bogs and fens. A bog is completely dependent on precipitation because it is isolated from the groundwater. No running water passes through it, which means that only species that don't need much nourishment can live there, primarily various types of sphagnum."

She looked at him.

"I'm just rambling; I'm sure you're not really interested in this."

"No, I am."

She gave him a skeptical smile.

"I'm not being sarcastic," he told her. "Go on."

"Okay, sphagnum has" she said, picking some up, "sort of like tiny holes in its leaves where it stores water. This way it creates its own reservoir above the groundwater level. As it dies, it turns into peat, which piles up and slowly raises the bog up over its original level."

Johannes was listening with interest.

"In general, wetlands are sort of like nature's kidneys," she went on. "They filter out excess nutrients from the water that passes through them; they slow down the flow when, for example, the snow melts or there's heavy rain. That's why it's a pity that so many of them have disappeared."

"Why did they disappear?"

"Partly because the climate used to be more full of moisture, and partly because the industrialization of farming led to people draining and drying out large swaths of wetlands." She brought her coffee cup to her lips and looked at her watch. "Shit, it's time for the next measurement!"

He seemed to have an almost insatiable interest in everything she said. It was a little suspicious, she thought on Sunday as they repeated the procedure on the north side. She had never experienced this before, being asked so many questions by someone outside the university.

Over and over they lost track of time and had to jump up to collect the samples.

"Something I've always wondered about," Johannes said once she thought he'd asked every possible question about mires and wetlands. "The stuff we usually call bog moss, like you use to decorate Advent candleholders or the space between windowpanes, it doesn't look like this at all. Why is that?"

"Good question," she said. "The plant that's sold in stores as bog moss around Christmas-time is actually a lichen. Saying that lichens and peat moss are the same thing is like saying that wood anemones and elephants are the same thing."

Johannes laughed. "How do you mean?"

"A lichen is two organisms, algae and fungus, living in a symbiotic relationship. The algae provides energy in the form of carbohydrates by way of photosynthesis; the fungus contributes water and nutrient salts it takes from rocks and so forth. Peat moss, on the other hand, is a single organism from the start."

"I'll have to tell Mum when she gets out the Christmas decorations," Johannes said. "She's going to feel duped."

When their work was done on Sunday, they went back to the cottage. Nathalie made dinner. She had bought the ingredients for the meal she always made on special occasions, the only one she knew by heart—lamb stew with mustard, peppers and potatoes.

"I've never eaten lamb this way," Johannes said. "It's really good."

They'd opened a bottle of red wine, and they talked about how Nathalie came to be a biologist.

"Actually, it all started with bang gas," she said. She told him about a chemistry lesson in junior school when she poured a little hydrochloric acid and magnesium into a test tube and put a match near the opening. And poof! It had formed hydrogen gas.

"I think that was the first time I felt like school could be fun," she said.

Later, when it was time to choose a course of study for sec-ondary school, the obvious choice was the natural sciences. She liked working in the lab; she liked the white coats, the order and cleanliness, making sure that all the safety equip-ment was close at hand. She loved the weighing and measur-ing, counting molecules—how many moles of an element you needed, how many grams that equaled.

On the first day of spring that year, as everyone else turned their faces toward the sun and enjoyed their coffee, Nathalie was gazing down at her cup instead—not just to feel satisfied by the way the milk and coffee truly blended, or the way the cube of sugar dissolved and vanished, but because she once again recalled the quiet joy she had felt when she under-stood for the first time exactly why this was.

In time, her entire life became setting up experiments, delving further and further into processes and sequences, deeper and deeper into the research that had already been done. It didn't make her feel exhilarated or even excited; she just felt calm. And slowly but surely, in a way that was as inex-orable as it was unconscious, this scientific structure truly became her new home. A safety net woven of fundamental axioms and delightfully diverse complexity that captivated her after the incomprehensible things that had left their mark on her childhood and eventually brought it toppling down.

But she didn't tell Johannes about that.

*   *   *

He said that his father, who was no longer living, had collected butterflies and other insects. He'd had a whole room full of identification guides and Latin dictionaries, just like Nathalie. Johannes had loved to spend time in that room as a child.

"Maybe that's why I'm"—he gestured towards her—"drawn to you."

"Because I remind you of your dad?" she said carefully, with a skeptical smile.

"Because you make me feel at home."

She fended off his words by pretending not to notice their significance.

"What about you?" she asked. "What's your story? Why do you want to become an artist?"

"I'll tell you about that some other time. But it's getting late," he said, rising.

"I'll sleep on the kitchen sofa," she said. "You can take the bed."

"I'll bike home."

"I don't think that's such a great idea." She laughed.

"It's fine. Maybe I'll see you tomorrow."

And then he held her close for a moment, kissed her on the forehead, and left.

The next day, Nathalie got up early and cleaned frantically all morning. She swept, dusted, mopped and did laundry with the sense that she had to get something out of her body—a restlessness, an itch. Around lunchtime, her phone beeped.

> Want to do something today? You got lots done over the weekend, so maybe you can take some time off? Hugs ☺

Her brain hesitated, but her fingers flew over the keyboard.

> Sure, that'd be nice. But don't you have stuff you need to do?
> I can get out of it.
> OK. Any idea what?
> Yup. I'll be over in a bit. Tell you then.

She was sitting on the steps and eating when he came pedaling up on his bike. It was a lovely, clear September day, and the sight of his gangly figure and his dark hair fluttering in the sunshine made something inside her feel buoyant.

"Hi there." He stopped next to her and put down one foot. "This weather!"

"I know," she said. "Nice day for some time off. I don't exactly feel like staying inside and studying diagrams."

He laid his bike on the grass, bent forward, gave her a hug, and sat down next to her on the steps.

"What's your plan?" she asked.

"I heard there's a little lake in the woods," he said. "I thought we could bike there."

Bytjärn, she thought, naming the lake silently. She pictured the thick old forest, large boulders and dark water. A body of water you could never see the bottom of, something she'd always thought to be normal and natural until she got to the west coast and realized that was just about the worst thing imaginable to people who liked the sea.

"Have you eaten, by the way?" she asked. "There's some food left inside."

"Just ate. But thanks. What do you say? Doesn't it sound nice?"

"Definitely. Let's do it. Should we bring anything with us?"

"Screw it, let's just go." He threw up one hand. "Unless *you* want to bring something, of course."

"I'll grab a couple of things. Be right back."

She went in and packed a backpack with coffee, water, nuts and what was left of her lunch, just in case they were gone for a while. A roll of toilet paper, a sweater and extra socks. It might well be wet where they were going.

"There!" she said when she came back out. "Now I'm ready."

An instant later, she caught something out of the corner of her eye, something disappearing around the corner of the house. *What was that? Like a shadow passing by.* She followed it. Her eyes searched the garden and the hedge that surrounded it, but...nothing.

But I could have sworn...

"What is it?" Johannes said. "What are you doing?"

"Nothing. Come on, let's go."

Side by side they jolted along the gravel path on their bikes. The smallholdings they passed rose out of Nathalie's memory like forgotten islands: *that's where Julia and I spied on the angry farmer; that house used to be falling apart, and now it's a middle-class dream home with picture windows and a huge porch. Right there I saw a tiny cat with a huge rat in its mouth. I was in the backseat of the black Volvo, Dad was at the wheel with his cigarette halfway out the window. "Look, Natti, that's a fat one!"*

Natti. She hadn't thought of her old nickname for so long. Much less gone anywhere near her memories of her biological parents.

"Nighty nighty, Natti." The bedroom door closing. The knots and lines in the pine ceiling of her room; long, narrow pictures to fix her eyes on when she couldn't sleep; the winding shapes of

women, like The Scream *in wood-grain form. A whole heaven of gaping mouths and eyes.*

"We should really have mountain bikes here," Johannes said, looking at her tentatively. She gripped the handlebars harder, nodded and looked away.

They turned on to an even narrower road and continued slowly on their way.

"I think the path is coming up soon," Johannes said.

"It's over there," she said without thinking.

Johannes raised his eyebrows. "Have you been here before?"

"I just thought I saw a path over there."

They left their bikes at the side of the road and began to walk into the forest. The sun fell on the soft moss in glowing streaks; the ground was criss-crossed by trees in various stages of decay. Johannes stopped and looked around, and up, at the light filtering through the treetops.

"It's like stepping into Sagrada Família," he said. "Have you been there? In Barcelona."

"Only outside it," Nathalie said, her eyes cast downward at the teeming ground.

They walked along the half-overgrown path and finally reached the small lake, a clearing protected from the wind by tall green walls of forest. Nathalie sat down on a soft, moss-covered rock and Johannes lay beside her, propping himself up on his elbows.

"God, it's so pretty," he said, closing his eyes and sinking down on his back. After that they didn't speak for a long time. Nathalie felt a little confused by the silence at first, but she soon relaxed. She had sat there so many times. They had often come here to swim when they took off on their own, she and Julia, and probably other children from around here as well. She remembered how they would dive in and play for hours, how the water closed in around them, moving around their slender bodies in heavy, glossy swirls.

A bird of prey soared high above them on outstretched wings as Nathalie cautiously glanced down at Johannes. His deep, arched eyelids. His long, straight nose. His mouth at rest, an almost invisible twitch of his lip. Rough stubble, open skin, a landscape.

She glimpsed something at the edge of her field of vision and turned her head. And there it stood, just a few meters away from them, so matter-of-factly that she was hardly even startled. A roe deer. She hadn't heard it approach. It was very close, so close that she could see her own reflection in its big black eyes. They looked at each other for a long time, she and the deer, and something inside her transformed. A veil was drawn away. A perspective shifted, a change took place, and everything became so clear and simple.

Somehow it was as if what she had believed was reality opened up and she fell down into the space between, down into a timeless expanse without words, a place she had never

known before. As if a construct burst and split and she realized that she was in fact one with the present moment and
everything around her. That she *was* that moment.

An instant later, a thought shot through her, like a harsh
reflex: *What is happening, what am I experiencing?*

A cloud glided by, blocking out the light.

"*Capreolus capreolus*," she managed to say in a faint, sharp
voice. The silence was broken. The deer leaped and disappeared.

"Huh?" Johannes said, sitting up and gazing in surprise at
the white rump as it bounced off into the forest.

Nathalie blinked and swallowed.

"Roe deer," she said softly. "In Latin."

~

Johannes often looked in on her once he had finished his run.
They would sit in the kitchen and chat for a while, and then he
would go home. Their good-bye hugs grew longer and longer, but
she always drew back in time, before a kiss became unavoidable.

She was reluctant to recognize that she looked forward to
his visits. That she had got herself into a situation in which she
risked falling for a man who passed by her house once a day,
and would probably continue to do so no matter what happened between them. This could easily become a complicated
element of her time at Quagmire, a threat to her independence
and relative peace of mind.

And besides, she should be focusing on what she had come to accomplish.

Johannes seemed to be considerably less concerned.

"I actually have tons of stuff to do at school," he'd said, "so if you need some time on your own to work it's fine with me. I promise not to bother you. Just hang a sign on the door." And then that smile that made her lose her breath, that reappeared in her mind when she had no intention of thinking about him at all.

She needed to focus.

One night he asked if she wanted to come back to his student apartment by the old factory. Two rooms plus a kitchen, large enough for a whole family in the good old days and barely sufficient for a young art student today.

The walls were covered in abstract charcoal drawings, a jumble of thick, high-contrast lines and mazes that made her feel both lost and exhilarated all at once.

He tidied up as they moved through the apartment, putting away piles of paper with one hand, moving an easel with the other, and shoving a stack of books ahead of him with one foot until it collapsed in a heap against the wall.

"If I had been planning to invite you over," he said as he wiped the coffee table with a dishcloth, "it definitely would have looked different in here."

He moved newspapers off the small 1970s-era love-seat.

"It's clean, at least," he apologized. "I may be messy, but I can clean. Really."

She shrugged and laughed. "Good for you."

"And maybe for you," he whispered, moving right up close to her.

"I see...what do you mean?"

He looked at her with a hesitant, searching gaze. "I don't know."

Silence.

"Would you like a beer? A drink?" he asked.

She hugged herself. "I have to be up early tomorrow. I won't stay long."

"Okay," he said, glancing at her. "Well, I'm glad you came, anyway. I hope I'm not scaring you off by showing my true self," he said mildly, gesturing at the room.

She froze. *True self...what did he mean by that?* But she reminded herself that he actually had no idea where she was from, or who she really was.

"I'm kind of hungry," she said. "Aren't you? Do you have anything here at home?"

Johannes disappeared into the kitchen. "I have two frozen pizzas, will that do?"

They played Yahtzee as they ate, and listened to Monica Zetterlund and Bill Evans Trio. "Come Rain or Come Shine" filled the room.

"A sprig of lingonberry in a cocktail glass," Johannes said as he rolled a full house of ones and twos.

"Woo, look at that!" she said. "What about lingonberries?"

"That's how Monica Zetterlund was described once. I think it was that tall redhead who said it. Tage Danielsson."

"Oh right! The guy who had that monologue about probability." Nathalie looked down at the dice. "Are you really going to use *that* for your full house?"

"Why not? Seven points. Works for me. How about you?" he went on.

"Me? What?"

"What would you be? If you were a plant in some sort of drinking vessel."

"No idea. Not a cocktail glass, anyway."

"I know," Johannes said. "A *guksi*. A drinking scoop. With a leather thong to hang around your neck."

"What about the plant?"

He thought about it. "A rose, maybe."

"A rose? Christ, how boring."

He looked at her, and his eyes grew serious. "My main reason for choosing a rose isn't because it's beautiful. Or because it smells good."

"Okay...then what?"

"It has lots of layers. And..." He hesitated. "Because it can be a little...how should I put it? Thorny isn't the right word. Reluctant."

"Reluctant?" she said, tasting the word and feeling her face grow hot. "What do you mean?"

"I'm sorry. Maybe that was a little too direct. We'll talk about it another time."

Nathalie caught her breath and shook the dice. "All right. I do have to get going. I'm pretty sure you won. Even with that terrible full house."

She stood up and went to get her jacket from the hall. As she put it on and wound her scarf around her neck, she walked over and looked at the pictures on the wall.

"Can't you tell me a little about your art, by the way?" she asked. "What you're working on?"

He stood up and put his hands in the back pockets of his jeans. "I mean, God only knows. I just do it. I have some sort of unfortunate...joy inside that has to get out."

She turned to face him. "What did you say?"

He looked down at the floor, embarrassed. "I know. That's not usually anyone's mental picture, exactly, of an artist."

"An unfortunate joy?" she repeated.

"I've always had this sense that life is one big happy journey from the start. Like everything that happens just makes it more and more wonderful. I don't know how I can manage all that joy if I don't let it out."

"Stop it," she said. "You're kidding me."

He shook his head. "It's true. That's me. Take it or leave it."

"My God." She wound the scarf one last time around her neck and tied it in a knot. "Have you ever analyzed yourself? Figured out why you're like this?"

"My theory is, it's because I was a few minutes away from not existing at all. So it feels like everything in life is a bonus. Every second. Even the difficult parts make me happy in some sense. Because I get to experience them."

Her eyes widened. "How were you a few minutes from not existing?"

"My dad ran out the door to buy cigarettes right after he and my mum had sex. He tripped and hit his head on a rock and died. So in other words, the sperm that fertilized the egg that became me just barely made it out. I swear, we're talking minutes. I wasn't even one cell-division old. Mum claims that Dad needed a cigarette so badly that she had to *convince* him to have sex first, instead of waiting until he got back. So…you could say it was a close shave. Then again, it's a close shave for everyone. It's really fucking improbable, that those of us who are alive should be the ones who are alive. It was just a little extra obvious in my case."

He shrugged.

"But what do I know? Maybe it's just genetic. Apparently my dad's family were all a bunch of happy folks. My mum's side, though, is full of schizophrenia and depression."

Nathalie realized where this conversation was going and felt the urge to end it.

"Anyway, it's nice," she said, raising her eyebrows, "to be so jolly."

"Ewwwww!" He made a face. "*Jolly. That* sounds sexy. Like Santa Claus."

He took a sip of beer. She looked at his hand, holding the bottle. Those long, slender fingers, how they could stroke her skin if she let them, cup her breasts, find their way inside her.

"What about you?"

"Huh?"

"What about you?" He put down the bottle. "What defects are you carrying around?"

She went back to looking at the pictures on the walls. "Well, I don't have quite this much joy inside me, that's for sure," she said.

Neither of them said anything for a moment. The only sound was her steps as she moved between the pieces.

"It doesn't matter," he said cautiously, walking up to her and placing a hand on her back. "I have enough for both of us."

She turned to him, and it was like something plummeted inside her.

They stood perfectly still for a long time, just looking at each other. His gaze didn't move away, didn't laugh anything off; he just let everything be as it was. A feeling of pureness, closeness, contact.

The light reflected in his brown eyes, sliding around,

waiting, turning. After a few seconds or minutes she brushed her fingertips across his arm, and then she pulled off his sweater and they undressed each other there, on the floor, dropping their clothing as fast as a chestnut tree drops its leaves in the autumn, and then they tangled themselves in a big knot of skin and hair and arms and legs. Afterward, they walked hand in hand to the bed and fell asleep.

~

The next morning, Nathalie woke early with a pressure over her chest and a feeling of deep aversion.

What have I done?

Johannes was sleeping with his back to her; she could hear him breathing deeply. She gingerly slipped out of bed, pulled on her clothes, and sneaked away. Images from the night before flickered through her mind.

Why, why?

She got on her bike and pedaled home through the dawn as fast as she could, vehemently and vigorously, as if to get away from the images and everything that had happened.

When she got to the cottage, she took a towel and went straight up to the manor for a shower. She stood under the warm water for a long, long time. She let the water rinse away every trace, every particle of vulnerability. Afterward she scrubbed herself dry. It felt better.

She saw both Jelena and Alex as she walked up the stairs, but she avoided them and hurried out.

Back in the cottage, she made a large plateful of oatmeal and sat down with her documents all day, her writings and test results.

That afternoon she went to Åmål to buy groceries. It happened to be about the time when Johannes usually came by, and maybe that was just as well; after all, they had seen each other every day recently.

When she got back to the cottage she made a simple pasta dish and tried to think of something other than Johannes. She didn't call; nor did she contact him in any other way. But it was crawling inside her, teeming under her skin.

The darkness seemed oppressive again. The chill clung to her from within.

When she finally went to bed around midnight, she looked at her phone for the first time all day.

One unread text.

Thanks. For yesterday. Yours whenever you want. ☺.

She lay in bed and listened to the sound of a gentle rain against the windowpane. She let several minutes pass without moving, without allowing herself to be caught up in thoughts of everything she should accomplish during the day. She just lay there listening to the rain, staring at the ceiling, as if she were *resting*.

It used to be that work and rest were the same thing. For her, resting was thinking about ongoing projects, what had to be done in the next step, what the results indicated—thought patterns that circulated through her system uninterrupted, helping her relax.

But now she realized that rest had moved. It had taken up residence somewhere else, in a place she could only imagine this morning as the quiet rain struck the window.

She decided to let go of everything that had to be done that day—to try to remain in this stillness. She was still taken aback by the explosion that had happened the other night at Johannes's place, but she had to admit to herself that, deep down, she hoped he would visit today.

Maybe she shouldn't be so overdramatic about what had happened, or what she thought had happened. Maybe this time she really could have a healthy relationship. It didn't have to be a dangerous thing, to open up as she had done—if she even had opened up. She didn't know. Maybe she and Johannes had simply *connected*, to use a word Harriet liked to toss around.

You never connected with us, Nathalie. Don't think I haven't noticed. But we have to be able to spend time together. We're your family.

After spending the better part of the day sitting in front of the tile stove in one of the easy chairs and trying to read a Norwegian crime novel she'd found up at the manor, she noticed that it was starting to get windy outside. At first the breeze swept lightly across the treetops; after a while it began to blow harder and harder until it was tearing at everything it could get hold of.

The dim light of evening settled in slowly, as if to cover over and mute the intensity, but it didn't succeed. This was truly a raw autumn storm, unusually harsh and ruthless. *Like there's something it wants.* Nathalie felt a vague sense of unease, a hint of something eerie and distant but also familiar.

Then she saw Johannes through the window. It was like receiving a gift: a brief flare of happiness in her chest, until she found the warmth of her spontaneous reaction turning into a sharp, burning pain.

He stopped at the car park up by the manor and leaned his bike against a lamppost. Though he looked down at the house, he didn't seem to see her.

He began to warm up, and she assumed he would come down and knock at her door. If not now, then later—after his run—and she realized that she truly hoped he would.

This was a desire of a sort she wasn't used to, and it was growing stronger and stronger, like a grass fire spreading unchecked in every direction, beyond her control. It was moving through unfamiliar territory, across foreign realms, deep down inside her. It felt true.

She might as well be honest; she couldn't keep fooling herself. It was an unusually dangerous desire and a destructive longing, and it threatened her very existence.

She hadn't expected that anything like this storm of emotions could happen out here in the middle of nowhere—quite the opposite, in fact; she should have been safe.

Now she wasn't sure if she was prepared for the consequences. Tears sprang to her eyes. Her thoughts were dizzying.

No!

She was not prepared. Full stop. She had to focus on herself at the moment, on everything she needed to do.

She wouldn't answer if he knocked. She would pretend to be asleep, and then she would take it from there. Their relationship could not continue—not as it was now.

She read for a while longer, then put the book aside. Despite the weather, she decided to go and get some water from up in the manor house.

She took a jug in each hand, opened the door with one knee, and walked out. A thought was nagging at her subconscious, but it took some time for it to reach the front of her mind.

When it did, it nearly knocked her over.

It's perfectly still out here.

When did that happen?

She dropped both jugs and hurried down to the path, in the same direction Johannes had run.

It was practically storming, thundered through her system as she ran as fast as she could. *Practically storming! Just a few minutes ago!*

She had to find him before it was too late.

TWO

Detective Leif Berggren looked almost exactly as Maya Linde remembered him, that time four years ago when he had rung her buzzer in Brooklyn although she'd had no idea he and his wife were coming for a visit. "We happened to be in the neighborhood. Do you have time for us to come in?"

He radiated the same easy-going slyness now, as he stood outside the door of her new house in Fengerskog. His hair a little thinner than last time, cool as a cucumber, in dark jeans and a thick knitted sweater with a zip at the throat.

"I know you weren't supposed to come in until Monday morning," he began after they shared a heartfelt hug, "but something has come up already...although I'm sure you have tons to do with the house and everything. You've probably barely had time to move in."

"No," Maya protested. "Tell me!"

"There's a probable crime scene not far from here. A guy seems to have been beaten unconscious. We have some pictures, but to tell you the truth, they turned out kind of shitty. It was pretty foggy when the team on duty was out there. So I was thinking, as I was passing by, maybe you'd want to join me? We need a real photographer."

"Where is it?"

"Out on the mire."

"Okay," said Maya. "The mire, of all places."

"Nice to see you, Leif," she said a little while later in the car. "It's so freaking fantastic that we're going to be working together again."

"Yes, for a little while, at least," he said. "I'm retiring at sixty-five, just so you know. Two more years."

"Okay, so I'll have to work on my own for the last thirteen years?"

He laughed. "The last thirteen? Unfortunately, your generation will never be able to retire. Won't be any money left."

"I guess I'll have to keep toiling away, then. But what are you going to do when you leave, since you're privileged enough to be able to retire?" Maya asked. "Listen to dance-band music and sell junk full time, or what?"

She was referring to his hobby, which was importing strange knick-knacks from Asia and persuading friends, acquaintances and anyone else who might possibly be interested to buy them.

"Junk? Is that the opinion of renowned artist Maya Linde?"

Maya Linde had had her big breakthrough fifteen years earlier at the Venice Biennale with an exhibition called *Rain*— and then she had moved to New York. Articles and profiles often brought up her unusual side job: she also worked as a forensic photographer. But the art world and the police world had been blended together within her since childhood: both her parents had been artists, and her mother was also a police officer.

Maya had come along to the police station in Karlstad many times as a child—it was an hour's drive from her home in Åmål. Later, in the mid-eighties, when she pursued post-secondary training in photography and landed an internship and summer job at her mother's workplace, she considered it to be at most a temporary departure from her plan to live as an artist, a necessary evil before she could create the life she wanted. But her work with the police gave her creativity a dimension she would never have predicted, and she didn't hesitate for a moment when she was offered a part-time position with the Karlstad police after art school.

To use her camera to depict a body that had taken its last breath was a deeply stirring experience. As was documenting a site where a crime had occurred.

She never ceased to be fascinated by the way a place that had previously been so ordinary, or an object that had been so inconspicuous, was suddenly imbued with new meaning and took on great value as evidence.

She had stayed with the Karlstad police for nearly twenty years. When she finally moved to New York at the age of thirty-nine, she managed to secure a part-time job with the ninth precinct in Manhattan's East Village, which allowed her to keep up her skills.

Now she was about to resume her position in Karlstad even though, from a purely economic standpoint, she didn't need it. They had agreed on two days a week, to cover for a colleague who was on sick leave.

"Junk?" Leif laughed again, turning to the backseat and taking out a plastic bag. "I'll show you . . . which color do you want? Blue? Red?" He held up a fistful of reading glasses encased in plastic.

"I have several pairs already," she said.

"Not like this." He ripped open the plastic and gave her a bright blue pair. The earpieces were connected at the back; they looped around the wearer's neck.

"But how do I put them on?"

"You open them here," he said, pointing to the bridge. "There's a magnet so you can split them in front."

She opened the glasses, put them on over the top of her head, and clicked the magnet back together. She opened them again and let go; they landed against her chest.

"See that? No more crumbs all over your glasses because they're hanging way down on your stomach. Or if you usually wear them up on your head, you always put them down instead, and then they disappear. Right?"

Maya tried it out a few times. Pop open, pop closed. Put on, take off. "I'll take them," she said. "How much?"

"A hundred kronor, but eighty for you."

"I'll give you sixty."

"Seventy."

"Deal."

After a ten-minute car ride with Lasse Stefanz on the stereo, they arrived at the scene of the crime. They turned off the road just where Dalsland ended and Värmland began, and the country road got narrower and narrower until it was just a pitted gravel path surrounded by forest on both sides. Then they saw the shabby old sign on the side of the road.

Mossmarken.

"Here it is," Leif said.

Mossmarken, the name of the area surrounding Quagmire Manor and the mire, had once been a destination for local school groups—she had been there herself, as a child—until a little boy disappeared without a trace on a field trip about a decade earlier. Maya had been living in New York at the time and her parents had told her about the incident. Afterward, all similar outings had stopped. It was too dangerous out on the bog, people thought; there were too many treacherous spots across too large an area.

And now a young man had been found unconscious next

to the jogging path. An examination revealed that he had a head injury, and the most likely scenario was that he had met someone out on the bog who had attacked him.

Leif parked in the little car park. Maya took her camera bag from the boot and they headed for an information board that stood at the very beginning of the bog area.

Mossmarken Nature Reserve

The nature reserve at Mossmarken is made up of diverse habitats and includes several different important biotopes such as old-growth pine forest and carr, but its main feature is the large peat bog. It is home to many threatened species. Some species that thrive here include the rare weissia moss and blemished lichens, as well as a number of amphibians and birds, such as the pool frog and the capercaillie.

The bog is also interesting from a historical perspective. There is reason to believe that it was used as a ritual site for sacrificing tools, food and even people during the Iron Age. Decomposition occurs very slowly due to the oxygen-deficient, acidic environment, and at the start of the twenty-first century a so-called "bog body" dated to around 300 B.C. was found here. It belonged to a girl of about seventeen; her hair, clothing and a gold amulet were preserved. She is called the Lingonberry Girl, and today she can be seen at the Museum of Cultural History in Karlstad.

An eight-kilometer jogging path encircles the bog. There are also boardwalks for those who wish to cross the bog. The area is extremely marshy in certain areas, and visitors are discouraged from straying from the marked trails. Enjoy at your own risk.

"Do you remember when they dug up that bog body?" Leif asked.

"Yes," Maya said hesitantly. "That rings a bell."

"It was a pretty big to-do, but it settled down quickly."

They began to walk into the forest. They could see the blue and white police tape about a hundred meters on.

And then the landscape opened up.

Maya stopped short. A serene, wide-open space expanded before her: waves of yellowed grass and moss under the great white sky. Here and there, low pines jutted up like skinny arms out of a sea.

It took her breath away. It was bewitching.

"Oh my God, it's beautiful," she said.

Leif glanced her way. "Beautiful? Yeah, maybe. In its own way."

They discussed the photographs she needed to take. She would focus on the spot where the man had left the path, and also the site where he had been found, on a boardwalk about ten meters into the bog. Beyond that, she would take survey shots.

"But nothing too artistic; these are documentary photographs, Maya."

"I didn't know you could tell the difference," she said.

"Of course I can. What are you saying about me? I saw your latest exhibition. Last spring."

"You did? What did you think?"

"We'll talk about that later. Time to work now."

She decided to start with the path. There was nothing remarkable about the ground at that particular site. There were a number of shoe prints all on top of each other, and they were quite difficult to make out, as one would expect on a jogging path. She took out a ruler for scale and placed it next to the prints. As she was adjusting the focus for a survey shot, she noticed a flash of something in the background, through the viewfinder.

"There's something over there," she said, heading across to it. She crouched down and soon discovered two gold ten-kronor coins in the grass alongside the trail.

Leif caught up with her. He pulled on some gloves, picked up the coins, and inspected them. They were perfectly shiny.

"Well done, Maya," he said, carefully putting them in a bag. "How did they miss these yesterday?"

This area seemed less untouched. The prints here were deeper, and the ground around them more disturbed. Several bushes and trees were damaged, and long sticks of various width were spread out among the bushes. They studied the broken ends of the wood. They looked relatively fresh.

"Take pictures here too," Leif said. "It's not out of the question that the actual attack took place nearby."

Then it was time to go into the bog to photograph the place where the man had been found.

They made their way out on to the walkways, which felt decently solid. Maya stopped and looked around.

The sun was back behind the clouds. The area felt less welcoming.

In certain spots, it looked like you could walk on the ground, or at least jump from tussock to tussock. In other places, it looked marshy, and in yet others the foliage was more compact.

She could make out a large, palace-like structure on the other side of the bog, half hidden by the pines. *That must be Quagmire Manor,* she thought.

She stepped cautiously off the walkway. It wasn't easy to walk here. The tussocks were firm and tall; the ground between them was soft and wet. All of a sudden, one foot slipped down between two tussocks. She had time to see the dark bog water close over her ankle and she felt the ground latch on to her foot and drag it down.

"Shit!" She tottered, but pulled her foot out and made it back up onto the walkway.

"Take it easy," Leif said.

"This isn't...walking around in here isn't exactly child's play," she said.

"This is where he was," Leif said as he pointed ahead of them.

Maya came closer. "Here?"

Leif nodded.

A hollow of water had formed in the part of the bog where the man had been found unconscious.

"I thought there was firm ground around here," Maya said.

"This might be what they call a floating mat," Leif said. "A carpet of dead and living plants that sits on top of the water and makes a quagmire. The ground must have sunk where the guy fell in, and then the water rose a little, I would guess."

Maya began to take photos.

"A messy situation," she said as she clicked away.

"Huh?"

"A quagmire, in a figurative sense. A predicament, difficult to get out of. A hazard. Seems like the whole world is one big quagmire these days."

"Oh. Heaven knows you're right about that," Leif sighed.

"Okay, so what exactly happened to him?"

"It's not clear. A woman from the manor house found him, and he had some head injuries, likely caused by some sort of blunt object. That's all we've got."

"No one saw anything around here?"

Leif shook his head. "No witnesses, just the woman who found him. Nathalie Ström is her name."

"And how did she find him—was she out for a run too?"

"No, I don't think so. She's a biologist or something, working on samples, so she moves around the area a lot. She knew him a little, too. Apparently he's a student over at one of the art schools."

"Oh!" Maya exclaimed in surprise, looking up from the viewfinder. "He is? I'll be damned. Maybe I'll recognize the name. Who is he?"

"Johannes. Johannes Ayeb."

Maya shook her head. "Never heard of him."

When they were finished, Maya wanted to spend some time taking photos for her own use. She was already there, after all, and it was such an unusual place.

"May I have half an hour before we go?" she asked.

"Sure," Leif replied. "Just be careful."

"I read the sign."

She ventured further into the bog, planning to take a few preliminary shots. She had already decided to return in her free time with her medium-format film camera.

It was so quiet and empty out on the bog. A little creak here, a little pop there. And then, after a while, the whoosh of an owl flying by; she recognized it by the rounded wingtips.

The minutes passed and Maya realized she would have to head back soon. She made her way up a rise, where she had a clearer view of the area. She could get a better look at the manor house in one direction and some sort of large works site on the opposite side. Maybe that was the old peat quarry she'd heard of. Just past that site she could see several smaller houses all in a line along one side of the mire.

She wanted to photograph a particular little pine further on in the bog. It looked like a bonsai tree with its knobbly branches and perfectly flat top. She just had to get a tiny, tiny bit closer.

All her concentration was on her lens as she cautiously stepped off the boardwalk and used her feet to feel her way forward. It was a little drier here, and easier to walk. But suddenly she tripped over something, lost her balance, and fell—equipment and all.

No, no, no. Why couldn't I just be happy taking pictures from the path? she managed to think before she felt the dampness.

There would be no more photos today.

*K*nock, knock, knock.

Nathalie placed her fingers at her temples as she sat next to Johannes's bed in the hospital in Karlstad. He hadn't woken from his unconscious state yet.

She reached out and gently touched her fingertips to his hand. Tubes ran from the respirator to his mouth. A monotonous, mechanical sound.

It looked serious, she thought. Not good.

A nurse was sitting half hidden behind a partition, reading a book. She had explained to Nathalie that she was there to keep an eye on the equipment and on Johannes, that patients in his condition were never left alone. "But don't mind me," she said with a wink. "You can pretend I don't exist."

Nathalie had been sitting next to him drowsing off and on for hours, losing track of time. Of orientation. As if something inside her had been shaken about and had begun to toss and turn. Memories surfaced from her childhood, ones that she had never opened up to before. Or not so much memories, but faces. Faces from the past. She saw her parents, as if they were deep down under water. She saw her friend from that time, a vague image of how she remembered her round cheeks and curious eyes.

It was scary, so she pushed it away. But somehow, she

73

realized, it had also calmed her. She didn't know if she was about to fall apart or into place.

After a while, Nathalie went down to the cafeteria and bought a magazine and a cup of coffee. She sat down and gazed out the window. Later she took the lift back up again.

When she returned to the room, a woman was standing beside Johannes's bed. She was fidgeting, as if she didn't know what to do with herself.

Nathalie stopped in the doorway. "Hi," she said at last.

The woman looked up. "Hi," she said, her expression confused. "Are you...Nathalie?"

"Yes, that's right."

"Maria," the woman said, approaching her with an outstretched hand. "Johannes's mum. I heard about you." Her handshake was surprisingly steady. "I only found out what happened this morning."

"I've been here all night, so he hasn't been alone," Nathalie said. "Or, I mean, he wouldn't have been alone anyway, but..."

She cast a glance at the nurse, who was taking notes and didn't appear to be paying them any attention.

"He fell in the swamp, is that right?" his mother continued. "He was out running? He's always running. But how could he have fallen in? One of the police officers said someone might have attacked him. Do you know anything about that?"

Nathalie looked at her. She had dark hair in a medium-length ponytail and was wearing simple clothes that gave the appearance of being well put-together.

"I don't know any more than you do," she said.

"Do you know Johannes well? Are you from the school too?"

Nathalie hesitated. "We had just started getting to know each other, you could say." She looked at the floor. "I live right next to the mire and... that's where I found him. Quite a way into it. Totally knocked out."

"But what could have happened to him? I don't understand. His ankle was swollen too." Her eyes grew shiny and her gaze seemed to swim anxiously about Nathalie, as if it were searching for something to hang on to.

"We might not find out until he wakes up and can tell us himself," Nathalie said.

"The doctor says," his mum said, swallowing, "that the next few days are critical, to find out whether they have to operate. If it swells any more in there, then... then they have to relieve the pressure. By... opening his skull."

Nathalie placed her hand on the woman's arm as she pressed on.

"Apparently the injury has affected an area that regulates consciousness and sleep. So even if it doesn't get worse, he might not wake up for a while longer. As far as I understand it."

She looked away.

Nathalie felt speechlessness settle over her. She felt distant, disconnected, as if none of this actually had anything to do with her.

"Okay," she said. "Then I suppose all we can do is wait."

She stood up and looked at Johannes and then at his mother. "I'm going to take off. I didn't want to leave him all on his own, but now you're here, so..."

His mother hugged her hard. "Thank you. Thank you so much, dear."

"If he doesn't wake up soon," Nathalie said, "I can come back and sit with him if you want. Otherwise maybe you could give me a call if he wakes up. I mean *when* he wakes up. The nurses have my mobile number."

She headed for the exit but turned around in the doorway.

"By the way," she said softly. "The police have his jogging gear. And a little bag... full of a bunch of ten-kronor coins. Must be a hundred of them."

Johannes's mother looked at her in bafflement.

"Apparently they were in his pockets when he was found."

The house Maya Linde had bought in Fengerskog was big and old and had originally been built to house a mechanic's shop. Bicycles had been built there in the 1930s, and since production stopped in the eighties, various owners had tried to create homely spaces, at least in parts of the building.

The house looked like an unusually spacious and imposing traditional Dalsland cottage: a two-storey wooden building painted red, with large mullioned windows and white lettering on the façade: *C.W. Haraldson Mech. Workshop.*

Maya herself was surprised, as she'd never expected she would settle in her old home district again—she had grown up in Åmål, only about twenty kilometers away. But then her dad became seriously ill and she didn't want to leave her mum on her own. What's more, one of her closest friends had moved to Fengerskog, just as so many other artists had done in recent years.

While people moved steadily and increasingly away from most of "Vänerland"—as Maya liked to call the area surrounding the border between Dalsland and Värmland, at the northwestern corner of Lake Vänern—the small community of Fengerskog was bucking the trend. Certainly the handicraft school had been there for several decades, but recent years had brought elements that made the district even more lively throughout the year, and sometimes throughout the day and night. A more progressive fine arts school had been started two years ago. With the school came student housing and a number of guest studios; as a result, new artists arrived every six months, not only from Sweden but from all over the world.

The schools had gradually taken over the abandoned paper mill nearby, thus gaining large spaces for exhibitions, theater and other performance shows—and, not least, parties. There had been a café there for a long time, but before long a bar and a small restaurant opened their doors too. More and more students—and teachers—were moving in. Other artists who, like her, had left the area years ago, were moving back, buying up the cheap property, and having families.

The schools attracted visitors year round: there was a craft market at Christmas-time, theater in the summer, an art crawl at Easter and various exhibitions between times. According to the latest estimate, the cultural center was the third-largest tourist attraction in the municipality.

Darkness had fallen outside the windows, and it was warm in the room. The glow from the candles and the fireplace flickered on the walls. Maya had invited her friend Ellen, who was also the rector at the new art school, to dinner along with Oskar, who had come to Fengerskog as a guest artist a few months back. Maya had met him at the bar in the old paper mill a few times, and the whole reason behind the dinner was that Oskar had offered to help Maya move in.

Now, after some box-carrying and the following dinner, he and Ellen were each lying on a sofa while Maya stretched out on the huge, worn Oriental rug.

"Have you two ever been out to the bog?" Maya asked, her eyes on the ceiling.

Oskar and Ellen turned toward her.

"No," Ellen said. "Are you thinking about what happened?"

"I was there today. First time in probably forty years."

"It was someone from the school, wasn't it?" Oskar asked, looking meaningfully at Ellen.

"Yes," Ellen replied. "It's scary when things hit so close to home. I suppose we'll have to have an assembly at school on Monday; a bunch of strange rumors have already started spreading. But isn't that why you were there?"

Maya nodded. "Although that's not why I was thinking about it; there was such a...magic isn't the right word—but such a *powerful* feeling up there. I took some pictures. For my own use, I mean."

"Anything we're allowed to see?" Oskar asked.

"Just sketches. Maybe later," Maya said. "But have any of the students been up there to paint or anything?"

"Not that I know of. That's a good idea though, Maya," Ellen said. "The basic course in painting doesn't actually have a theme this autumn; maybe we could do something around the idea of nature."

At that moment Maya regretted having brought up the bog. The last thing she wanted was a bunch of art students there.

The wine was almost gone and Ellen had got on to the topic of how she had met her future, now ex, husband in New York by mistake.

"Or more accurately, it was Maya's mistake," Ellen clarified for Oskar. "We were there visiting Maya in New York the same week, my ex and I. That is, before we were together, or even knew each other. Not only did Maya forget she'd invited me, she also invited him the same week. And as if that wasn't bad enough, she herself was booked solid."

"Okay, so what happened?" Oskar said.

"Well, she didn't have much time for us, so I guess it's lucky we had each other," Ellen said, throwing an acidic look Maya's way.

"Yeah, it was lucky!" Maya said.

"So we went to museums and galleries for a week," Ellen went on, "and then I moved in with him in Stockholm. We ended up with a son and almost ten years together. It didn't end until four months ago, when I found him at our summer cabin with a man. I probably could have lived with that too, for what it's worth. If it hadn't been for the fact that he was truly in love."

"Now what?" Oskar asked.

"It might end with me moving in here."

"You're welcome to." Maya smiled. "I have to atone for my mistake. You can vacuum and polish the windows instead of paying rent. I do have a hell of a lot of windows."

"Maybe I'll move in too," said Oskar. "The guest houses are so small."

"All joking aside"—Maya said—"I think I prefer to live alone."

"What about Vanja?" Ellen asked. "Where's she going to live?"

"Who's Vanja?" said Oskar.

"That's my assistant, from New York. We're not going to live together; she bought a cheap house not far from here."

"Oh right, I think I heard something about that," said Oskar.

"She's arriving tomorrow. But I suppose I'll need extra help in the next few days," Maya said, turning to Ellen. "Would one of your students be interested? Mostly just to get things in order. I was planning to put up a notice on the bulletin board."

"Don't," said Oskar. "Don't put up any notices. I'll do it."

"You? But it's unpaid."

"That doesn't matter."

Maya brought her glass of red wine to her lips and smiled.

"Okay." The alcohol was starting to make her sleepy. "Is there any cheese left, do you think?"

Oskar stood up and went to the kitchen.

Once Ellen and Oskar had left, Maya took a quick shower, pulled on her nightdress, and crawled under the blankets. She read a few pages of the paper before setting it aside and gazing out at the room.

An idea had taken root in her mind. An idea about doing a series of photos from the bog at Quagmire Manor: quiet, simple images of the varied landscapes. Wide-open spaces. Maybe a few houses. As scaled back as possible, so that the atmosphere up there would shine through in the pictures.

She took out her laptop and brought up one of her photographs in full-screen view. It showed how the open bog met the sky, two fields with differing structures. Maybe it had no artistic merit as it was now, but at least she had got the idea and knew how to bring her intentions to fruition. Black and white, a square format. It would be suggestive and lovely.

She brought up another picture, then another. She was just about to close her laptop when something on the screen caught her attention.

The picture had been taken from the walkway, straight across the bog. A few trees were visible on the right. But there, quite far back in the image, partially hidden by the trees and bushes—it looked like someone was standing there.

She flipped through the other pictures from the same series. In the first few, it looked like the person was moving forward, only to have stopped and turned toward the camera in the later ones. The body was vaguely hunched. As if it were stooping. It could be a woman; it could be a man.

In the following pictures, the person was gone.

She looked through the series once more. Maybe it was just someone out enjoying nature. Or exercising, she thought, because who else would have any reason to be out there?

S orry if I'm intruding," said Agneta, the manor house manager. "I just wanted to hear how you are doing. And find
out what's going on."

Agneta was standing outside the cottage door, calm and
collected, yet eager somehow. She was clearly anxious to find
answers to what had happened out in the bog. And for Nathalie to give her those answers.

"I don't know much," said Nathalie, "just that he's still
unconscious. But come in. Would you like anything?"

She had just sat down at the table to eat a few open-topped
sandwiches with hard-boiled eggs. She gestured at the kitchen
table, at the coffee, the bread, butter and a box of juice.

"There's something familiar about you," Agneta said as
she stepped in. "I thought so from the very start."

"I get that a lot," Nathalie said. "Would you like something
to eat?" she repeated.

"No, I'm fine, thanks," said Agneta. "But won't you tell me
more about what happened when you found that man? You
knew him, didn't you?"

"No, not really. He liked to jog by here; beyond that we
only saw each other a few times."

"But you sat with him at the hospital?"

Yes, it had ended up that way.

They sat down on either side of the table and Nathalie saw no other option but to tell Agneta how she happened to be out there on the mire. To explain how nervous she had become and how she had set off to look for Johannes.

"If you hadn't acted so quickly, he might have died," Agneta said gravely. "You saved his life."

Nathalie looked away. "Well…" she said. "Maybe. It was mostly just luck."

"There's something I don't quite understand," Agneta said, her gaze sharpening. "He wasn't really out there long enough for you to start worrying, was he? You had a feeling, didn't you? That something had happened?"

Nathalie hesitated to answer the obtrusive question.

"I don't really know…or, okay, maybe. I just got it into my head that something wasn't right. And the weather was so terrible."

"Well, in any case, we'll cross our fingers that everything will be fine," Agneta said. "He's come by on his run just about every day for over a year, no matter the weather. I was so impressed," she went on as she stood up. "Anyway, outstanding job, Nathalie, really—just sensing something like that. That's what I call intuition."

"I don't know," said Nathalie.

"By the way," Agneta said, lowering her voice as if anyone could overhear, "we don't want any incidents to give the area a bad name, do we?"

So that was what she was after, Nathalie thought once Agneta had left.

Business as usual.

As if Mossmarken wasn't already tainted, after everything that had happened.

The most important rooms were furnished, the office among them. Handymen would be coming this week to start the renovation of the remaining areas: she had plans to build a darkroom for developing traditional black and white photographs, as well as a photography studio with an exhibition space, plus a small bar.

Maya glanced at her computer, which was on the floor next to her bed. She would have liked to pick it up and take another look at the photos from the mire—the yellowed landscape, the stooping figure—but she felt drained. A journalist and photographer from a monthly magazine had just interviewed her about her return home and her future. Fengerskog versus New York.

It had been an interesting meeting. The journalist, Tom Söderberg, was well-read and familiar with most of the projects she had worked on in recent years. She was flattered by how deeply he had analyzed her images and pleased at how sharp his observations were.

She also approved of him because he hadn't just stuck to flattery—at one point he had also challenged her with some well-founded criticism in a manner she wasn't used to. It had sparked her interest, at least in his intellect, and at least temporarily. She could take his criticism with ease, with a smile, maybe because she understood that he was already enamored with her. And that those feelings had probably appeared even as he read about her art and career.

This wasn't the first time that had happened.

The photographer arrived near the end of the interview. She had seemed a little tense and uncertain, and she wanted pictures of Maya from various spots in the house but also out in the middle of the cow pasture and on her way into the barn. Tom came along; they smiled at each other and exchanged quiet glances as the photographer's camera buzzed and clicked.

When it was all over, she offered to let Tom borrow a couple of articles about her he hadn't been able to get hold of.

Once she was on her own again, she put together a lunch out of some deli items she had in the fridge. She sat down at her large dining table and looked out at two brown cows who were staring at her from their field. She caught sight of herself in the big mirror on the facing wall, and was reminded of a few lines from a book she had read some time ago, a description of a person who appeared to have "a body full of food, drink, and years lived."

She had her father's round face and short neck. His narrow lips and nut-brown hair; his, too, had begun to go gray after fifty. Even her wrinkles were in the same places as his. Her father's face rested inside hers, like an image sinking below the surface of the water.

She remembered almost to the day when she first felt the

line-graph of her body swing downwards, like an elegant movement in the eternal cycle. The process had actually begun much earlier, of course, but she remembered when she noticed it: everything from the way her vision started to get worse to the realization that her skin was abandoning its former posts and beginning to sag. She could see the way her neck formed an accordion of folds when she turned her head and observed her reflection at the same time.

She remembered how she had been filled with the awareness that her body was a compostable organism like any other plant or animal on earth. It had given her a feeling of total freedom. Like a whisper from above, from inside, of letting go. In that moment, she felt like a leaf falling from the branch, only to float to the ground, where the decomposition process would take over.

Free to fall.

Like an uncomplicated leaf.

Teach me to decay like a simple leaf, as a poet once wrote.

Maya hadn't even needed to learn how. She was a natural.

Nathalie stood at one of the windows in the cottage, watching the landscape; the forest and that familiar desolation.

So much was coming back to her now.

But so much was different, too.

She could tell that she was more jittery. Or more open. Movement in every layer. Something had awoken, wanting up, wanting out. It was as though she were no longer in charge. If she ever had been.

The glow from the kerosene lamps made sharp shadows that streaked across the walls, hard and fast with the tiniest movement, like bats at night.

The indoor warmth creaked through the timber walls; there was scratching at the floor, probably mice who had returned from their leaf piles and holes in the ground.

She had never responded to Agneta's question; she had been nonplussed, but of course they had met before. Many times, years and years ago, up at the manor house. But that wasn't all. She also hadn't told her the real reason she had gone out to look for Johannes. That it had been because of the weather. But not because it had been so stormy—because it had stopped so suddenly.

She knew what it meant from personal experience, and

from the thousand times she'd read the book she'd been given by her neighbor, way back when, words about changes in the weather echoing in her ears. It was these words, and nothing else, that had caused her to act so quickly.

Samples, she thought to herself. *I need to take samples.*

She needed to find something measurable, send it in for analysis, and receive an answer. She needed that document with that text to still the rough seas inside her mind. The letters, the tables. The conclusions she could draw from them. She needed to do something to take back control, at least to feel like she had taken back control.

Her hand shook as she spooned a bowl of plain oatmeal into her mouth. The dryness parched her tongue. She downed a big glass of water, pulled on a thick sweater, hung her sampling equipment over her shoulder, and headed out into the damp air.

A thick fog had settled over the bog. It was as if the path formed as she walked on it, and she could only see a few meters ahead.

She went the same way she'd gone when she was following Johannes, and she soon arrived at the place where she'd found him. There had been fog that time too, but not this thick.

This was where he had lain, moaning, looking at her without truly being present. She remembered his eyes, veiled by exhaustion and resignation. Confusion, maybe surprise.

She had watched him slowly sinking and felt reality

collapsing in on itself, twisting, crumpling, dying. And then expanding again as if it were gasping for breath. In the nick of time she had yanked him up on to the walkway, checked to make sure he was still breathing, and dashed to the cottage for her phone. Then she had run back with the emergency dispatcher on the line.

By the time she returned to the walkway, Johannes had completely lost consciousness. She had been struck by the dizzying, deafening sense that she was about to lose someone—someone she loved. The sense that nothing else mattered if he did not continue to live. That the world would shrink down to a forgotten window that no one had bothered to close, and she was the thin curtain that would be whipped about by the wind and rain until everything was ripped to shreds and destroyed.

Nathalie kept walking; the fog had let up a bit. The boardwalk split in two and she went to the right. She needed to take two core samples to check the bacterial activity, which would in turn give information about the rate of decomposition. She needed to shake off her uneasiness and focus on concrete facts.

After a minute or two, her GPS indicated that she was in the right spot. She put down her bag, took out the corer, and plunged the first section in. Then she screwed on the next piece, and continued in this manner until the corer was deep enough in the earth. At last she pulled it all back up, removed the peat sample, and placed it in a tube.

The next site wasn't far off, as she recalled. She began to walk and was just about to enter the new coordinates when she caught a glimpse of something right next to the walkway, in a drier portion of the bog.

It was as though her body knew what it was before her brain could register it.

It wasn't deep, and it was empty, but it had to be two meters in length and there could be no doubt what she was looking at.

Someone had dug a grave in the bog.

N athalie Ström, the woman who found Johannes, found something else out in the bog," Leif said. "We're going to meet her there."

They were in his car on their way to Mossmarken again.

Leif was the one who had called her. A pit had been dug in the bog; it was discovered not far from where the unconscious young man from the art school had been. Leif wanted to check it out, and he wanted her to come. Which was fine with her.

"She's pretty quiet," he said. "Doesn't say much more than she has to. I met her for a little while yesterday as well. If you want to get anything out of her, you have to work for it."

They didn't say anything for a moment, until Maya spoke.

"What about the pit, it was out in the bog itself?"

"Yes."

"What do you think it's for?"

"Not sure. Maybe someone was planning to bury their dog there or something."

"That's not what you think," Maya said. "You wouldn't be checking it out if you did. And you wouldn't ask me to come along, either."

"She said it was at least two meters in length. So there's that."

"Okay, so it's a grave," Maya said. "The bog sure is an interesting place. From a historical perspective, I mean. I don't know, I'm starting to think about the Lingonberry Girl and all the graves that might exist out there."

"Yeah…"

"If a person were to start digging around in the bog today, that person might find some interesting things, don't you think?" Maya said.

"And?" Leif looked at her.

"I'm only saying that people might go digging out there just to see what they can turn up. Maybe someone was only trying to dig up historical objects."

"I wouldn't put my money on history stuff at the moment, Maya. Let's talk to Nathalie Ström and check out this pit. Then we'll keep working out who Johannes is; why someone knocked him out. And above all, why he was out in the bog so late, and in that storm."

"Okay, but it isn't necessarily strange that he was out there; he was there just about every day," Maya said. "I've been asking around at the school a little too; he's a perfectly ordinary art student, his permanent address is in Örebro, and he's been attending art school for a little over a year… there's nothing unusual about him at all."

"I know," Leif sighed. "And yet someone knocked him out."

Nathalie Ström was waiting for them in the car park next to the bog. She was between twenty-five and thirty and dressed in serious outdoor gear.

As they followed her into the bog, she told them what she had seen that afternoon: a grave, dug not far from the place where she'd found Johannes.

"Have you figured out what might have happened to him?" she asked anxiously.

"Unfortunately I can't discuss that just now," Leif said. "Do you have any ideas yourself?"

"I don't know. I think it's strange that he left the path. Of course, he wasn't that far in when I found him, but still."

"Maybe he had decided to run half his route and was taking a short cut across the bog," Leif said. "After all, it was already getting pretty dark."

Nathalie nodded. "But it still seems unlikely that he would have decided to run on the slippery boardwalks when it was so wet and windy; it probably wouldn't have been any faster than staying on the path."

"Are you thinking he was out there doing something else? That he wasn't just out for a run?"

Nathalie shrugged. "No, I don't know. I'm thinking some-one moved him, maybe."

Leif and Maya followed her as she left the path and walked into the bog. They didn't speak as they passed the spot where Johannes had been found. After another minute or two, Nath-alie stopped and looked around.

"It should be right here." She spun around. "Hold on... Maybe it was a little further in," she said.

They kept walking. There was no grave to be found, not even a tiny hollow, and Nathalie seemed to grow increasingly frustrated.

"Shit. I should have taken the coordinates." She looked beseechingly at Maya and Leif. "I swear, it was here before."

"It's fine," Leif said. "Why don't we spread out a little and see what we can find?"

After another half an hour, they gave up.

"I wouldn't have thought it would be so hard to find," Nathalie said.

"Something else just occurred to me," Leif said. "Maybe someone who lives nearby dug up some peat to use at home. I think I've heard something about that, that the farms around a bog might each own a strip. Although in that case the hole should still be there, of course."

"To use at home?" Maya said.

"Yes, as bedding for the animals, for example."

"That can't be," Nathalie said. "Partly because this is a nature reserve and digging up peat isn't allowed. And partly because it wouldn't be done that way. It's a point of honor to dig holes with sloping sides so that animals can get a foothold and climb out if they fall in. This pit wasn't dug like that."

Leif stopped and looked at her in surprise. "You're awfully knowledgeable," he said.

Nathalie blushed a little, then turned around and began to walk away. "I have to get back now."

"Hey, I'm sorry. I didn't mean any offense," Leif said.

Nathalie shrugged dully. "None taken."

"Listen, here's what we'll do," Leif said. "Give us a call again if you come up with anything. Don't hesitate. Okay? It's not so strange that it turned out this way; it's a large area."

Without looking at them, Nathalie raised a hand in farewell and left.

Leif and Maya got back in the car.

"Well, that's that," said Leif. "Stuff happens. Let's head back to the station."

Maya pulled her computer on to her lap.

"She's not from here, is she?" she said.

"No. Not that I know of, anyway. She's renting up at the manor for a few weeks."

They drove in silence for a while, until Maya spoke.

"Do you think she seems strange?"

"Nathalie?"

"Yes."

"Not really," Leif said. "But she is the only person who has been seen out on the bog with tools for digging recently. On the other hand, she was the one who contacted us."

"That's true." Maya gazed at the road.

"But I suppose you're right," Leif said. "I should probably

talk to her a little more, under different circumstances. Find out what she's actually researching out here, and so on."

They drove in silence once again, with the dark forest looming close over the road.

"You know those coins," Maya said, "that Johannes had on him?"

"Yes?"

"I've been thinking about it a lot—why would someone have a whole pile of ten-kronor coins with them when they were out for a run?"

"Robin ran with a full backpack every day for six months before he headed off on whatever adventure he was training for," Leif said, referring to his youngest son.

"Yes, okay. But coins? It must have some special significance."

"Yeah, maybe," said Leif.

Maya sighed. "There's something very odd about this whole bog saga," she said quietly, looking out the window. "About this place."

Leif chuckled. "Yes, that's how it usually goes when you don't quite know what you're dealing with."

"At the beginning of an investigation, you mean?"

"Pretty much."

Maya looked at him and turned on her computer, opening one of the image files.

"But there's something else I wanted to show you too, something I discovered yesterday. Look at this," she said, pointing at the blurry, stooping figure in the background of one of the pictures. "There's someone there, see?"

Leif glanced at the screen as he drove. "I can't see it just now. But it's probably outside the cordons. There's no rule against walking around out there."

"You're certainly right about that," Maya said, clicking on to the following images. She inspected them carefully, and suddenly she saw what she had missed earlier.

The person hadn't vanished from the frame in the last few exposures, as she had first thought. He or she had simply crouched down. In among the bushes.

Perhaps there were other explanations, but she had a gut feeling she knew what it was.

Someone had been trying to hide from her.

Since Nathalie had spent so much time in the woods and fields during her studies, she had come to feel at home in nature. But where others sought silence and tranquility, she found satisfaction and a deeper meaning in her very knowledge of the natural world. Her knowledge of various species. Understanding behaviors and traits on the basis of the laws of evolution. Her entire existence seemed to be grounded in Latin names, classification terms, complicated organic processes and other scientific facts.

She found it reassuring to know that all life on earth is divided into three so-called domains—bacteria, archaea and eukaryotes—and that these were based, among other things, on the comparison of DNA. Or that eukaryotes in turn were further divided into the kingdoms of plants, animals, fungi and protists. Within each kingdom were divisions first into phylum, then class, order, family, genus and species.

Her therapist, back when she saw one, had pointed out that it seemed she was determined to fill her brain with information. The therapist had suggested that this was either because she was trying to avoid confronting emptiness, in the sense of the absence of information, or else because she wanted to keep other information out: information that was impossible to manage, information that most likely had to do with her former life.

Personally, Nathalie thought she had found a useful way to deal with her emotions, and even if those around her sometimes thought it didn't work, she herself didn't have any major objections.

But now everything felt turned upside down and she was starting to wonder if her decision to return to Mossmarken was a huge mistake. She was beginning to lose her grasp on reality.

Had there ever even been a grave? If she was so convinced she had seen it, why couldn't she find it? Why wasn't it there?

And Johannes. She couldn't think of anyone else who had ever managed to rob as much focus from her work as he was doing now, despite the fact that he wasn't even conscious.

Her intention was to keep working out in the bog, but her thoughts kept going back to Room 11 at the hospital in Karlstad. At night when she went to bed, she saw his eyes in her mind. His smile and his honest desire to help her out on the bog.

It had been a long time since she'd felt the blessing of love.

And the curse.

Was it because of Johannes she had lost focus? Or was it something else that had taken hold of her?

The past?

But it was as though she only had one choice: to let it happen. Because there was no point in fighting it, anyway. The more she tried to keep the past at bay, the stronger it seemed to get.

Her memories from that last summer were closing in on her. Including the knocking in her head. It was harder now. Louder.

She had sought medical help for it throughout the years. But when no physical problems were found, she was referred to a psychiatrist who suggested that she was stressed, that something was agitating her.

"Some people hear voices," the psychiatrist told her, "and others hear other sounds. You hear knocking. There are medicines we can try."

Maybe it was around that point that she decided, out of sheer rage, to stay away from the healthcare system and behave as if she were healthy.

But had she even decided to travel up here?

She couldn't remember making the decision. Or whether it was her decision. Suddenly she had just found herself here. Again.

Here at Mossmarken.

After so many years.

So if I'm understanding you correctly," Ellen said, "you're envisioning a whole exhibition of photographs from the bog?"

Maya was sitting in her studio with Vanja, Ellen and Oskar. They were sharing a pot of ginger tea as they looked at her draft photos from Mossmarken.

"Nothing huge, but...I already have an exhibition planned; it's just that I'm not as eager to put up those pictures from New York as I was expecting. This feels more interesting, although I'll have to work pretty fast to finish in time. It's so fascinating— the bog, the dampness, the mist. You should come out there with me."

"It's not the strange events out there that you find attractive?" Ellen asked.

Well, that too, she couldn't deny it. Yes, it had all started with what happened to Johannes Ayeb. Then the grave that was there one minute and missing without a trace the next. And then there was the stooping, shadow-like person she'd caught in her photographs, who had apparently been trying to hide from her.

They were all inexplicable—and she had always been attracted to the inexplicable.

"But there are other interesting things about the bog too,"

she began, a sort of plea in her own defense. "A long time ago, people were sacrificed out there. And there's always been talk about how people vanish without a trace around Mossmarken. Whether that's idle chatter or straight-up ghost stories, I don't know, but I remember how we used to frighten each other with stories about it when we were little."

"I think it sounds exciting," Oskar said.

Maya had looked up information about the Lingonberry Girl online. Maybe, it occurred to her now, she could photograph some real bog bodies at museums to accompany the landscape photos. Maybe her bog project could become an exhibit about death and the dream of eternity. Something along those lines.

She recalled seeing similar portraits in a book a long time ago. Portraits of embalmed bodies in varying conditions from underground burial sites, catacombs in Italy and France.

The last person to be buried in the catacombs in Palermo was a little girl by the name of Rosalia Lombardo. She was two years old in 1920 when she fell ill with pneumonia and died. Her grieving father sought out a professor named Alfredo Salafia, who embalmed her body with a technique that proved especially successful. His recipe was apparently a combination of, among other things, formalin to kill bacteria, glycerin to prevent desiccation, salicylic acid to stop fungal growth and—the most important ingredient—zinc salts to keep the tissues from collapsing. Rosalia lay there to that day, in her open coffin, with soft, round cheeks and an apricot-colored bow lovingly tied at the top of her head. It was as if she might stand up and walk away at any moment.

Maya had pondered what it was about preserved bodies that struck a chord in her, whether the embalming was natural, as in the bog, or done by man, as with Rosalia. In the first instance, it was the mystique surrounding historical events and the fascination of a place that wouldn't let go of her.

With the latter, perhaps it was the act of preservation itself that interested her, an act that rose out of the desire to make sure those we love don't disappear.

In the United States an industry had sprung up out of preserving house pets; she had once watched an interview with a previously devastated master who had got his dog back. Once again he could see his companion lying in her basket like always, her head resting on her paws. His voice was full of joy as he talked about how alive she looked, how he could almost see her peeking at him out of one eye when he walked by.

There was something about that despair, Maya thought, that demonstrated how humans elevate the physical body to a status it doesn't deserve and was never meant to have. That reveals our inability to see who we truly are, beyond the bodies we inhabit. Our inability to let go, in life and in the face of death.

She thought about the art of photography, which was, at once, a melancholic reflection over the past and a manifestation of the present. A click of her finger stopped the flow of change. Crime scene photos, in their own way, embalmed the dead. The image as evidence. *This happened. This existed. This is what it looked like.* A body on the floor in a kitchen. In the sink, a plate that never got washed. On the table, a well-used cast-iron casserole with what remained of dinner—meat stew. Details that usually passed unnoticed.

It was always the everyday details of a crime scene that worked their way into Maya and made her feel dizzy. If there had been a showdown in the underworld, it was never the bills or the cocaine or the weapons that affected her: it was the observation that the man in the pool of blood on the floor had put on mismatched socks that morning. She would imagine him sitting on the edge of his bed or looking in his drawer, probably without the slightest clue that it would be his last morning.

"I'm planning to take you with me next time I visit the bog, whether you want to or not," she said to Ellen.

"I'd love to come too," said Oskar.

"Sure," said Maya. "Please do."

At that moment, the studio doorbell rang. Oskar went to answer it. After a moment he returned, a vague plea in his clear, blue eyes.

"It's a journalist. Tom Söderberg. He says he wanted to return a few books. Should I just take them, or...?"

"No," said Maya. "I'll get it." She rose and continued: "What do you say, isn't it time for a little wine?"

Maya welcomed Tom with a big hug and effusive words about how much she liked the text he'd written—she had been allowed to read a first draft. The others seemed a bit self-conscious about having a journalist among them, but Maya invited him in without hesitation.

He wore a tentative smile on his lips, and he ran his hand through his messy, longish hair. She didn't know if it was the wine, but he seemed to be radiating eroticism more strongly than last time they met—that sinewy, trim body, relaxed and comfortable in its own skin. She could picture it without clothing, the skin taut over his chest and legs.

She put on "Crosstown Traffic" and felt the energy level in the room rise. Jimi Hendrix was a force of nature, she thought, or an element all his own. It was beyond good or bad. You couldn't declare fire to be good or bad, or water. It was what it was.

"Will you send out some texts, Vanja? It would be fun if a couple more people came over," Maya said, placing her arm around Tom and leading him out of the studio and into the sitting room.

"Come on, let me show you something," she said in a low voice, as if to emphasize that the words were meant for his ears only.

She didn't actually see the looks Oskar was sending her way, but she could feel them burning on her back. It was a pleasant sort of pain. It was like good whisky or strong liquor; it intensified the feeling of *now* and made her look forward to a really nice evening.

Vanja's texts got things moving. One person after another showed up, and the night turned into an impromptu inaugural party for Maya's new studio.

Tom knew several of the new arrivals, and this seemed to help him feel at home. He conducted himself with ease, Maya thought; he didn't appear to have to make an effort to fit in among the artists.

A few people, Oskar and Ellen among them, continued to discuss aspects of Maya's art and her latest touring exhibition—a series of head-on photographs of everyday objects and beings. A stone, a tree, a house, a dog. A person, plain and simple; a gate, a wall. Straightforward clips lifted from the physical world. The exhibition was called *No Thing* and what Maya had attempted to do was depict each object's underlying unity and eternity. To focus not on the describable, distinguishing features of each motif, but on the transcendental power that united them.

"It's probably your strongest work," Ellen said. "As I wrote in the foreword to the exhibition catalog: *It's as though a breeze has swept through all the pictures and blown away everything but the impression of being and dignity that unites them deep down."*

"I saw that exhibition in Oslo," Oskar interjected, "and I agree. I still think about those photographs pretty often. There's something free about them."

Maya gave him an appreciative look.

"It's fascinating," said Vanja. "There're so many levels to it."

Tom turned to Maya and placed a hand on her back.

"There's something about the way you describe reality," he said in a lower voice, right next to her ear, "that makes me think about longing. Longing to unite with someone on a deeper level. To come together."

She felt the warmth of his body. The presence of her other guests only made the spark stronger.

"When lovers unite," she whispered back, her lips to his ear, "it might generate such strong feelings because it is a glimpse of the ultimate unity: between our inner nature and eternal being, when we die."

He pressed gently against her.

"That sounds tempting."

"Which part?" she whispered.

"Death can wait. The other part."

He let his gaze rest on her own. She didn't respond, just looked at him. This was the best phase. When everything was still undone, and all roads open.

*   *   *

In the morning, when the worst of her hangover had dissipated and she had said good-bye to Tom with the promise of seeing each other in the next week, she sat down on the sofa with her laptop and a big cup of strong coffee.

She visited the website of the Museum of Cultural History and looked up contact information and opening hours, but purposely avoided images of the Lingonberry Girl.

I want to see the real girl, the first time, she thought.

Nathalie had taken a few hesitant steps earlier, but now she was ready to go all the way. She was going to head westward on the path along the bog. She would follow those electrical poles back to the place where it all started. She would follow those wires backward. There could be no return; this was something she was driven to do. It wasn't even a choice any more.

Her backpack was full of food and drink. If everything went according to plan, she would be back in the cottage early this evening.

She didn't want to rush. She wanted to linger for once. Make room, create space to exist in. That scared her too, but in some strange way it felt like she wasn't alone. It was as if some new sort of consciousness was following her. A presence that followed her like a shadow. Or perhaps the opposite—it was leading her.

At the edge of the woods on one side of the path, the trees were mostly pine, but there were also some aspens, crab-apples and heather. The ground was scattered with half-rotten apples that had been stabbed by what appeared to be sharp beaks. They often flocked here, jackdaws and crows going about their vociferous business.

On the other side, the bog spread its yellowed panorama

under the pale gray sky; shades of color gradually melting into and away from one another. In between, the sharp reefs of dark silhouettes: fir trees in the distance.

Like a sea of grass and moss.

At this stage, in the beginning of its development, it was so clear that a bog was no more than an overgrown lake; there were still few trees and the ground was covered in hard, high tussocks and treacherous pools of water. It was a challenge, to say the least, to travel across such wilderness—but from a distance, the landscape appeared dreamy, almost seductive.

She had probably been expecting to find that more growth had occurred in the vegetation, although she knew that processes moved particularly slowly in pine bogs of this sort. Nothing seemed to have grown much at all, in all these years. It looked just as she remembered from back when she visited so often.

A bit further on, the bog gave way to open water. Once, as a child, she had found an old object on the lake bottom. It turned out to be an Iron Age fibula, a type of clothing fastener that had been replaced by buttons a few centuries later.

Her discovery had sparked her interest in the people of that time. She remembered feeling as if she had something in common with those people—just by virtue of living in the same place as they had, because they had walked the same ground, seen the sun travel the same path in the sky, followed the changes of each season in the same, changing landscape.

She felt a pang deep down inside.

She closed her eyes and let the memory float up to the surface. Her biological mother, Jessica, had noticed Nathalie's awakening interest. She had borrowed a book from the library about a boy in the Iron Age and began to read it to her. In the story, the children were warned about the dangerous wetlands, which were said to be a refuge for different kinds of mystical spirits.

Her voice. Her mother's voice as she read. *She liked it. She liked it as much as I did.*

The Iron Age boy lived in a small village with several farms, in what was called a longhouse. In one part of his home there was a large fireplace and people shared that space with piglets, chickens and the dog and cat; the animals helped keep everything warm. Even larger animals like cows, horses, sheep and pigs lived under the same roof, in an attached room.

Nathalie had begun to beg her parents to keep pigs in their own house. Or at least chickens. In the end she was given a budgie. It was pale blue with a white breast and she named it Jackie. "Now we're a family of four," she'd said happily. She had always wanted a fourth family member. She had always wanted a sister. An older sister.

After a few days, the bird bit her right index finger badly. After two weeks, it flew out of the open kitchen window and was never seen again. Nathalie was never able to shake the feeling that it had *fled*.

The story about the Iron Age people ended with a sacrifice to the gods for good harvests or success on the battlefield—or to give thanks for having already received it. They put food, tools and beautiful objects into the nearest carr.

Sometimes they sacrificed people.

She was almost there, the place where they had lived their lives together, she and her parents. Jessica, Jonas and Nathalie.

Was the house even still there? Did someone else live there now?

She passed the enormous fallen oak that lay alongside the path; the roots rose from the ground like a wall, knobbly tubers pointing in every direction. She had been so happy the first time she managed to climb up and sit on its trunk; it had felt like she was sitting on top of the world.

She was close; she kept walking.

Until suddenly, there she was.

The windows gazed emptily past her. Some were still whole; others were broken and had jagged edges.

She had never had any expectations about this moment, because she had never been able to picture it. She hadn't even approached it in her mind; never thought she would find her way here.

The house was deserted.

Leaves everywhere.

*   *   *

Her parents had always worked best together in the autumn. Her mother could rake for hours. She dressed in loose, comfortable clothing and sang "Billie Jean" and "Man in the Mirror" as her dad stood by the barrel, legs planted wide and cap on backward, laughing at her. With her. She recalled his sun-bleached hair, combed back and falling to his shoulders. How he seemed to enjoy standing there and poking at the fire, watching the garden piles vanish into the barrel and up to the sky. As if each autumn brought fresh opportunities for something better.

And the house. The pale gray, horizontal wood siding, which had been newly painted back then. She remembered the scent of turpentine in the evenings that last summer; now a layer of grime covered everything and there was a damp smudge of filth under each window. The gravel path they had laid before her mum lost her job at the beauty salon and the money began to run out—shining whitish-pink stones, swallowed by the ground, eaten up, gone.

Nathalie gasped for breath. She had forgotten to breathe. Her vision went black for an instant, and she collapsed, falling into a crouch; she was forced to steady herself with one hand. She sat like that for a moment, perfectly still, as the blood returned.

As everything returned.

She stood up again on shaking legs. She pressed on, in.

No one lived here, apparently. And no one seemed to have inhabited the house after them. She didn't know if that felt natural or just sad. An ash tree had twisted its fingers in through Nathalie's old bedroom window; the blackberry bush in front blocked the entire kitchen window. And out in the garden—could it be?—was the family's old Volvo, the black one.

She cautiously approached the car. One window was broken. The seats were ripped up and full of trash and twigs; apparently feral cats had used it as shelter from the wind and weather.

She was bombarded by fragments of memories. Mum and Dad, it was like they were still here, like they still existed here. She could see them moving through the garden. Pale and light as air, like weightless figures, but still present. In and out of the house, a window opening, a door closing.

She thought about her old life; it felt so foreign and yet so close. She thought of winter, skis on the roof of the car. Summer, with sweaty, sticky legs and a melting popsicle in her hand, on the way to the swimming spot. The expanse of the backseat, and her longing for a sister to sit beside her. Her dad at the wheel, her mum constantly turning around to check on her. Her short blonde hair. Her lively eyes.

The car was still here. Had always been here. As if it were waiting for her.

It was to the car she had fled when everything happened.

First she called the emergency number and then she went out to sit in the Volvo, where the police eventually found her.

Now the back door gave a screech and dropped from its mountings when she opened it; it fell to hang askew.

Each movement ached inside her; every breath carved deeper and deeper down. She cautiously got into the car, brushing away a few twigs, and sat down with a hard thud.

The buzzing in her ears. The present, drained of air; time, leaking, struggling for breath. She fell against the backrest, closed her eyes, and let her surroundings inspect her. The cats prowling around, the insects crawling over her legs. The wind nosing at her.

She must have fallen asleep, because the knocking woke her up. Knocking, blessedly real, from living hands against solid material in the physical world.

A face. She recognized him immediately.

"Göran," she whispered.

He had his hand on the roof of the car and nearly had to bend over double to see in. His hair had gone gray and his face was furrowed, but his eyes were the same. Sharp, warm. Welcoming.

"Nathalie," he said. "I'll be damned. I wondered when you would be coming back."

THREE

Bog bodies, that's what they were called—people who had been buried in bogs during the Iron Age, and whose skin, hair, fingernails, innards and clothes had been spared, to varying degrees, from decomposition.

Back in those days, it was typical for the dead to be burned. So the question was, why were some people apparently exempted from that norm? One common theory was that they had been sacrificed to the gods to bring prosperity in some form, or at least to keep bad luck at arm's length. Other theories said that they had committed a crime or a sin against the values of the time—infidelity or perhaps homosexuality. But the science was insufficient and in certain cases these assumptions were based more on guesswork and biases than on research.

What was certain was that bogs had, throughout time, been surrounded by an enigmatic, mystical air and thus made a natural site for rituals and communication with the spirit world. In more recent times, bogs were considered the perfect burial place for outcasts—a nutrient-poor, unusable place at the edge of both society and the public consciousness, and, more importantly, a place people seldom had reason to visit.

One priest in medieval Germany even spoke of the marshy wetlands as hell itself and consequently refused to bury a man who had drowned in a bog. *He who is taken by the bog stands hand in hand with the devil*, he argued.

After doing quite a bit of research on her own, Maya arranged to meet Samantha Olofsson, an archeologist at the Museum of Cultural History in Karlstad where the Lingonberry Girl rested. Maya had introduced herself on the phone and told it like it was: she was an artist who was interested in the bog as a site of mystery, and especially in bog bodies as a historical phenomenon.

The museum was down by the water and consisted of a Falu-red addition beside the severe, temple-like original building. It wasn't far from the former dance restaurant Sandgrund, where, these days, the artist Lars Lerin exhibited his own work and that of others.

Samantha Olofsson was around sixty and had white hair like an angel's halo; she was wearing a substantial white tunic and was obviously eager to share her time and knowledge.

Maya's eyes were drawn to her earrings, a large ring of twined filament and leather hanging from each ear. *A vulgar take on classic Sami handiwork*, she thought.

Samantha noticed her attention.

"It's pewter thread and reindeer hide," she said, fingering one earring. "Sami crafted."

Maya smiled.

"So, I'd like to begin by asking you a question," said

Samantha. "Do you know of a single culture in the history of the world that didn't have a relationship to the spirit world?"

"I guess that would have to be our own culture," she said. "Since way back."

Samantha laughed out loud. "Not really—there is no culture we know of, no people that has lived completely devoid of any such relationship. Humans have always sought contact with another dimension in various ways. To differing degrees, humankind has been guided by the notion of a spirit world; we have made use of prayer and sacrifice. That's one of the things that unites people through time. The museum's goal with this display is to give examples of the ways this relationship may have manifested itself in our part of the world during the Iron Age."

The display was divided between two dimly lit rooms. A few objects said to be sacrificial gifts were on display in glass cases: a pair of hazel walking sticks, some crumbling ornaments and a clay vessel whose purpose was unknown. Large screens showed illustrations of how the Iron Age people and their surroundings might have looked.

The Lingonberry Girl was presented in a large case in the far corner of one room. She wasn't at all what Maya had expected. The body was a puzzle of loosely connected, blackish-gray parts, and it was slightly curled up in a hollow in what was supposed to represent part of a bog. The tissues of her face were practically non-existent. The only remains that were decently well-preserved were her hair, which was swept up on her head; a tattered medium-length brown wool dress with a braided leather belt at the waist; and an oval-shaped gold amulet she had once worn around her neck but which now lay in a case to the side.

"When it comes to bog bodies, Sweden's contributions to history are extremely limited," said Samantha. "In comparison to other important European discoveries, the Lingonberry Girl is just a side note. But in Sweden, she is absolutely unique."

The other Swedish bog bodies were from a more recent age—the Bocksten Man in Varberg was from the Middle Ages—or else they were not considered "real" bog bodies, since in most cases only the skeleton was preserved. When the Lingonberry Girl was named, it was with a nod to one such example, the five-thousand-year-old Raspberry Girl who had been found during a peat harvest outside Falköping in 1943. The only surviving "soft parts" in that case were seeds from the sun-ripened raspberries that were assumed to have been her last meal.

"The Lingonberry Girl was in good shape when she was found," Samantha said, her face lighting up. "But unfortunately, too much time passed before she was handled properly. This type of find is destroyed by air, you see. The bodies can remain in the ground for thousands of years with no change, but up here they decay in no time. Quick action is crucial."

A sturdy oak pole ran through the clothing and remaining body parts, a reconstruction of how the girl was believed to have been pinned down in the earth.

"It's likely that poling served the practical function of keeping the body from floating up, but there are more superstitious theories as well," Samantha said.

"Such as?" Maya asked.

"That the pole was meant to keep the buried person from haunting, for instance."

"Does that have anything to do with the belief that vampires can be killed by a stake through the heart?" Maya asked.

"No, there's nothing to suggest it does."

One illustrated image depicted a man and woman helping each other stab a large pole through a dead body that lay in a pit.

"We're extremely pleased and proud of our Lingonberry Girl, of course," Samantha went on. "But as I said, she isn't much in comparison to what our colleagues in places like Denmark have. Have you been to the museum in Silkeborg? Where the Tollund Man is?"

Maya shook her head. Samantha sighed again and looked at the Lingonberry Girl.

"Come on," she said. "I want to show you something."

She led Maya to a small office, pulled down the blinds, and turned on a projector. A square of light appeared on a screen on the facing wall.

And then Samantha told her the stories of the Grauballe Man and the Huldremose Woman, her voice so full of passion that it could almost be mistaken for bliss.

She told Maya about the Tollund Man, whose millimeter of stubble was still intact after more than two thousand years, and about the teenage Windeby Girl who had been found in a bog in southern Schleswig, Germany, in 1952. She had a band of braided wool over her eyes; it had been tied so tightly that it carved into the bridge of her nose and the back of her neck. At first it was believed that the left side of her head had been shaved by a sharp knife—a sign of shame, they assumed.

"Many people felt that she had been killed following a crime of infidelity," Samantha whispered in the darkness. "That this child was taken into the bog with her head shaved and her eyes blindfolded, and drowned there."

A few days after the Windeby Girl was dug up, another body was found just a few meters away—the body of a man. The discovery was thought to support the infidelity theory, that the two of them had been lovers whose story came to a brutal end. Part of the reason for this was that German archeology at the time was influenced by Nazi ideology. With SS commander Heinrich Himmler at the helm, the German bog bodies were held up as evidence that Germanic people had always purged socially deviant individuals.

Later research showed, however, that the girl was in fact a boy, and the two "sinners" hadn't even lived during the same century. Perhaps the blindfold was a hair band that had slipped down, and maybe the "shaved hair" had in fact disintegrated.

"But exactly what makes it possible for so much to be preserved so well?" Maya wondered.

"It's partly because a bog is oxygen-deficient, which prevents bacterial decay. But a bog is also acidic. When sphagnum dies, it releases a substance that transforms into a brown humic acid, which binds calcium and nitrogen, among other things."

She brushed a silvery lock of hair out of her face.

"When the calcium is leached out of a dead body, the bacteria that cause decay can no longer use it to reproduce. And in the long term, the binding of nitrogen causes the skin to be tanned in a series of complex chemical reactions. Beyond that," she said, taking a deep breath, "we can say that there are basically three crucial factors: the temperature in the bog must not exceed four degrees Celsius when the body winds up there—if it does, the body will begin to decompose immediately. The body must also lie deep enough so wild animals can't reach it, and it must immediately be covered with peat."

Samantha smiled and nodded as if to confirm the information she had just shared.

"And then there's the fact that the specific conditions are different everywhere. No one bog is exactly like any other."

"No, of course," Maya said. "But why is the Lingonberry Girl a 'side note,' or whatever you called it?"

"I suppose because she's neither well-preserved nor restored, but there are other explanations as well."

Then she told Maya that most bodies had been discovered during the post-war period when the lack of coal and other energy sources led to the increased harvesting of peat. The bodies were often initially mistaken for current-day homicide victims: in one case in England, a man had confessed to murdering his missing wife when he was confronted with a body that had been discovered, though that corpse had later turned out to be over two thousand years old.

Later on, as peat became less important as an energy source, and as manual harvesting gave way to mechanical peat-cutting, the number of discoveries—and the interest surrounding them—dwindled as well.

"By the time the Lingonberry Girl was found at the start of the twenty-first century, the interest in bog bodies had fallen off considerably." Samantha's voice grew deeper as she looked at Maya through the dim light. "But of course that doesn't necessarily mean that there aren't more corpses out there. Maybe it just means that they haven't been found yet."

Not much had changed in Göran Dahlberg's home. It was bohemian and full of trinkets, but it was still neat and clean.

The living room was open to the rafters and the walls were covered in books. Two fans turned lazily on the ceiling. One corner contained a sofa and a dark leather easy chair. The wooden blinds were lowered halfway down the large windows.

"I always did like being here," Nathalie said as she sat down in the chair.

"I liked having you here."

They didn't speak for a moment.

"I missed you a lot," Göran said. "I missed you the most."

"I thought about coming many times," she lied.

Göran waved this off with one hand. "I understand why you wouldn't want to set foot here."

It felt like she was standing at the edge of an abyss. As if something had carried her here while she slept, and that she was only now waking up to see the depths before her.

What am I doing here? she thought. *How am I supposed to handle this?*

"But you stayed, all these years?" she said instead.

"I'm the one who bought your house. Maybe you knew that?"

She shook her head. Harriet had told her that eighty thousand kronor showed up in her account after the sale, but she had never bothered to find out who the new owner was.

"Why? Why did you want the house?"

"I just couldn't imagine someone else living there. I decided I would rather watch the place fall down. Hope that doesn't seem strange to you."

"I...I don't care," she managed. "I truly don't care. I've moved on. I really have. I moved on right away."

"And yet I just found you in the car?" Göran said, with a gaze that saw right through her. "How are you doing these days?"

"I don't know. I suppose I'm thinking about some stuff. Things I haven't been able to let go of, after all."

It was a peculiar feeling, sitting in the home of her old neighbor as a grown woman. She would have preferred to find that everything was in the past, that it was all gallons of water under the bridge of her childhood. But now it seemed rather the opposite. As she sat there in Göran's house, she realized that instead all the water had been frozen, just waiting to thaw, waiting for her to stick her feet into it again.

She told him about her education in biology and the dissertation she was currently working on.

"Wetlands," he said with a small smile. "Interesting choice of subject for someone from these parts."

She smiled uncertainly, not quite sure she understood what he meant, but she told him about the cottage she was renting at Quagmire Manor.

Somehow she could sense the question hanging in the air above them, invisible. Neither wanted to touch on it, because both knew what it might mean.

"He's not the first," Göran said at last.

"Who?"

"You know who I mean. The man whose life you saved."

"How did you know?"

"I talk to people, Nathalie. And I read the papers. I put two and two together. He's not the first," he repeated, his voice grave. "And you know it."

Nathalie looked at him.

"He was lucky," Göran said. "You found him. But there are a lot of people who have vanished here since you left."

He looked out the window without saying anything for a moment, then went on. "More than usual, in fact."

Just as Maya got in her car to leave the museum, her phone chimed. It was a text from Tom. He thanked her for the day before and quoted art critic John Berger.

The relation between what we see and what we know is never settled. Each evening we see the sun set. We know that the earth is turning away from it. Yet the knowledge, the explanation, never quite fits the sight.

～

To be desired is perhaps the closest anybody in this life can reach to feeling immortal.

She closed the text and decided she would have to remember to answer later, when she wasn't as tired.

They had spent a few nights together—always the same set-up. He came to her house around six and left his car there, and they took a walk over to Slaughterhouse, a restaurant just beyond the factory area.

The restaurant only had five tables, and it was in a newly renovated hotel that had previously been a slaughterhouse, which was how the restaurant got its name. The functional industrial style was reflected in every detail of the décor, and there was only one item on the menu: a vegetarian dish, as if in response to the history of the building.

They stuffed themselves full and drank themselves drunk, became absorbed in some metaphysical discussion, walked home. He had spent the night each time. It had been nice, no question, but an invisible veil of expectation had begun to settle over everything. Their sexual encounters had become increasingly strained and uninspired.

It pained her a little to see how much effort he was expending to keep what was happening from happening. How much he was struggling to stop their relationship from losing its spark, even though that only made everything worse. He had started to seem servile, and his intellectual sharpness lost its rigor as it turned into chewed-over bait he tossed out time and again with the aim of getting her to stay, keeping her from swimming to fresher waters.

Yesterday's conversation had revolved around Schopenhauer's critique of Kant's transcendental idealism. She didn't recall whether they had reached any substantial conclusions, but she was still a little exhilarated about the meal: a large bowl of roasted red sweetheart cabbage stuffed with goat's cheese, deliciously spiced spinach and chopped walnuts. Dessert had been blackcurrant parfait followed by an aged cognac from France, which the restaurateur had purchased on a personal visit the summer before.

Now she was driving home, her thoughts elsewhere. The radio was playing Arvo Pärt's *Für Alina*. First came the dull tones of the prelude, then two minutes of notes composed with absolute perfection. The silence between the notes was the important part; the space between musical molecules, the fraught emptiness.

Pärt's music embodied what every form of gifted art sprang from: serene presence. Timeless being. The space deep down in every human—the part that found itself reflected in the silence between the tones in Pärt's compositions.

She thought of it as *nothing*.

Of what *was* nothing, not what was *nothing*. A keen void that could be likened to openness rather than desertedness. Which was everything. And nothing. All at once. A single life-force of space that expressed itself through constantly shifting shapes in the physical world and which clearly possessed both humor and a fondness for variety—after all, there were three hundred and fifty thousand different types of beetle. Some of them rolled balls of dung with their hind legs as they moved forward; others had big horns on their foreheads or antennae that looked like feathers.

So, as she saw it, these physical expressions were only the outermost layer of reality, a shifting veil of illusory variety that concealed the true, fundamental unity of reality. Within Hindu mysticism, this veil was called *maya*, and it was from this concept that she had chosen her artist name, which soon came to completely replace her given name, Magdalena.

She thought of the physical forms she had just witnessed at the museum. The bog bodies. Which had lain there in layers of earth while eras shifted above them. Which were now on display in airtight cases, as empty of life as they were protected from mortality. It became so obvious that *this* was not what a human was at the most basic level.

That was how she felt every time she saw a dead body. And every time she met grieving family and friends, she wanted to shout: *But wait, you don't understand—only the body is dead!* And at the same time, the care bestowed upon this particular body, this particular flicker in eternity, as holy as every other form around us that rises and falls, that flares up and goes dark.

If only we knew how we shine.

When she returned home, dusk was not far off. She stepped out of the car and walked slowly through the garden. Both chestnuts had dropped all their broad leaves in just a few days, creating an enormous golden blanket. She observed the ground for a long time, wondering whether she should let the leaves rot where they lay or ask someone to take care of them. Having a house and garden was a new experience for her. There were many things she wasn't prepared for.

She sat down on a long, worn wooden bench that stood along one side of the house, thinking of all the workers who had probably sat there throughout the years, maybe taking a break in the sunshine before returning to the workshop. She twisted the ring she wore on one middle finger, back and forth, back and forth. A friend had given it to her many years ago; it was a thin silver snake that coiled around her finger and then extended upward, toward her knuckle.

The snake has bitten you, Maya. You'll never be the same again. Now you will become who you are, who you have always been.

She felt herself opening up, her brain starting to rest as impressions from the day began to flow through her, stories of soft ground and hard blows; she could almost hear the sound echoing through her without knowing why, where it came from, what it wanted to tell her. She just heard the blows ringing through her body.

Thud, thud, thud.

In the next instant, realization spread out like sunlight in a glade.

The pole.

When she was out taking photographs, she had tripped over something sticking out of the bog and fallen headlong into the dampness. It hadn't quite seemed like a branch or a root; it had been more substantial.

More like a pole.

It had taken hours for the thought to surface, and now that it had she didn't have the patience to wait. She had never had that sort of patience. She needed answers now.

The Lingonberry Girl was poled, over two thousand years ago.

She stood up and went to the garage. *Are there any tools here?* She realized she hadn't even checked to see what the previous owners had left behind; she just remembered that there had been a few objects stashed in the back.

In the corner she found a few rakes, a pitchfork, an ax, and...there. A shovel. She picked it up and hurried back to her car.

In no time she was turning into the car park next to the bog.

His eyes moved under his delicate eyelids and Nathalie noticed his upper lip twitching. She had been sitting with him for over two hours.

Johannes's mother had drawn up a schedule so that someone he knew would be with him for the better part of each day. A few friends from school were helping out as well.

She had looked both anxious and relieved when she told Nathalie he wouldn't need an operation. The doctors had said all they could do was wait for the swelling to go down, and then Johannes would wake up, hopefully without permanent injury.

In the meantime, the doctors could only support his various bodily functions: temperature regulation, water and salt balances, kidney and lung functions, blood circulation. Make sure his organs got what they needed, that his blood received oxygen and carbon dioxide was removed.

Nathalie's routine involved coming to Room 11 of the ICU at Karlstad Hospital for three hours at a time, three days a week.

She spent the first few days sitting at his bedside in silence. She just sat there, looking at his face. She would stand up and walk to the window. Look out at the car park. Sit down again. Now and then a nurse would come by to change an IV bag or check a value; sometimes there were two nurses so they could

turn him over. They moved through the room like quiet spirits, without demanding any attention at all, as if they kept an
almost holy reverence for the integrity of visitors and patients.

After a few days, her silence ended. She couldn't keep it up
any longer.

"We didn't really get to know each other," she whispered,
the beginning of a conversation. "But I very much enjoy your
company."

The only sound came from the machines around the bed.

"I haven't felt that way about many people before."

She swallowed hard.

"Not many at all," she reiterated.

Then she didn't know what to say, so she started to tell him
about everything that had happened. Why he was lying there
in a room at the Karlstad Hospital. How she had dragged him
out of the marshy bog. About the grave she had seen, which had
later vanished.

"The police don't understand..."

She sighed.

"I met an old friend, a man from the area. He says I saved
you from..."

She closed her eyes and sank down on to the chair.

"Oh, Johannes, you have no idea." She took a deep breath.

"He says that people have been disappearing from the bog
forever. That you were..."

She looked at him: his face, his forehead, his pale skin.

"Your friends," she said instead. "They've started planning the party they'll throw when you come back. But maybe you already know about that. They're here almost every day."

Then she talked about the progress she had made on her work, her latest measurements. At the same time, she thought of how interested he had been in her research, or at least she wanted to believe he had been. He had seemed to be.

"Did I tell you that you can find out the ages of different layers of wetlands by analyzing seeds? Once I found a seed from the Stone Age. The fact is, you can even estimate the ages of objects buried in bogs by identifying pollen from the same layer of peat. If you can determine the age of the vegetation you can also pinpoint what climate period it was from and, thus, the time period. Although the Carbon-14 method is a little more precise, of course."

She fell silent again.

Why am I telling you this? You nearly lost your life out there; you're still fighting to come back.

She sat quiet. And after a while, again, faces came floating up to the surface of her consciousness, faces from the past. Her parents, her friend, people she knew. They had voices but she couldn't distinguish the words, only the melody and the tone—if it was warm or cold, caring or stressed. Her body tightened a bit at first, but relaxed again when she focused on Johannes and his closed eyes.

She bent forward and lowered her voice to a whisper.

"Johannes, I never told you this, but I grew up in Moss-marken. I lived in a house by the bog until I was twelve. I would like to tell you what it was like, what it was really like. I would like to tell you about what's actually going on out there."

Maya stopped the car and climbed out. The car park was empty; everything was quiet and still. She put on a headlamp, took the shovel from the boot, and began to walk into the forest.

She went the same way as last time—down to the jogging path, out across the bog, past the spot where they had found the art student. The veils of mist swirled at her feet like diffuse lights.

Deep down she knew she was blinded by eagerness. She shouldn't be out here—not alone, not at night, not after what had happened. But she couldn't help it.

She wanted to see if she could find what it was she had tripped over. When it happened, of course, she'd thought it was a branch or maybe a root, but now she had the definite feeling that she had been mistaken, that it could have been something else. Now she was looking for the little pine that resembled a bonsai tree, short and knotty with a perfectly flat crown. She'd had it in perfect sight when she fell, when she lay in the damp ground, cursing herself for being so inattentive.

The whole area was so different in moonlight. The shadows at night were unlike the daytime shadows, naturally. They changed the proportions, distorting them.

She left the boardwalk and began to step across the bog.

From a distance, the grassy ground seemed so soft and beautifully billowy, but it was a completely different sensation to be in the midst of it. It was difficult to balance as she took giant steps from tussock to hard tussock, each half a meter high, trying to keep from plunging her feet straight into the water that waited between them. She was out of breath within thirty seconds. The tussocks bobbed and swayed under her feet, as if they wanted to get away, as if they did not wish to be trodden upon.

She stopped for a moment to catch her breath, then got a second wind and stumbled toward an area further on where she could see more trees, where the ground was probably more solid. When she reached it, she crouched down and exhaled. *There's nothing weird about this place*, she told herself. *It's just a regular old bog.*

But all the words she had read recently echoed in the back of her mind. How for thousands of years the bog had been considered a place possessed, so difficult to define and categorize. A waterlogged, unusable nowhereland beyond the control of humans. Where hidden sources of power ruled and seduced, taking what they needed and giving what they wanted.

A borderland between land and sea, between dry and wet, soft and solid. *Between life and death.*

A bird cawed, breaking the silence. She closed her eyes and caught her breath.

When she looked up again, she saw the pine. The knotty one with a flat crown. It was straight ahead of her, fifty meters on. She tried to shake off the uneasiness she had just felt and made her way forward, aiming her headlamp at the ground nearby. Nothing odd.

I'm being overdramatic, she had time to think, but an instant later she found it. She had been right.

The thing she had tripped over was neither a branch nor a root. Rather, it did appear to be a pole—a hefty, cylinder-shaped piece of wood, a few centimeters in diameter, poking out of the ground a little bit.

She gathered her thoughts, letting her eyes sweep the desolate landscape.

The light of her headlamp was cold and white, and she thought she heard noises from every direction. She felt small in a way she wasn't used to—vulnerable and watched and surrounded by darkness. Fear crept across her skin, under her skin, with tiny, gentle steps. Then it began to sink its claws into her. Slowly, firmly. She yelled at herself, in her mind: *If I got this far, I am sure as hell not...*

She pulled on a pair of gloves, grabbed hold of the pole, and tried to dislodge it. When that didn't work, she began to clear away the vegetation around it instead. She yanked at grass, branches and peat and then took the shovel and began to dig, hard and with determination. Time seemed to vanish, and she let go of it, let it go on its way. When it returned, she had dug a pit around the pole just over half a meter in diameter and depth.

Her shovel struck an object. She cautiously switched to digging with her hands, and a moment later she was thrown backward as if she had received an electric shock. There was something down there. *There was something...*

She bent over to see what she had felt, something cold and stiff and narrow, like...

Like fingers.

One, two, three, four.

A human hand was sticking out of the earth.

As a child, Nathalie had had two clues about who Göran Dahlberg was. For one, her mother had told her that he was "a professor or something charming like that," and for another, she had peered through his living room window to discover that there were taxidermied bats on his bookshelf. This prompted her to imagine him as a mix between Count Dracula and Professor Balthazar.

But then she met him in the flesh one rainy spring day when she was eight. Her parents were having a fight; her dad had slammed the door and taken off in the car at just about the same time as her mum pulled on her coat and walked into the forest. Neither of them realized they were leaving Nathalie behind.

She was sitting on the steps outside the house, scraping bark from a stick, when Göran came to ask if she wanted to come to his house. He didn't say "poor little girl" or even "what's wrong, honey?" He just asked if she wanted to come in for some tea while she waited. She had never drunk tea before; this was the first time.

It didn't take long for her to forget she'd thought Göran was strange, and by the time summer arrived she was at his house all the time, bringing injured birds and earthworms in glass jars. He treated her as he would anyone else and spoke to her as if she were an adult. She could tell he was different, that he wasn't like her mum or dad or other grown-ups, but he was kind. Sometimes he would stop short in the middle of a conversation and appear to be thinking about something. She liked that. His strange ways made her feel free to be herself.

Then came the day when she'd just started fourth year and her mum mentioned, for the first time, Göran's interest in ghosts. A middle-aged German tourist had vanished while on vacation in Tösse, near Lake Vänern. There were indications that she had visited the mire that same day, so the police had knocked on doors in the area. Just after Nathalie's mother spoke to an officer, she sat down on the patio with a friend and lit a cigarette.

"Oh, they're knocking on Göran's door now," she'd said. "I suppose he'll tell them the ghosts took that German."

"The ghosts?" Nathalie asked.

And her mother had received a *look* from her friend.

"Well, of course. He believes in ghosts, our dear neighbor." She blew thick rings of smoke and turned to her friend. "He says the ghosts took his wife too. He thinks *that's* why she disappeared." She put out her cigarette and went on: "If you ask me, I bet she's sitting in a bar in some nice, warm country, having drinks with a man who *didn't* give up his university career to start chasing ghosts."

Her friend laughed.

That same afternoon, Nathalie went to see Göran; he was working at his desk. His back was to her.

"Do you believe in ghosts?" she said.

He froze and looked up, but didn't respond.

"Mum says you believe in ghosts. Do you? Are ghosts real?"

He turned around, took off his glasses, and considered her for a long moment. Then he turned back around and kept writing.

"No, Nathalie. They aren't," he said.

"Mum says that *you* say that ghosts really exist."

Another silence.

"But ghosts don't exist, Nathalie. That's the whole point of ghosts," he said. "That they don't exist. The question itself is contradictory."

"It's what? Don't talk so weird. Why didn't you ever tell me you've seen a ghost? Are they dangerous? What do they look like?"

He turned around again. Then he took his pen and a piece of paper from the desk and drew a flying ghost with a sheet and chains.

"Like this, maybe?"

"That's the kind of ghost you saw?" Nathalie was clearly disappointed. "You're just making things up. Tell me the truth."

He crouched down in front of her and looked her in the eyes.

"Do you really want to know?"

She nodded eagerly.

For a few eternal seconds the air in Göran's office seemed

electric. It felt like she was about to gain a great knowledge: the truth about the ghost world.

But Göran looked away, dropping her gaze as if it were worthless, and turned back to his desk.

"It doesn't matter what ghosts look like, Nathalie. The important thing is how you deal with them."

And that was all.

She stood there for a long time, staring at his long, narrow, mute back, but she knew the conversation was over.

From then on she realized that there was no point in trying to get a straight answer out of Göran, at least not when it came to ghosts. She had to accept that his words would never be anything but as flighty and elusive as the ghosts he spoke of—or *didn't* speak of.

It must have been a year before they had another conversation about hauntings, this time initiated by Göran himself. It happened when they were out on the mire together. She wasn't allowed to go there alone, but she could visit if Göran came too.

"I'd like to talk to you about something," he said as they sat down to drink coffee and hot chocolate from their Thermoses. "Since you've shown interest in... ghosts and so on."

Finally, she thought, nodding silently.

"This place we live near, you and I..." he began. "It... how should I put it? There are certain things you should be aware of."

He took a book from his bag.

"I want you to have this; read at least the fifth chapter. But maybe you shouldn't show it to anyone. They won't believe what it says anyway."

He looked at her gravely.

"But promise me you'll do that, you'll read it."

In under two hours, Leif Berggren had arrived at the mire with a colleague, a medical examiner and two technicians. Maya herself had just returned to the discovery site. She had sped around in her car while waiting for the others, stopping at a hot-dog stand and buying some food that she barely touched, just so she could sit in the well-lit seating area for a moment.

"Now tell me, why did you come here?" Leif asked in a voice full of both worry and a certain degree of irritation. She knew he wasn't happy that she had come out here alone, but he also didn't want to have that discussion quite yet.

So she told him how she had visited the Museum of Cultural History and heard the stories of the past, of human sacrifices pinned into the earth by poles. And how, as a result, she came to realize what she had really tripped over in the bog.

"You're saying it was a pole?" Leif asked, looking at her with narrowed eyes.

She nodded. "It was a way to pin down the body, but apparently it was also a common trick to prevent the dead from rising again," she said with a tired smile, to mitigate the strangeness of her implication. "Whether it works, I don't know."

"Well, you learn something new every day," Leif said. "You'll have to come in tomorrow and give me more details." He glanced at the area around the pole, which was now half hidden under a protective tent. "I suppose the question is whether we're dealing with a corpse from the Iron Age this time as well. I spoke to an archeologist at the museum, and she'll be here as soon as she can."

Samantha, Maya thought.

The medical examiner, who was bent over the emerging body, heard Leif's words and straightened up. "I think you can tell that archeologist we won't be needing her."

A pause.

"And I think you'll have to read up on more current superstition," she went on. "This person is wearing a leather jacket from H&M."

A flock of birds lifted from a tree. Maya watched as Leif's face changed color.

"Well then," he said. "Well then."

One of the technicians fished something out of the pocket of the leather jacket. Leif took a step forward.

"What's that?"

A stiff, damp breeze struck the canvas of the tent as the technician took off his mask, held up his find, and weighed it in his hand.

"A bag of ten-kronor coins. Must be almost half a kilo of them."

The book Göran had given Nathalie was called *Sacrificial Bogs, Now and Then* and described, among other things, how Iron Age people buried their gifts to the gods in bogs. According to the book, the ritual lived on in many locations until well into Christian times. But there was a problem, though the people of the time were probably unaware of it: because the bodies never decayed, those who were buried never came to peace. They were said to hunger for fresh sacrifices, which might also explain why people suddenly vanished without a trace—even in modern times.

For these reasons, sacrificial bogs were considered both holy and dangerous. A place to fear and to worship.

Nathalie learned the words in chapter five by heart. She could recite them with the same ease with which she listed the vowels, or the local rivers.

When a sacrifice is desired, the weather becomes enraged.
When a sacrifice is chosen, the rage turns to peace.

One evening, a week or so after she received the book, she found Göran in his kitchen. Potatoes were boiling on the stove; steam rose from the pot and drifted out the open window. Göran himself was sitting at the kitchen table and invited Nathalie to join him.

"As you may have realized," he said, "there is reason to believe that Mossmarken is one of these sacrificial bogs, where... lost souls hunger for fresh sacrifices."

At first she couldn't make a sound. "Why?" she whispered, her voice cracked. "Why do you think that?"

"People have vanished from here without a trace," he said, his voice solemn. "Throughout time."

Then he told her about an old farmer in the nineteenth century who never returned from the autumn harvest. But there were also more recent stories of tourists who had disappeared after a visit to the area.

She wanted to ask about Göran's wife, but she didn't dare—she was scared of how he might react.

"The German in Tösse," Göran said, gazing at her for a long time.

According to the book, it was important to be on the alert if a storm subsided suddenly. It could mean that the undead had selected a victim, so it was crucial to find a safe place. Above all, it was crucial to avoid being out in a sacrificial bog.

The book was written in a surprisingly matter-of-fact tone. As if there could be no doubt that this was the way of the world, or at least the way of the bog.

According to Göran, people in this area had lived with

that knowledge for centuries. It had been passed on from generation to generation, and there were even stories of how the inhabitants had desperately tried to appease the undead. To keep them satisfied. But of course, it wasn't the sort of thing people discussed out loud. Because it meant sacrificing others. Sacrificing strangers, visitors. There was talk, for example, of how locals had together taken the life of a persistent tax collector and buried him in the mire.

As a child, Nathalie considered that book more valuable than all her toys put together. She lay under the covers reading by flashlight at night, and hid the book as soon as her parents appeared. The only person she told was her friend Julia.

Julia lived with her family on the other side of the bog. They were in the same class and played handball together. And Julia was there the first time she experienced something strange out on the bog. A particular sort of presence, something...different.

It happened one afternoon when they were in sixth year. They had agreed to meet at the hut they'd built out on the bog. Their parents didn't know about it—had they known, the girls would have been forbidden to play there.

On that day, a Saturday, they were sitting quietly among the trees, eating cold hot dogs and drinking chocolate milk.

After they ate, they each leaned against a pine tree and Nathalie dozed off.

When she woke up, the wind was blowing hard in her face

and at first she didn't know where she was. When she turned around, Julia was gone.

Nathalie gazed out across the landscape and got the feeling that...well, she couldn't put it into words at the time, but it had felt like she had dissolved and become one with her surroundings. She sensed an energy filling her, an energy that wasn't entirely benevolent.

And then, just as it said in the book, the wind died down as suddenly as it had come up. At that instant, she caught sight of Julia walking off across the mire. She called and called, but Julia didn't seem to hear; she just kept moving toward an area that was far too marshy to walk on.

"Julia!" she screamed. "Stop!"

She ran after her friend and caught hold of her arm, yanking it with all her strength.

"Wake up!"

Julia blinked. "Wake up?" she mumbled. "What do you mean?"

"You can't walk there. It was...it was like you were asleep."

"I must have been...I don't know what was happening," Julia said.

It was at the very beginning of that summer, the summer that changed everything.

That last summer.

When she was twelve.

One week later, the Lingonberry Girl was found in the bog.

Larsson's peat quarry had enjoyed its heyday in the seventies, but up to twenty-five men were employed there during the brief, intense harvesting period even into the twenty-first century.

A young worker from town had happened upon the ancient body, and he called for Julia's father. They all started digging together. The police were called, archeologists arrived, and the circus was under way.

It turned out to be a body from the Iron Age. Researchers would later guess that the woman had been sacrificed to the fertility gods in the hope of a good harvest. Hazel wands and clay pots were also found nearby.

Nathalie had felt a certain amount of pride. Göran was right—people really *had* been sacrificed and buried there once upon a time.

Shortly thereafter, near the end of summer, came the tragedies.

First one, then the other.

Before it was all over.

Leif and Maya were sitting in the café at police headquarters, deep in thought. The sound of clattering dishes and pots came from the kitchen, and on the other side of the frosted glass they could see the vague shadows of passers-by on the pavement.

The corpse in the bog was a man, Stefan Wiik, forty-eight, from Brålanda. He had disappeared in the early hours of 15 March 2012, after a visit to his girlfriend, who lived only a few hundred meters away.

It was remarkable enough to have found a body in the bog, but the fact that the body was from the current day and had been poled had brought an extra dimension to the case. What's more, a cloth bag of ten-kronor coins, identical to the one found on Johannes, had been discovered in Stefan Wiik's clothing.

Ten-kronor coins, again.

In other words, Johannes Ayeb and Stefan Wiik were not two isolated incidents. Although four years separated the crimes, they had probably been committed by the same person, or people.

The biologist who was staying in the cabin next to the manor house had probably spared Johannes from meeting the same fate as Stefan. The pit she thought she'd seen was apparently meant to be Johannes's grave—but someone had had enough time to fill it in again.

Leif had a grim look on his face.

"We've asked Trollhättan to find out who Stefan Wiik was. All I can imagine is that this has to do with some sort of underworld deal; it's the only thing that would explain this type of brutality. But the question is, how does Johannes fit into the picture? Drugs? Are there lots of drugs at the school?"

"Not that I know of," Maya said. "And like I said, Johannes seems to be a perfectly normal student. You really should talk to that girl, Nathalie. I heard she's been keeping vigil at his bedside."

"Yes, I suppose we do need to have a real conversation with her," Leif agreed, scratching the back of his neck. "And all those coins," he said in a low voice as he distractedly watched the blurry movements outside the window. "What's the deal with those?"

Maya leaned back. She wondered if she should say what she was thinking. But Leif beat her to it.

"Say it," he said. "I can tell you've got some idea."

She looked across the café, then back at him.

"I'm not sure you're going to like it; I'm not quite thinking along the same lines as you."

"Go on."

"Sacrifices," she said.

Leif looked at her. "What do you mean?"

"Well, that's what people did a long time ago," Maya said. "Made sure what they buried was as valuable as possible, to satisfy the gods. Food, tools and that sort of thing was furthest down the list. Number one in the ranking was people. To really be on the safe side, you made sure to bury them in really nice clothes, too, or..."

"Or?" Leif tried to get his index finger into the handle of his cup, but at last he gave up and gripped it with his whole hand.

"Or else maybe you filled their pockets with items of value."

"Did you learn that at the museum?" Leif asked. "You're not just letting your imagination run away with you?"

"Well, it's only a guess," Maya admitted. "But Stefan Wiik's grave looks like it belongs to a sacrifice."

Leif nodded. "So you're suggesting we're dealing with a... superstitious individual? Someone who believes in sacrificial gifts?"

"Yes, someone with a specific goal in mind. Just like in the past, when sacrifices were made to win wars or have good harvests, or to escape evil powers. Someone who's prepared to kill for it."

They fell into silence once more.

"What are you really saying, though?" Leif looked like he would prefer to avoid coming to the obvious conclusion. "That people are sacrificing to the gods still today? Is that what you mean?"

Maya looked at him. "*Someone* is, anyway," she said. "We can't turn a blind eye to the obvious link."

"You mean the Lingonberry Girl?"

"Yes." Maya took a sip of her coffee. "I mean the Lingonberry Girl. After all, she was poled. It can't be a coincidence that we found a modern-day corpse poled in the same bog."

The Åmål marina looked just as she remembered. They had come to the café there to celebrate the end of each school year. Waffles and ice cream. She always chose the same flavors: blueberry, chocolate, pistachio. Or strawberry. Never vanilla.

Back then, she was a perfectly average girl.

Someone completely different.

In a different time.

Mum and Dad got coffee, poured milk out of tiny, round plastic cups with foil lids. Dad always had trouble opening his.

Could you give me a hand, sweetie?

There had been tenderness in that. It was in his voice, that broad, patient voice that emerged sometimes. She remembered wishing she could lie down and rest inside it.

And the emotion in her mother's eyes, because Nathalie had completed another year of school, because they were a family that stuck together no matter what. It was a warm, loving gaze—but it also contained something left unsaid. As if, through her eyes, she were giving Nathalie space to fill with her own possibilities.

And the sun. Always the sun. That was how she remembered it.

It was the same now, as the autumn sun made fireworks

in the water between the anchored boats. They had moved the ice-cream counter to a different corner, but otherwise everything was the same. The chairs and tables were probably new, though; she didn't recall.

The marina. The pride of the city. "The loveliest in Sweden," someone had once written somewhere, and since then it had just been true. This was where you came in the summer, here or Örnäs, the nearby swimming beach.

Summer was over now. But this was the only place Nathalie considered when she decided to visit Åmål and have coffee. She had no idea if there were any other cafés—there probably were, probably ones with milk steamed in shiny espresso machines rather than poured out of tiny, round plastic cups with foil lids. But she didn't know about them.

So she ended up here, in the city where she'd gone to school and where she might have lived now if what happened had never happened. Or maybe not.

She probably would have moved anyway.

Knock, knock, knock.

Not now.

Be calm, breathe.

Her thoughts were interrupted when she felt a shadow approaching her table.

"Nathalie? Is that you?"

She looked up. It was that police photographer, Maya.

"Hi," she said.

Maya was wearing black jeans, red trainers and a beige T-shirt under a tailored black jacket. She was holding a tray with a bottle of water, an enormous Danish, a mug and a carafe of coffee.

"Nice to see a familiar face," Maya said. "I used to live here, but now it feels like all the residents have been replaced."

"I know exactly what you mean," Nathalie said.

She noticed herself feeling as she had last time—Maya somehow made her feel at ease.

"Would it be a bother if I joined you?"

"No, no, that's fine."

Maya put down her tray and sat in one of the chairs. The background noise was commercial radio: top forty and insistent sales jingles.

"Did you hear what..." Maya appeared to be choosing her words carefully: "...what we found out in the mire?"

"You mean the body?"

"Yes."

"Yeah, I heard."

Maya looked at her. "A lot has been going on out there recently. And I don't think you were seeing things or making a mistake; I think you really did see that grave."

Nathalie lowered her head. "Thanks. That's nice of you to say."

Maybe, she thought, *Maya is serious*. Or maybe she just

wanted to be nice and make sure Nathalie didn't feel so silly for dragging the police out to the bog for no reason. Seldom had she felt so embarrassed.

"I don't suppose you've spoken more with Leif Berggren?" Maya asked.

"No, not since the last time I saw you, although he called and said he'd like to meet me. It's just that I don't quite understand what he wants."

"Leif has been speaking to Johannes's friends too . . . we're a little curious about him, ever since we found this new body. We'd like to know what sort of life he lived."

"I don't really know what to say," Nathalie said. "I don't actually know much about his life. We only met a few weeks ago, so we don't know each other very well."

"But you've been sitting with him at the hospital?"

"Yes, it sort of just happened, I don't know . . . so he doesn't have to lie there all alone."

Nathalie's body felt heavy, as if something were dragging her down. Why hadn't she stayed home in Gothenburg and let everything be? Why hadn't she chosen another site, any other wetlands? She should have stuck to the scientific world, where everything could be classified and a wetland was a collection of well-documented chemical and biological reactions that behaved according to established patterns.

Where wetlands were just wetlands.

Not seas of dead and lost souls.

People disappear out there.

Was she the one who'd said it? Or had she only thought it?

She realized that Maya was leaning forward and resting her chin in her hand. Gazing seriously at Nathalie.

"Disappear?"

"What?"

"You said people disappear out there."

"I did?"

"Do you know something, something you should tell us?" Maya asked.

Nathalie squirmed. Could she handle a discussion about what was gnawing at her?

"There are folks who say people have always disappeared out in the mire."

Maya's eyes were fixed on her.

"If that's true, wouldn't people have realized it earlier?" Maya said.

Nathalie felt a pressure in her chest, a sudden flare of anger mixed with deep exhaustion and possibly a certain amount of confusion.

"You're thinking about that little boy who disappeared— when was that? Ten years ago?" Maya asked.

"Yes, but it's not just him. There are more..."

Silence fell between them.

"Folks, you say," Maya repeated. "Like who?"

"There's someone you should talk to. He's given several

tips to the police, advising them to search Mossmarken for missing people. But nothing has come of it. Until now."

"Is that true?" Maya asked.

She nodded. "His name is Göran Dahlberg. He lives up there. You can tell him I sent you."

"Okay," Maya said, looking surprised.

She took a bite of her Danish, bending suddenly over her plate when crumbs rained down.

"Where do you live?" she asked then, as if the topic of Mossmarken had become too touchy. "When you're not renting that cottage, I mean."

"I live in Gothenburg," Nathalie said. "But I'm from here, originally..." She hesitated before pressing on. "Or at least, I grew up in Mossmarken. Göran is our old neighbor. *Was* our neighbor, for many years."

"I see," Maya said. "Did you go to school here in Åmål, then?"

"Yes, until I was twelve."

"Which one?"

"Södra. Then I moved to Gothenburg."

Maya smiled. "I went to Södra too. But that must have been twenty-five years before you did. And I stayed here, at least for a while. My parents still live in Åmål—I was actually visiting them right before I came here."

Then came the reaction. Maya's face froze; her gaze cut through the air.

"Hold on, you lived in Mossmarken...you weren't the one..."

Nathalie didn't respond.

"The one whose parents...?" Maya looked at her, eyes wide.

Nathalie nodded slowly. "You might be thinking of my dad," she said with surprising ease. "How he...shot my mum. And then himself."

Maya closed her eyes. "Oh my God. I remember it so well. I was just about to move to New York. I think it was that same year. I thought about you a lot back then, how you were left all on your own. I thought a lot about what that was like for you. And wasn't there some accident out there too, right before what happened with your parents? A young woman died?"

"*Yes*," Nathalie heard herself saying. "*That was Tracy. My best friend Julia's older sister.*"

She really didn't mean to sound so emphatic. Suddenly she found herself standing up, taking her jacket, and leaving the café, Maya's frantic apologies drifting after her like a cloud.

Ellen was speaking to a colleague when Maya stepped through the entrance of the art school. The building had originally been the People's House, the local meeting place, and consisted of an auditorium, offices and some classrooms.

The walls were covered in paintings and posters advertising exhibitions and lectures. One corner was full of half-finished sculptures in twisted positions, waiting for someone to have mercy on them.

Ellen's curly hair was in a big bun on top of her head, and her eyes were circled by a thin stripe of black eyeliner.

"Hi there," Maya greeted Ellen and her colleague.

"Hi, Maya."

Ellen finished her conversation and turned to Maya.

"Should we head over right away? I'm hungry."

"Yes, Vanja and the others are already at the bistro."

The path through the old industrial area ran from the gravel entry where the workers had once passed through the gates up to the factories with a chimney pointing at the sky. Here and there small groups of people stood, chatting in various languages; the colorful lanterns in the café's outdoor seating area swayed lazily in the autumn breeze. The notes of a bossa nova floated from an open window.

"I heard you were up at the mire again," Ellen said.

"Yes, I know rumors have been going around the school. Actually, I'm the one who found the body."

"Are you serious?" Ellen stopped and stared at Maya. "Jesus, that's creepy. What do they know about it? Or are you bound by confidentiality?"

"Yeah, there's not much I can tell you. On the other hand, there's also not much I know."

"Naturally, like I said, our students are feeling pretty spooked. All kinds of rumors are running rampant."

"Understandable," said Maya.

Once a month there was a concert in the bistro, and as always it was a full house. Lots of people came from Åmål, Säffle, Mellerud and other nearby towns.

Maya and Ellen took a seat at a table already occupied by Vanja and one of her friends. Daniel Lemma would take the stage in an hour.

Maya and Ellen each ordered a glass of red wine and a sourdough pizza with pesto and prosciutto. The others had eaten already and ordered espresso and cognac instead.

"We're talking about the place where we ended up," Vanja said.

"The place?" Maya asked.

"This place. Fengerskog."

"Well, don't blame me," Maya said. "It's all Ellen's fault. I just do as she says, and she said *move here*."

"Things are definitely a little unsettled at the moment," Ellen said, "but it's not because there's anything wrong with Fengerskog."

"That wasn't exactly what we were talking about," Vanja said. "We were talking about the school, this arts-and-crafts stuff we can't quite put our finger on. We don't understand what the movement is all about."

"Oh, that. It just wants to have a good time," Ellen said. "It's satisfied with itself in a way we can never allow real art to be."

"Real art?" Vanja's friend asked, her forehead creased.

"Yes, exactly," Ellen said. "Real art doesn't quite mesh with this cozy organic lifestyle concept you find all over Fengerskog. It doesn't thrive when placed side by side with the broader, more accessible handicraft movement that makes regular people feel *arty*, even though they're not."

Ellen smiled, revealing her dimples.

"It could have been a big mistake to try to make them coexist in such a small area," she went on, "but for some reason it works in Fengerskog. In my opinion. At first I was a little nervous when we opened the school here. I thought we might lose our soul and our direction."

Maya took a sip of wine and considered her friend for a long moment, an amused smile on her lips.

"Just so I've understood you correctly," she said. "*Real* art, that's what you and your school represent, I assume?"

Ellen gave her a meaningful look. "What kind of a question is that? Of course it is. And so do you!"

All four of them laughed.

"If I can share what I think," Vanja said, "all the different kinds of art are necessary. Or, more accurately, there is space for everything."

"I agree. Everything except elitism," Maya said.

Ellen gave a loud laugh and raised her glass. "Hypocrites. I know you agree with me. Cheers."

"Hello there!" Oskar had approached their table. He rested his hand on Maya's shoulder and bent down so she could hear him over the loud restaurant. She placed her hand over his.

"Come and sit down," she said, making room.

He squeezed in next to her. They hadn't seen each other for a while and she felt the sudden urge to kiss him. He looked so...open somehow. So new. So unspoiled and vulnerable.

"It's my birthday today," he said. "Next round's on me."

This was met by loud protests.

"Not on your life," Maya said; she beckoned a waiter and ordered five tequilas.

"How old are you?" she asked.

"Twenty-seven," Oskar said.

Maya sighed lightly, bent toward him, and placed her lips near his ear. "Then you're too young for me."

His gaze faltered, as if her forwardness had almost knocked him off balance. Then he shook his head slightly and moved his leg a little closer to hers until they were touching.

At that instant, Maya's phone rang.

It was Leif. He sounded eager in his own low-key way.

"Maya, I was thinking about those pictures you showed me."

"Oh, right," she said. She stood up and moved to a corner where she could talk undisturbed.

"I'd like to take a closer look at them," he said.

"Yes, I was thinking the same thing. I can send them to you, but I'm not at home just now so it'll have to be later tonight."

"That's fine. Just do it as soon as you can."

"Listen," she said, "I happened to run into Nathalie today. Have you spoken to her yet?"

"No, I haven't got that far," Leif sighed.

"She had some remarkable things to say. You and I really need to talk *about* her, and you need to talk *to* her."

"Sure, let's meet up tomorrow. I'm heading up to Quagmire Manor in the morning, and I can pick you up on my way."

"Good. I'll get back to you about the pictures soon."

"Great."

"Who was that?" Ellen asked curiously when Maya returned to the table.

"Nothing special, but I'm sorry—I have to head home now," she said. "Hope you all have a nice evening."

She turned to Oskar. "And you—have a terrific birthday."

Then she took her jacket and moved through the crowd and out of the bistro as the band came onstage and the intro of "Haze" filled the room.

It had become a routine. Nathalie arrived at the hospital and spoke to Johannes's mother for a while before relieving her with a promise to call if anything happened.

Nothing ever happened.

Johannes's condition was perfectly stable but unchanged. Sometimes she tried to imagine what it would be like when he woke up. It was impossible. What would they say to each other? Who would they be?

She leaned back in her chair and looked at Johannes, who was still on his back with his eyes closed, tubes and wires everywhere. Then she leaned forward and began to speak in a voice that was almost a whisper, the way she had grown used to doing although she doubted the nurse across the room had any interest in listening.

"I thought I would tell you about the first thing that happened that summer," she began. "We basically only hung out with each other, me and Julia. I think the reason I wanted to spend so much time with her was really her big sister . . . Tracy. Just that. Just her name. I was so jealous."

She had slept over at Julia's, as she sometimes did at weekends, and she woke up very early on Sunday morning. Maybe it was because she needed to use the bathroom, or maybe there was some other reason she got out of bed and walked downstairs so quietly that no one heard.

Maybe she hoped the door next to the bathroom, the one to Tracy's room, would be ajar as it sometimes was in the summer, so that her spying could occur more naturally.

Tracy was seventeen and had had several boyfriends who often slept over. She was on the Pill and partied at weekends— at the park in the summer and at the disco in Vikenborg in the winter. This was a world Nathalie was moving toward, but it was still foreign to her.

Tracy was the poster child for that world; she hinted at lands yet undiscovered. She was perfect. She had wavy, medium-brown hair, a year-round tan, pretty makeup, brilliant blue eyes and jeans that were ripped in exactly the right way. She was cool. Unattainable, and gifted besides. She wrote poems about love and sex and liquor and cigarettes; Nathalie and Julia read them in secret. They seemed sad somehow, although Nathalie didn't understand much about them. Tracy almost never smiled. It was like she was above that sort of thing.

Nathalie and Julia themselves completely lacked any of this mystique. They had known each other since first year, and now they were on their way to becoming perfectly average teenagers. It was clear that they would never, ever come even close to being like Tracy.

One time Nathalie found herself witness to a fight between Tracy and her mother, Yvonne. She had been sitting on the stairs to wait for Julia and caught a glimpse of the ongoing conflict in the kitchen.

"You are not to go there again, do you hear me?" Yvonne hissed, her voice sharp.

"You can't stop me," Tracy said with the same explosive rage.

"Oh yes I can."

At first there was silence, but then Tracy's tone changed and grew gentle and pleading.

"Please, Mum, I really want to go."

There was another silence as Yvonne tried to orient herself. Then an embrace, as they came to a compromise they could both accept—a compromise that meant the finale of the short play: a fleeting, highly concentrated drama about teenage conflicts, stormy feelings and power.

That Sunday morning, Nathalie approached the bathroom. Tracy's door was slightly open, as she'd hoped. A narrow crack. The pale morning light forced its way through the blinds and settled on the floor in waves. She had little trouble catching a glimpse of Tracy's bare, brown back through the narrow crack. White lines where her bikini top had been. They were both asleep in there, half tangled in each other. Almost naked.

Something sucked at her. From underneath. From inside.

The desire to be like Tracy. Her life would never be complete if she didn't reach that goal.

She never told Julia how much she admired her sister. Maybe it was understood that everyone felt that way. It was self-evident. On the other hand, they often talked about how Tracy had sex in her room sometimes, and a thought like that led to endless ruminations on how they could catch a glimpse or hear some of this activity. On a few occasions they had sneaked down at night and pressed their ears to the door, but with no results.

That morning, Julia woke up early as well. She came down the stairs silently and stood beside Nathalie. They didn't speak; they just stood at the little gap.

Then the bodies began to move and all the naked skin disappeared under the covers; instead came sounds, heavy breathing that turned into something else. Soft at first, then hard.

Then silence. Muffled laughter.

Was this something she would eventually take part in? She looked at Julia. It felt absolutely unreal. It couldn't be possible.

Yet they went back to Julia's room that morning and lay down close to each other. They ran their hands over one another's bodies. Their skin, the smells. They swore never to tell anyone else about any of it.

After a short walk around the area, Maya and Leif entered the doors to Quagmire Manor. The chandeliers cast a glimmering sheen over the soft, dark red carpets, over the easy chairs and the sofas across the salon.

"Does she know we're coming?" Maya asked.

"Yes."

They walked around to have a look. The restaurant was to the left and the salon to the right; the rooms were divided by a wide foyer with large arches in either direction. On the far side of the salon was a fireplace, and in front of it, four easy chairs and a table full of books and magazines.

They approached the bulletin board and read a sheet of paper tacked to it.

Create the life you've always wished for

Do you want to live a truer life? Do you want to get that job you've always desired, be cured of an illness, or find your dream partner? Or do you simply want that gorgeous sports car so you can enjoy the jealous glances of your neighbor? Whatever you want, it can become reality. You are in charge! Your thoughts can make it happen! Nothing, and we mean NOTHING, is impossible.

179

MatrixMind will teach you how to use quantum physics and the miracle of the law of attraction in your everyday existence to create the life YOU want.

～

Please contact Agneta von Sporre—yoga instructor, personal development coach and certified instructor in applied quantum physics.

～

(Price: 1,200 kronor per hour for personal counseling and a customized strategic action plan.)

They exchanged glances. Maya raised her eyebrows and put her hand to her mouth to hide a laugh. Leif's eyes narrowed.

"It's not even funny, damn it." He bent down to her. "Everywhere you go nowadays there's a new-age fool bringing out quantum physics like fucking ketchup and squirting it all over their favorite spiritual movement. Believing you can change the physical world with your thoughts. What utter drivel. It's madness."

Maya looked around and whispered with a smile, "Although now that you mention it, you're no better than *Lady Agneta von Certified Flimmity-Flammity*. When you claim that something you know nothing about is made-up craziness, you're playing on the same field as she is. You're opponents on the same team." Maya winked. "Just so you know."

He turned to her. "The same team? What do you mean by that?"

"Rhetoric, Leif. You need to think about your rhetoric. Just like Lady Quantum-Sporre. She and her ilk wallow in assumptions; they roll around in cheap turns of phrase. You do exactly the same thing."

"I'm sorry, but what am I supposed to say?"

"A more proper way to express yourself, or at least a way to position yourself in this matter, would be something along the lines of *Given my limited knowledge, and considering what we know today about how the universe works, I judge the power of thought to be bullshit.*"

She sauntered away from him, then turned around.

"There could actually be a kernel of truth where you least expect one, or want to see one, so it would be stupid to throw the baby out with the bathwater, so to speak."

"A kernel of truth..." He rolled his eyes and looked at her, sighing. "Maya, you're just the same; I can barely tell you've been in New York for so long...but everyone knows the whole concept is total crap."

Maya watched as a tall woman approached and lowered her voice to a whisper. "Your rhetoric, Leif."

"Are you Leif Berggren? With the police?" the woman asked.

"I certainly am," Leif said, putting out his hand.

"Agneta von Sporre," Agneta said, her upper body canting downward as she greeted him. Then she turned to Maya and repeated the same solemn greeting. "Agneta."

"Maya."

"And you are?" Agneta asked.

"A photographer. I know the area. I've been showing Leif around a little bit."

"Okay. And I see you're looking at my course." She turned to the bulletin board. "That's my little enterprise on the side, you could say."

She looked at them with an expression Maya suspected was meant to signal sincerity.

"You know, now that I think about it," Agneta went on, "maybe it could be useful for the police!" She closed her eyes. "It's coming to me now, how you could learn to...sort of *picture* yourselves solving all the crimes. And then the powers of the universe come in and"—she waved one hand around in front of her—"it must be so. That's called the law of attraction. It's a power of nature. Pure science."

Leif cleared his throat. "We came here to talk to you and possibly your employees," he said gruffly, as if he were calling on every ounce of self-control he had. "And we also wanted to take a look around the manor."

"Oh, it's so lovely here," said Agneta. "We have two large conference rooms and we can offer—"

"Thanks," Leif interrupted, "but I was also wondering whether any of your guests happen to be in."

Agneta knitted her brow.

"Not at the moment, I'm afraid. It's possible that the girl down in the cottage is home."

"We've already been in contact with her," Leif said.

"Oh? Well then! Why don't we head to the office to talk."

~

"There, there, take a deep breath," Maya said, placing her hand on Leif's back as they reached the car park. "Are you sure you don't want to *create the life you've always wished for*, Leif?"

"Don't think so," he said.

"No, at least not with her help, maybe," Maya said, looking down at Nathalie's cottage. "It looks dark down there."

"Maybe she's at the hospital," said Leif.

"Yes," said Maya. "So, have you been reading up on her?"

"Yes, I checked her out. I have to say, I was surprised that it's her. I suppose we'll have to be a little cautious with her."

"What do you think about what she told me?" Maya asked.

"Which part?"

"Don't you listen?" She sighed. "About all the rumors. How people just disappear here in Mossmarken. Without a trace?"

Leif shot her a skeptical glance. "Those rumors have always been around."

"But there was some man called—"

"Göran Dahlberg!" Leif chuckled. "Yes, I know of him."

"Nathalie said he tried to get you to listen."

"Yes, he certainly did," Leif sighed. "And we *did* listen; we checked up on his information. We know the schoolboy was here when he went missing, but aside from him, only *one* of the missing people can be said with certainty to have been in Mossmarken around the time of their disappearance."

"Who's that?"

"Göran's own wife. And she's been living in Australia or New Zealand, or somewhere like that, for decades now. She had explicitly told her friends that she couldn't stand him any longer. You have to understand, Maya, that all this malarkey started with the Lingonberry Girl. We'd hardly ever heard of Mossmarken before the Larssons dug her up. But it was like a dam broke."

Maya pulled on a pair of thin gloves.

"You are planning to talk to Göran Dahlberg, though, aren't you?" she asked.

"You've never met him, Maya, he's a...how should I put it? An original. There's a lot going on in that head of his. Just like..." He gestured toward the manor house.

"But I still don't get it," said Maya. "Now that we've found Stefan Wiik, that has to bring all this to a new level, doesn't it? Stefan vanished from Brålanda four years ago and now he pops up here. You have to admit that's a little odd."

Leif gazed out at the bog. "Sure, but let's take a look at the connection between Stefan and Johannes before we dig our way back through the malarkey again."

"Okay," Maya said, "but did you get a chance to look at the pictures I sent? Of the crouching figure?"

"Yes." Leif rubbed his hands over his arms as if to get warm. "I agree with you. It really does look like someone trying to hide, or spying on you. But like you said, it's hard to make out any details."

"Yeah, I tried to enlarge it," Maya said, "but it only got blurry."

"I'll have to assign someone to ask around about it," Leif said.

Maya shrugged. "I can do it; I was planning on going around and taking some pictures for my own use anyway. I can say I want to take pictures of people who live around here or something, as an excuse, so we don't have to send your people all the way out here."

"You're not a police officer, Maya."

"That's the whole point."

"But you're employed by the police. You can't just do whatever you want."

She shrugged. "This much," she said, holding her fingers a centimeter apart. "I'm only employed a tiny bit. I won't mingle with any suspects, I promise."

Leif smiled. "I'm not going to sanction anything like that. But whatever you do, be careful. And most importantly," he said, looking at her with a stern gaze, "only tell me stuff I want to know."

Maya put her hand over her heart.

"I promise."

The summer before that last summer, Nathalie and Julia created a secret club, the Ghost-hunters' Society, and decided to build a secret hut out on the bog. There was a lot of construction material at Julia's house, and it seemed unlikely that anyone would miss it; her dad was a big collector and although he was good at sorting all his scrap materials, they assumed it was impossible for him to keep track of every nail and board.

One day, Julia and Nathalie were all alone at Julia's house. Their parents had gone to Åmål and would be away all day. They were going to do homework and watch movies. At least, that's what they said. Instead they went straight to the workshop and the storage sheds, where there were stacks of construction materials, piles of electronics, mountains of appliances and shelves of odds and ends.

"Check this out," Julia said, gathering up some nearby boards. She tied a rope around them so they would be easier to transport. She made three more identical carryable loads so they could each take two.

"And here's a hammer!" Nathalie raised the tool. "There are at least ten more, so we might not even have to put it back."

She kept browsing, gathering nails of all sizes in a box, which she put in her backpack.

They exchanged pleased looks and set out. But the material was too heavy.

"Hold on, I know," Julia said. She found a wagon to load everything into, and together they pulled it into the bog. They had packed a bag with juice and chocolate bars in case they got hungry, so they could spend all afternoon in the bog.

"Let's start by putting up a wall here, okay, comrade Ghost-hunter?" Julia said when they arrived at the site they'd selected, a grove of low pines. She held up a board to show what she meant.

"Looks good, comrade Ghost-hunter," Nathalie said, and they started hammering. It echoed across the landscape.

A few hours later, their little hut had walls and a roof. They considered their handiwork.

"I guess I'd imagined it would be a little bigger," Nathalie said.

"Me too," said Julia, looking up at the roof. "And it's not watertight; the rain will get in."

Then they heard a voice behind them.

"I can help you, if you want."

Nathalie and Julia were startled. It was Göran. They hadn't heard him approach.

"You're doing a nice job." He knocked on one wall and raised his eyebrows in appreciation.

Julia shot Nathalie a frightened look. "We ... we have to go home now."

"I'll take care of the last little bit. Just tell me how you want it," he said.

The next time they visited their hut, it was perfect. Exactly as they'd imagined. It was just the right size, with stable walls and a watertight roof. On the floor they spread a cow hide that had been stashed away in one of the sheds at Julia's house. They put up a clothesline for wet socks and arranged baskets of paper, pens, food and games into a small cabinet Göran had built in one corner.

They peered through binoculars; they discussed their observations; they kept a log of suspected ghost activity.

6.40 p.m. A cold wind, four minutes. Believed to be a malicious spirit.

And they read from the book Göran had given her.

It was so innocent, so harmless. Until all hell broke loose the next summer. When it did, Nathalie had the feeling it was all their fault. That they had tempted the spirits, woken them up.

FOUR

The gravel road that led past the houses curved around the north edge of the bog. Maya had driven a few slow passes of it earlier, hunched over the wheel, her eyes on the surroundings like the flitting beam of a flashlight.

Several of the houses were empty; their occupants seemed to have suddenly abandoned them to the forest and the vegetation. Letterboxes were open at the side of the road, stuffed with circulars and newspapers that had swelled in the rain. In her world, homes were of great value; here they seemed like something you should be happy to have escaped.

She was only a ten-minute drive from Fengerskog with its bulgur salads and spirulina smoothies served by the baristas at the café, and yet these were two wildly different worlds.

She had done some research. Four of the houses along this road were supposedly still inhabited. She had a decent idea about two of them: Göran Dahlberg's house at the far end, by the turning circle; and the Larssons' near the start of the road.

The other two houses were owned by a moonlighting farmer in his fifties and a family who raised beef cattle, respectively; those two houses weren't visible from the road. She intended to visit each house and farm, including the abandoned ones, and decided to start with the Larssons'.

The house was pretty if past its prime, set on a small rise with a view of the bog. At the edge of the road was a white metal sign that said "Larsson's Peat" in worn letters. The property sloped down to the large peat barn: a decaying monstrosity of graying wood with a small railroad track that ran up a steep slope on one side. That was where the turf had once been carried in to be unloaded, she assumed.

The gravel drive up to the house was edged with statuary of dogs and gnomes. A window was open on the first floor.

Maya parked the car in the middle of the yard. She stepped out and approached a big storage shed; its door was ajar. She could hear sounds coming from inside, someone hammering.

"Hello?" she called.

No response.

She walked in and looked around. There were tools and gadgets from floor to ceiling, in quantities she couldn't recall ever having seen before. The sound seemed to be emanating from a room behind a door on the other side of the shed. Her eyes roamed the walls and piles of stuff; she was having a hard time taking in the sheer volume.

Someone in this family was clearly a thing-finder or a junk collector, or both. In one spot, several bathtubs were stacked on top of one another. Bicycle tubes and chains hung one after the next from the ceiling; it was hard to imagine how anyone could ever find a use for them all. Refrigerators, ancient ovens, boxes, tins, jars, barrels. It was almost disturbing.

"Are you looking for someone?"

She hadn't realized that the noise had stopped.

A man in overalls was standing in the doorway and watching her with reserved suspicion. He had a lightweight hat and a neat beard.

"Hi," she said, hurrying over to introduce herself. "Apologies for intruding. I called out, but maybe you didn't hear me."

"Oh. Sure, sure."

"My name is Maya and I'm from Fengerskog; I'm an artist. I'm working on a series of photographs in the area, and I wanted to start by just introducing myself. In case you were wondering what kind of shady person was sneaking around."

"Photographs? You're saying there're things to take pictures of out here?"

"It's a very beautiful place. In its own special way. It's peaceful and a little mystical," Maya attempted.

He didn't appear to agree. "Peaceful isn't the word I would use. Does this have something to do with all the devilry that's been going on out here recently?"

"You mean—"

"One person beaten and another found buried," he interrupted. "It's not exactly fun to be living in the middle of it. Who knows what might happen next? So you're not a journalist?"

"Definitely not," Maya said.

"Good. Because I've had enough of those." He considered her. "An artist, you say?"

"Yes. A photographer."

The light of the fluorescent tubes painted his face in chilly tones.

"You harvest peat here?" Maya said, steering the conversation in a different direction.

"A long time ago. This area became a nature reserve, so we had to stop. We have the forest instead. We work with that." He wiped his forehead with a handkerchief.

"I see." She looked around. "This is an impressive collection of stuff you have."

"Forty years," he said, raising his eyebrows and coming close to a smile. "Without cleaning it out even once. And before that, my parents—they were also good at collecting. You can find just about anything, if you don't mind looking around for a while."

"I can believe that," Maya said, gazing at all the junk.

A brief pause.

"Listen," she went on. "I was thinking of taking some portraits for this project too. Of people who live around the bog."

"Portraits?"

"Yes. Pictures of the people who live here."

"Really? What would be interesting about that? It's just us. Those of us who're left. Me and Yvonne here; Göran, Texas. And Laila and her family. We're not very interesting."

Maya smiled. "People always say that. But it's almost never true."

"So it's not for some newspaper article?" he said, still suspicious about journalists.

"No, what I'm working on is a photography project, you could say."

He grinned. "So you want to take pictures of me, you're saying?"

"I'd love to. What's your name, by the way? If I may ask?"

"Peder. Now?"

"Not necessarily. I could come back another day if that's better for you."

He bent down, picked up an empty soft drink can, and tossed it into a pile of other glasses and cans. "No, I don't know. I don't think I'm..." He paused for a moment. "Do you have your camera with you?"

"Yes, I do."

"Did you want me to go and get my wife too, or...?"

"That would be great."

Peder's wife, Yvonne, was a stout woman with a steady gaze and a firm handshake. Maya quickly told her about her photography project and, if anything, Yvonne seemed flattered.

It never ceased to amaze Maya that the people she wanted to photograph often took such a benevolent view of her. They almost always wanted to participate and they seldom had any demands or objections, even though they didn't know her and had no real idea of what she planned to do with the pictures.

What's more—and perhaps this was the strangest part of all—it was extremely rare for anyone to refuse to sign the release form she'd drawn up to give herself free rein to publish the images or show them at an exhibition.

"Is this okay?" she asked, holding out the paper. "I have a few books in the car, if you want to get an idea of things I've done in the past, before you sign."

"No problem," they both said. "I'm sure it's fine."

When the formalities were over, she asked them to stand in the center of the storage shed and she selected a wide-angle lens to capture as much of the interior as possible. It really was a beautiful mess, a liberating chaos yet with a hint of order. That collection of bathtub taps was sorted by type, after all, even though they were buried in a pile of carburetors and bike pedals.

When she was finished in the shed, she wanted to take some pictures outside, with the peat barn and the bog in the background.

"Can we see the pictures later?" Yvonne asked, putting her chubby hands on her hips.

"Of course. I'll even come by and drop off a copy of the best one," Maya said.

"That'll be nice," Yvonne said, glancing at her husband. "Maybe we can make it into a Christmas card and send it around to our friends."

"Definitely," Maya said. "It might not be all that Christmassy, but it would still be fun."

Afterward they followed her to her car.

"I'm also interested in the history of this area," Maya said. "From what I hear, Peder, you were the one who found the old bog body here?"

"Oh, yes..." Peder looked at the ground. "There was such a damn fuss after that."

Maya's hand was on the car door.

"I can imagine," she said. "By the way, I met someone you know around here the other day. Nathalie. She was best friends with your daughter Julia, wasn't she?"

They looked at her as if they thought they had misheard.

"You met Nathalie Nordström? She's here?" Yvonne asked.

"She's renting over at the manor for a few months while she finishes a dissertation in biology. Otherwise she lives in Gothenburg."

"Is that so? Well, we did wonder how everything turned out for her," Yvonne said. "She just disappeared. Everything happened so fast. Oh, I'm sure you know about all that... what happened to her parents and so on?"

Maya nodded. "Yes, I lived in Åmål at the time and there was a lot of talk."

"Okay, well, I need to get back to work," Peder said, heading back for the shed.

"Just one more thing," Maya said. "Did you happen to be out in the bog last Thursday, near where the unconscious guy was found? Over there." She pointed.

"On the bog? No, not that I recall," Peder said. "Right, Yvonne? Why do you ask?"

"I was taking pictures out there and I accidentally caught someone in the frame; I just wanted to know who it was, and I thought you might—"

"We seldom have any reason to be over there. We mostly stay along this edge," Peder said. "So, if that was all...?"

"Okay. Thanks," Maya said, smiling.

"He gets so pouty when he can't potter around in there," Yvonne said once Peder had left. "Anyway, what was I going to say... right, are you planning to take pictures of the bog itself too?"

"Yes, I was planning on it."

"Then you have to be careful. We had a daughter, Tracy, I'm sure you've heard about it. She drowned in the bog. There are some parts of it that aren't safe. Keep to the walkways, is my advice."

Maya was taken aback by her frankness. "I remember that," she said. "That was also such a terrible thing."

"Yes," Yvonne said, looking tired. "And now they found a man buried there. And the guy you mentioned, the one who was found unconscious. You start to wonder what sort of place you're living in. Who will want to buy our farm now? No one."

She looked up at the house.

"Then again, no one wanted to before either. We've put it on the market three times. It won't sell. We'll never get away from here."

Up at the house, two girls were peering out of the front door. One was about five; the other was maybe eight.

"Those are Julia's girls," Yvonne said, smiling at them. "Say hello to the lady out here, you two," she called.

"Hi!" the girls called in unison.

Maya said hello back. "Are you babysitting?" she asked.

"Babysitting?"

Yvonne didn't seem to understand at first, and Maya nodded toward the two girls.

"Oh, that's what you meant. No, they live with us, to all intents and purposes. Almost all the time. Julia has...she works at the bank in Åmål and...she has enough to deal with on her own. And their dad isn't much help. He's not exactly the dependable type."

Maya couldn't stop herself. She realized that she was

taking advantage of Yvonne's willingness to get personal, to share intimate information.

"I told her from the start," Yvonne went on, shaking her head. "You should stay away from that type. It will only bring problems. He did hash and...I'm afraid he beat her too. But he won't be able to get at the children. We've made sure of that."

"Do you have custody of them?"

"No, not really. But neither Julia nor their father can even take care of themselves, so they know that Nova and Lilly will do best here. Peder spends most of his time working, of course, but I have plenty of time. It would almost seem too empty around here if there were no kids to take care of."

It all started with the discovery of the old corpse. It happened during a period of intense work in the peat quarry; school had just finished and a bunch of boys from town were working on Julia's farm.

Nathalie was there when it happened. She and Julia had recently turned twelve and they were sitting on a blanket in the sun and playing cards for acorns. Nathalie had just lost her last acorn when Julia's dad came up to the yard. His face was red and shiny with sweat. He walked up with a rag in his hand and stopped next to them.

When Nathalie looked up, his gaze was somewhere else entirely.

"We found something," he said.

"What?" Julia asked.

"Where's Mum? I think I need to call the police." He walked into the house.

A police car showed up straightaway, and then people came from the cultural center and soon they called in staff from the museum in Karlstad. Even the newspaper showed up eventually, and with that there was a complete hullabaloo at the farm. Julia's mum made coffee and put out tray after tray of pastries. Nathalie heard a man being interviewed by the local paper.

"There's no way to be certain yet," he said, "but signs indicate that it's the body of a young woman who lived a very long time ago. Perhaps as long ago as the birth of Christ. There are long-standing theories that this site was used as a sacrificial bog, and now we may have found concrete evidence. We've found clothing and some sort of gold amulet. It's a fantastic discovery."

It took several days for everything to calm down. Nathalie practically lived with Julia during that time; it was exciting to be at the center of the action.

Julia's father was less amused. He wanted to keep harvesting his peat, keep working.

"Enough is enough," he said. "All this fuss over an old body."

The museum took possession of the body and eventually it found a home there and went by the name "Lingonberry Girl."

Around the same time, Tracy had met a new guy, an older one. People said he was almost thirty.

"It's disgusting," Julia said. "He's an old man."

"It's exciting," Nathalie taunted her.

"Nah, just disgusting."

But they hardly saw Tracy any more. Her new boyfriend almost never came out to Mossmarken. And Tracy herself had rented a room in Åmål to be closer to her school.

But one Friday night Nathalie was in Åmål with her parents. They were going to have dinner with friends and she packed a bundle of comics and came along.

"Is it okay if I go out?" she asked after dinner.

"Where are you going to go?" Her mother's voice was softened by wine. In the background she could hear the others playing records and discussing songs. Someone opened the patio door to let out cigarette smoke.

Nathalie shrugged. "Dunno. The kiosk."

Her mother smiled and took out her wallet. "Of course you can go to the kiosk. Here you go." She pressed a bill into Nathalie's palm and closed her fingers over it. Then she brought her own index finger to her lips in a shushing gesture and winked.

Nathalie didn't open her hand until she got out to the street. Fifty kronor. She did the maths in her head. A nougat bar, a Fanta, a bag of cheese puffs—and money left over.

A number of different gangs had gathered down on the square. Some seemed drunk, reeling around and yelling at each other, laughing loudly; someone was crying.

Nathalie was hesitant. She felt out of place, almost frightened, and she headed for the back of the kiosk to avoid attracting attention.

It stank of urine and beer and rancid grease there.

Then she heard muffled voices on the other side of the refuse bins. She peered through the gap. A guy and a girl were holding each other. She heard the girl give a sob, and then she realized who it was.

Tracy.

"I don't *want* to stop seeing you. I don't know what I'll do without you," Tracy said, tears in her voice.

"Don't say that." The man stroked her hair, brought his face to hers. "You'll be just fine," he whispered. "Maybe better, even. You...your life isn't like it used to be, Tracy. I'm not good for you."

And they stood like that for a while, their faces so close. Then their lips moved closer and they kissed. First tentatively, then wildly, hungrily. At last he shoved her away and caught his breath.

"Shit, I can't."

"Why not?" she heard Tracy's voice. "Are you already together, or what?"

Silence.

"Are you? Have you slept together?"

The guy didn't say anything; he just looked at her.

"Fuck you," Tracy said. "Go to hell. I never want to see you again."

She stalked off, sat down on the slope that led down to the river, and waved him off dismissively.

"Tracy," the guy said, beseeching.

"Get lost."

He ran his hand through his hair and looked at her for a long time. Then he turned around and left.

At first Nathalie didn't dare move. But after a while she came out cautiously from behind the bins and started walking along the slope. She pretended that she had just arrived.

"Tracy? Is that you?" she asked.

Tracy snuffled and whipped around. She squinted, as if to get a better look. "What the hell…is that you, Nathalie?"

"What are you doing here?" Nathalie asked.

Tracy raised her eyebrows. "I should be asking you that."

"My parents are over at—"

"Screw it. Come and sit down and we'll have a smoke."

Nathalie felt a thousand birds take flight inside her chest. They flew out over the expanses inside her; in an instant she was bigger than she'd ever felt before.

Come and sit down and we'll have a smoke.

She walked over and sat down on the dry grass.

"Have you ever smoked before?" Tracy asked. She had smudges of black mascara under her eyes.

Nathalie nodded.

"Liar. Whatever, just take one."

Tracy used her lips to catch a cigarette straight out of the pack, which she then held out to Nathalie. She took one and hoped her fingers wouldn't tremble. Tracy held up the lighter, brought her cigarette to the flame, and inhaled. Nathalie did the same. The tips lit up like two burning eyes staring at each other.

She held the smoke in her mouth for a moment, then blew it out.

They sat there without saying a word, side by side on the slope, and then Tracy began to speak.

"There was a guy here just before you came. That's why I was...crying. We've been seeing each other for the last year or so, but now he wants to break up."

Nathalie blinked hard. She had to choose her words carefully. "Are you in love with him?"

Tracy gave a deep sigh. "It's more than that. It's like every cell in my body is completely...obsessed. He's, like, dug his way into my brain, my body, you know what I mean? Taken over. I hate it." She burst into tears again. "I feel so fucking awful."

Nathalie shifted a little closer and placed a hand on Tracy's back. She didn't know quite what to do.

"It's been that way ever since the first time I met him," Tracy went on. "For a whole fucking year. We see each other at night, but in the daytime we lead different lives. He never wanted me for real. It's so degrading. I feel like a...a fucking flavor of the week."

She sniffled and wiped her nose with the back of her hand. "He met someone else. Angelica saw them together in town."

She turned to Nathalie and emphasized her words. "*In town*. He had his arm around her. He never did that with me. We never even went out together."

She stopped talking and looked at the ground.

"It hurts so goddamn much. It feels like I don't exist any more."

Nathalie held her breath. Her thoughts were going a mile a minute. "But you do," she managed.

But you do. Jesus, what a comment.

Tracy forced herself to smile, flicked her butt away, and stood up.

"It's fine, Nathalie. You're nice. But I have to go now." She ran her hand over Nathalie's hair. "See you. Take care of yourself."

Nathalie stayed put for a while, then she stubbed out her cigarette on the ground, stood up, and gazed out over the square.

Did that really happen? Had she—Nathalie—really just been sitting there with Tracy, smoking cigarettes and talking about guys?

She straightened her back and headed for the kiosk. This time she wouldn't shrink away from the loud teenagers. She walked straight up to the window and bought what she'd been planning to buy, plus a pack of peppermint gum.

One night a few weeks later, when most of the fuss over the Lingonberry Girl had settled down, Tracy came home. She slid through the front door, acknowledged Julia and Nathalie with a nod, and disappeared into her room. She didn't say a word about her talk with Nathalie.

"That guy broke up with her," Julia said later, as they were sitting on her bed and listening to music. "If they were even together in the first place, I don't know. He met some other girl, apparently."

"Oh," said Nathalie. "That's a shame."

"No, I think it's a good thing."

She twisted her hair and put it up in a bun. "She's been so grumpy ever since she met him. And she hasn't been eating anything either; have you noticed how skinny she's got?"

The weather had been nice for several days, but on that particular evening a sudden storm blew up at dusk. Julia had fallen asleep right away, but Nathalie couldn't settle down. She lay there staring at the ceiling and listening to the wind outside. The whole house was shaking.

Then she heard it all stop suddenly.

A thought spurred her to get out of bed and walk to the window.

She could see Tracy outside, not far from the house, barefoot in her gray and white striped nightdress. She seemed to be stumbling off in the moonlight, heading for the marshy part of the mire where it turned into open water. The part where they were warned never to walk.

Soon she heard Tracy's mum from an upstairs window, a cry that cut through the air: "Tracy! Where are you going? Be careful, come back!"

Then her father's heavy steps, hard thuds through the

house. Nathalie opened her window and woke up Julia, who immediately ran down the stairs and across the yard.

Tracy kept walking as her parents' increasingly desperate shouts echoed through the trees in the late evening. She made no attempt to stop; she just pushed further into the marshy land. Nathalie watched her path from the upstairs window; she may have seen better than anyone what happened.

After a while, Tracy began to sink. First to her knees, then even further. The fog seemed to envelop her body and made it pale in the moonlight, almost shimmering.

As if it were receiving her.

As if it were embracing her.

As if it were pulling her down.

And then she was gone.

What Maya had really wanted to know as she chatted with Yvonne at the Larssons' farm was more about her daughter's death. But she was hesitant to ask. She didn't want to reveal just how interested she actually was in that particular incident.

Now she was driving along the small gravel road with the forest on her right and the bog on her left. After a minute or so she passed a deserted property on her right, and just after that another one, its drive blocked off. She parked at the side of the road, hung her camera around her neck, and stepped out. The sky was bright, almost white.

She couldn't tell whether these houses were begging to be seen or trying to shield themselves from sight. The garden she was approaching now was absolutely miserable. The ground was dug up here and there, and upon closer inspection she realized that the pits had been used as toilets.

She walked around taking photos and tried to peer in through the partially drawn blinds. She could see filthy wall-to-wall carpet, bookshelves full of trash and cheap trinkets, and a large, dirty corner sofa covered in piles of clothing.

Human beings certainly do their best to decay without dignity, she thought.

She went back to her car and got in. The sky was darkening, and in less than a minute raindrops were striking the windscreen. She was about to turn on the radio but stopped herself. Instead she sat in the front seat and stared straight into the rain as it formed rivers on the glass.

Then she put the key in the ignition and started the engine.

She drove another half-kilometer and as the rain let up she turned off at a hand-made sign that simply read "Texas."

Sheep and horses were grazing on the property. Hens, geese and a rooster ran around the garden. She could hear loud music coming from the house. She recognized the initial tones and phrases. It was Kris Kristofferson, singing "Sunday Mornin' Comin' Down," with a familiar melancholy.

She stopped the car, turned off the engine, and looked around. The mood here was different, to say the least; it was a farm full of life and energy.

A man appeared on the front steps and approached her. His hair was longish and streaked with gray; his mouth was framed by stubble, and he was wearing jeans, a T-shirt and a dirty black apron.

She got out of the car and went to meet him.

"Hi, sorry to bother you," she said. "I'm from Fengerskog and I'm a photographer. I'm working on a project about the area and I just wanted to introduce myself to everyone who lives around here."

"Okay," Texas said with a certain amount of reserva-tion. "Well, you're the third this week. But I have nothing to add, I can tell you that right away. I just think this is all very unpleasant."

"No," Maya said. "That is, I'm not from the media. I'm an artist working on a project; I want to photograph the area. It doesn't really have anything to do with the recent incidents out here."

He appeared to relax a bit. "Oh, well, that's a relief. That's nice then." He extended his hand. "Texas."

"Nice to meet you," Maya said, taking it.

He gestured down at his body. "I apologize for my get-up, by the way. I'm putting in the week's hygiene hours. That means cleaning out the cats' rooms here in the house. Just has to be done sometimes. I should do it more often. What did you say your name was again?"

"Maya. The cats' rooms?"

"Yes, they have three rooms of the house. It's like their own apartment. It just happened. They're in the process of eas-ing us out entirely, you could say."

"Us?"

"Yes, my partner and me. Marie. Although she doesn't actually live here."

Maya told him more about who she was and what she was up to. Texas ran his hand through his hair and listened, pay-ing close attention.

"Well, you're welcome to take pictures of the animals at least. It'll probably take a little more convincing for me, and I don't know about Marie. She's at work. I'm on disability benefit for the time being."

"What do you do?"

"I'm an aide at a mental hospital. But a few weeks ago I was attacked; I got hit on the head by a guy who weighs a hundred and thirty kilos. Ever since I've just been tired for no reason. It probably really shook up my brain. Just how it is."

The rooster approached Maya rather insistently, as if it had some important issue that couldn't wait. She looked at its shiny feathers, small eyes and giant claws.

"His name is Morgan. He's probably wondering if you have any food. He'll eat right out of your hand."

"Morgan?" Maya asked, amused.

"Yes, after that guy from Ullared, if you've seen him, on TV? The chickens are Boris and Ola-Conny. Among others. The ducks belong to Marie. They were a package deal. They're nice animals, I have to say. Swedish ducks."

Texas took a piece of bread from his pocket and held it out. The rooster hopped into the air and caught it.

"Well done," Maya said. "It would be fun to get a picture of the two of you. If that's okay."

"You think so? Well, we can give it a shot. Just tell me what to do."

She asked him to sit down on a bucket next to the root

cellar, and working together they convinced Morgan to stand still beside him for a moment. They were almost the same height when Texas sat down.

"You make a very charming couple," Maya said as she took pictures.

"Aren't we?" Texas said. "My therapist says all my progress is thanks to the rooster."

"That's the first time I've heard of someone discussing his rooster with his therapist," Maya said.

"Someone's got to do it. Morgan has lifted me out of darkness. We have a very fine relationship." He patted the rooster.

"Darkness?" Maya repeated.

"Yeah, what can I say? Life is hard. Haven't you noticed?"

"Oh, certainly," Maya said. "But...what did you mean, more specifically?"

Texas shook his head and glanced over at the forest. "Sometimes it feels like the whole point of everything is not to booze too much. And sometimes it feels like the point is *to* booze. It just feels like everything is always about booze, and then what does it all matter anyway?"

Maya nodded. "I know what you mean. I think. And getting hit on the head by a hundred-and-thirty-kilo guy can't make things any easier."

"It doesn't. You're right about that. Then again, people get knocked on the head all the time."

They continued their small talk as Maya took pictures and Texas began to chat about the recent incidents on the bog.

"I try not to think about what's going on out there. I can't deal with it. The police have been around to ask questions, sure, and the papers...yesterday I set Morgan on a photographer who was lying in the bushes. He ran after her with his wings out like this." He lifted his arms and took a few big steps forward.

"Is that true?" Maya asked.

"It's true."

"What a sight." Maya laughed and started down a new track: "By the way, have you by any chance been digging out in the bog?"

"No, for God's sake. Why do you ask?"

"There was a pit. But then it disappeared."

"A disappearing pit?"

"Yes, you could say so."

"How did you hear that?"

"I...also work as a police photographer," Maya said reluctantly, bracing herself for a negative reaction, but Texas just raised his eyebrows and nodded.

"Oh, I see. There you go."

Almost an hour later, after a cup of coffee and an apology that he didn't have any whisky or beer to offer, she was ready to leave.

"Great music, by the way," she said. "My dad listened to Kris Kristofferson when I was little."

"Yes, you know, a person needs some Kris at least once a day. Otherwise you'll never get anything done. But you hardly do anyway, as I like to say."

He held up a tin of snuff and offered it to Maya, who shook her head. He took some and tucked it inside his lower lip.

"Otherwise I mostly listen to country. Waylon and Willie and the boys. Townes. Sometimes I listen to other stuff, Lars Demian for a while. But then you have to go right back, back to reality, so to speak." He began to head up toward the house. "Have to make sure you don't get too far from the stock price of a pig, as a Center Party MP once said."

"The stock price of a pig?"

"Sure, you know. What use are you in real life, if you forget the market value of a pig?"

He placed his hand on the stair railing.

"Well, listen, I suppose I need to get back to my cleaning before my lady gets here. So I have something to show for my day. But what was I going to say? Right, if you want to know more about Mossmarken you should talk to Göran Dahlberg. He's got lots to say. More than I do, anyway."

They were too late.

Nathalie stood in the upstairs window, watching as Peder and Yvonne ran out into the marsh after Tracy, in only their underwear. Their cries of despair, the way they tripped and fell and got back on their feet, but at last were forced to watch as their daughter vanished under the surface. They threw themselves right into the water and they too nearly went under.

Nathalie closed the window as she watched Julia fall to her knees; she looked like she was screaming. But she couldn't hear anything any more. It must be the new windows they'd put in last year. Triple-glazed, she remembered her dad had said. That if they could have afforded it, they would've got the same. That they could really make a dent in the electric bill.

Nathalie cautiously walked down the hall and dialed her home number. Her dad picked up, half asleep.

"Something happened," she whispered, a sob in her throat. "You have to come and get me."

Later, her parents turned their black Volvo on to the gravel drive just as the police and ambulance arrived; they ran into the house and embraced her as if she were the one who'd been in danger.

Then came divers, and some relatives of the family. Peder and Yvonne had to show them where their daughter disappeared. For a few, quiet hours, the divers battled the cloudy water.

But they didn't find her.

Yvonne rushed about, apparently trying to get the mud off her body with persistent, rough strokes. Peder crouched nearby, his back to them and his head drooping between his drawn-up knees.

Nathalie experienced all this as if reality were behind glass. As if she were watching it all on a screen with no sound. She didn't come to until one of the police officers started asking questions about what she'd seen.

"I don't know," she said in a thin voice. "Tracy was walking around, and then she fell in. She was pretty far off. I couldn't see very well. She just walked right in."

She didn't understand why, but she didn't quite want to say how determined Tracy had seemed. Maybe because it seemed too inconceivable.

"She fell in?" the officer asked. "Do you think she could have tripped?"

"Yes, I think so. It looked that way, almost."

Then the short, silent drive home in the car. Her dad's desperate grip on the wheel, her mother Jessica's deep, gasping sighs, and the air that didn't seem to be sufficient.

When they got home, they held one another for a long time and then fell asleep snuggled close in the double bed.

But Nathalie couldn't stop thinking about Julia. Who would hold her? What would happen now?

Tracy's body was never found. It was assumed to have vanished into the dark marsh. It had been difficult for the divers to see and move, and although they expressed surprise that they didn't find the body, it wasn't entirely unexpected given the tricky circumstances.

Later, a collection would pay for further searches, private ones, since the authorities no longer considered it possible to continue in any meaningful way. In the end, the family would be forced to realize that these efforts wouldn't lead anywhere either.

Weeks passed before Nathalie and Julia spoke. She never understood why. She wanted to go over there, or call, but her parents said that Julia's family needed time alone.

And then handball camp started; both of them had planned to attend, but Julia never showed up. This gave rise to a great deal of talk about what had happened to her sister. No one seemed to know that Nathalie had been there when it happened, and she didn't mention it.

When Julia finally called and they started hanging out again, Nathalie did her best to make her feel as comfortable as possible. They tried to get together and just talk; they went running together, did all sorts of things. But nothing was the same between them.

She knew they were both thinking that their ghost stories and games out on the bog had become reality.

The memorial service was so sad that Nathalie couldn't eat for several days afterward. Tracy's friend Angelica's rendition of "Amazing Grace" made even the pastor weep.

It was also the first and last time Nathalie saw her father cry. It frightened her and made her feel like the end of the world was coming. And in some ways it was, at least for her, although she had no idea at the time.

Instead of a coffin, a table stood at the front of the church, displaying a photo of Tracy. Peder and Yvonne had trouble walking; they seemed to have trouble even breathing and had to support one another. Julia walked several steps behind them. She looked so lonely. As if she were expected to make it on her own, in contrast to her parents, who had each other. They had been given sedatives, Nathalie had heard. To make it through the service. She wondered what would help Julia make it through.

"There he is," Nathalie heard a man next to her in the pew whisper as a man of around thirty approached the photograph to say good-bye. "The one in the dark green shirt. That's who she was dating. Apparently he met someone else, but she doesn't seem to be here. Thank God."

The guy was the only person up there who didn't cry; his pain seemed to be of a different variety.

After the memorial service, Julia pretended they didn't know each other. She spent more and more time with a different girl, who seemed overjoyed to have become friends with Julia. Nathalie saw them on their bikes together sometimes.

Nathalie grieved. For the first time in her life she felt truly alone. It was as if her life had turned its back on her, as if something huge were blocking the light of the world and turning everything cold and dark.

She didn't know that the tragedy of Tracy was only the beginning.

She didn't know that this was only a foreshock, a distant rumble.

Maya was already exhausted when she woke up. The previous day had been a long one. Today she would pay another visit to Mossmarken—to see Göran Dahlberg. *Finally.*

Last night, nine of them had sat around Laila Börjesson's kitchen. Aside from Laila, her husband Johnny, and their children plus partners, there was an acquaintance from the next town who was helping lay gravel in the garden. Apparently one of the many favors Laila had earned throughout the years.

Maya had brought a kringle from the bakery in Fengerskog and they gathered around it. Then they let her take some pictures and after just over an hour she headed back home. Laila and Johnny got up at five every morning to take care of the animals, and then they went to their regular jobs, and then it was time for the animals again. That was their life.

Maya reached across the bedside table and checked her phone. She thought she'd heard it vibrate a few times during the night. She had four texts from Tom.

She sighed.

The first contained a quote from Susan Sontag's book *On Photography.*

> *Thought of you when I read these. Feels like something you might have said.*

She probably knew every important line in that book by heart, but she read it anyway.

> *Photographs are a way of imprisoning reality...One can't possess reality, one can possess images—one can't possess the present but one can possess the past.*

The other two texts questioned her silence with rising degrees of accusation.

She leaned back. She simply hadn't had time.

What do you want with me? Why are you acting like this? he wrote in the last one, which had been sent at 3.14 a.m.

Maya composed a response.

> *Sorry, there's been a lot on my plate. Want to make it up to you. Maybe you can come over some night for a glass of wine? Just the two of us?*

Just the two of us. She knew he would eat that right up. She knew he would interpret those three words as some sort of promise, as a whole world of meaning to his own advantage.

Maya hadn't gone grocery shopping for weeks, but others had filled her fridge. It contained various spreads, fresh veg, cooked beans, aged cheeses and preserved delicacies from spontaneous late-night parties.

She toasted a piece of bread, spread it with olive tapenade, and placed it on a plate along with a sliced avocado and alfalfa sprouts. Then she poured a cup of espresso, topped it with frothy milk, and sat down in the living room with the newspaper.

Man Ray came slinking across the room—he was a Norwegian Forest Cat Ellen had given her as a housewarming present. She found that the cat made her happy.

An hour or so later, she packed her equipment in the car and took off for Mossmarken.

Just before she reached Göran Dahlberg's house, she slammed on the brakes and reversed.

A letterbox. She could easily have missed the drive. One had once existed here, but now it was overgrown with scrub. Yet beyond it she could see a house. And a rusty car. Nature had taken over.

The name "Nordström" was painted on the letterbox in faded script.

This must have been where Nathalie had lived; her name had been Nordström as a child. Maya had read the police report on what happened, the murder-suicide that had occurred in the house. She'd read about how Nathalie was sitting in the car outside when the patrol arrived. How her mum and dad had been lying, shot and bloody, on the kitchen floor. How her father had had a rifle in his hand.

The event had been described by the newspapers as a family tragedy, with no further details. But Maya still recalled the shock and the aftermath the story caused throughout the region. People had wondered what could cause a father to make the devastating decision to take the lives of himself and his wife—and leave a little twelve-year-old girl behind.

She put the car in first gear and continued to the next driveway. *Mossmarken is a tormented place*, she thought. Stories like that one never leave the people who experienced them, especially not if they were children. That sort of thing must shape a person. Blast new paths into one's consciousness.

Göran Dahlberg lived in a dark brown, two-story wooden house with a large garden full of wilting growth. A white van stood in the drive, and a bike leaned against a post.

Maya felt a chill as she stepped out of the car. Soon autumn would fade into winter.

"Hi."

Maya was startled. He had been standing beside the house all along: a tall, thin figure in an old knitted cardigan and trousers the same shade of brown as the house.

"Hi," she said. "I'm sorry, I didn't see you there." She approached with her hand outstretched. "Maya."

"Göran," he said, taking a step forward and separating himself from the background.

"I'm a photographer and I'm taking some pictures in the neighborhood," Maya said. "I'm going around and introducing myself to the people who live here."

"Okay," Göran said.

"It's so lovely here," Maya said, looking around.

"It is what it is. The end of the road. The end of the *world*, some would say."

"Seems like lots of people have moved away?" She nodded at the road. "Lots of boarded-up houses."

"Yes," he said. "Anything else would be strange."

She looked at him, perplexed.

"This is no place to live," he clarified.

"But you live here."

He shrugged. "Yes, I do. I'm like my garden—run wild. I wouldn't be able to function anywhere else." He observed her. "How come you're interested in photographing out here?"

"I work part time as a police photographer and I recently came out here on assignment. You know about what happened, I assume."

"Of course. But as a police photographer, surely you have no reason to go on house calls like this."

She felt her cheeks burn and immediately regretted bringing up her side job. She was too used to moving forward unhindered with a relatively vague motive.

"No, that's true. But I'm also an artist and I'm working on a project. I find Mossmarken intriguing, and all its history too. I've been to the museum in Karlstad to check out the Lingonberry Girl, and I wanted to know more. So you were the right person to talk to."

"And you don't have me confused with Peder Larsson, who found the Lingonberry Girl...?"

"No, I spoke to Nathalie and she tipped me off about you."

His gaze sharpened. "You know Nathalie?"

"I wouldn't say that; I only met her a few times. Nice girl."

He nodded, apparently debating with himself. "Would you like some coffee?"

Maya flashed him her friendliest smile. "I'd love some."

Göran showed her into the house, into a room with dark wood-paneled walls and substantial bookcases.

"Have a seat."

He went to the kitchen and Maya soon heard the sound of a coffee-maker. She looked around, her eyes exploring the spines of books. She spotted titles in Arabic, Hebrew, Spanish and Russian; she also saw English titles like *The Anatomy of a Ghost* and *A Study of the Unknown*.

After a while, he came back with two mugs and a plate of biscuits.

"You know that Nathalie lived just next door?" he said.

"Yes."

"And you know what happened to her parents?"

"Yes. I lived in Åmål at the time. There was a lot of talk. But you knew them, didn't you?"

"Yes, of course, at least a little—we were neighbors, after all. But Nathalie was the one I talked to the most."

"Pardon me for asking," Maya said, "but were you at home that day? Or night?"

"When it happened, you mean?"

"Yes."

"I sleep soundly," Göran said, "I always have. I didn't wake up until the next morning, when it was all over. Nathalie had already been taken into care and she never returned, until now." He wiped his mouth with a napkin.

She would have liked to ask more about Nathalie and the incident, but she didn't want to risk destroying the affinity that was building between them. Instead she kept talking about her photography project and her meeting with the Larssons. They discussed the importance of collecting or shedding belongings. Then she nodded at his bookcases.

"So you're interested in...the supernatural?"

"Oh, I suppose you could say so," he said curtly, taking a bite of a biscuit.

"Have you always been?"

He cocked his head. "No, not always. Once upon a time I was a professor. Of theoretical physics."

"Aha," Maya said in surprise. "What was your specialty?"

"String theory. Quantum mechanics."

"Exciting," she said. "Is it true that at least 99.99 percent of matter is empty space?"

He smiled. "You're in the know."

She wrinkled her nose and shook her head. "Not really."

"Well, you know more than most, anyway," he said, setting down his mug. "But the fact is, it's closer to 100 percent empty space. Not even the atomic nucleus, which I imagine you're making an exception for, has any real volume on a fundamental level. But perhaps it's important to point out that it isn't an *empty* void. It's boiling, bubbling, fluctuating; stuff is happening all over the place all the time. The so-called empty space contains unlimited *potentiality* for particles to arise. It contains everything and nothing all at once. But it's a little hard to...relate to. In everyday life, so to speak."

Maya smiled. "I think I understand. Emptiness not as the desolate nothingness our rational mind likes to think about, but an aliveness at the core of all things. All beings. Of everything. As if our entire existence is an expression of this one seamless, constantly transforming emptiness."

Göran went quiet.

"That sounds like quantum mechanics in a nutshell," he finally said. "Although better than I could put it."

"Actually, it's my description of emptiness as fundamental reality," she said. She paused. "In Buddhist philosophy."

"Ha, ha!" He pointed at her and laughed. "You got me!"

"And you can get in touch with that reality by quieting your senses," she continued. "With meditation, for instance. So maybe you have to look *inside yourself* to have a direct experience of the laws of quantum mechanics and the basis of existence."

"Maybe," Göran said, raising his eyebrows and taking a sip of coffee.

"In any case," Maya said. "Go on. How did you come to quit physics?"

"We moved here. And my focus...how should I put it?... shifted. This was in the late eighties. God, how time flies. That was almost thirty years ago."

"What happened?"

"What happened? Well, what can I say? After living here for a while I noticed...well, that something wasn't quite right."

"How do you mean?"

"At first I suppose it was just a feeling. But then things started happening. More concrete things."

"Such as?"

Göran threw up his hands. "The disappearances." He glanced at her. "That's why you're here, isn't it? Isn't that what you really want to talk about?"

Maya stirred her mug and nodded slowly.

"I've suspected for a long time that all the disappearances that have happened in this area of the country have something to do with Mossmarken," Göran said.

"Yes, I heard you had such suspicions."

"I've called the police countless times. But they won't listen. I suppose I'm on some list of crazies. A red light probably starts blinking when my number pops up. Or it has until now, because as it happens I tipped off the police some time ago that they should check for Stefan Wiik here."

"Who else do you claim vanished here, and how did you come to believe they vanished in this particular place?"

He stood up, left the room, and soon returned with a thick envelope.

"Look at this," he said, spreading a couple of dozen sheets of paper across the table.

Each page contained a name, age and date of disappearance, neatly listed, as well as a photograph and newspaper clippings. Maya bent forward and let her eyes wander across the table. They were captured by one of the images.

Stefan Wiik.

Several years in the ground, but he was still recognizable.

"I'm sure you've heard of this boy," Göran said, picking up a piece of paper with a picture of a little boy with a big smile. "He disappeared on a field trip to the area ten or eleven years ago and has never been found. Several years before that, a middle-aged German woman went missing; she was believed to have visited Mossmarken just before she vanished, but after a while the search was called off and it was decided that she probably went back home. And it just keeps on like this. Mossmarken has been on the fringes of an interminable number of cases, but no one has bothered to pay attention to the pattern."

He paused for a moment and went on in a low voice.

"But for me, the pattern has only become more obvious. I've studied it, growing more and more interested in...what can I say? Old superstitions. Stories of the apparently unexplainable. I've read up on theories about evil spirits, ghouls—ghosts, if you prefer. If you just believe in a tiny little snippet of all this, maybe these disappearances are no longer as inexplicable. But of course, I made trouble for myself. This interest stands in direct opposition to my academic position, and I haven't set foot at my institution for many years. My reputation is probably considered quite low."

Maya bent forward. Among all the papers and documents in the envelope was a thick folder he hadn't touched.

"What's this?" she asked, indicating the folder.

"That's...research I've conducted about...my wife. She disappeared too. Right after Nathalie and her family moved here."

"Oh yes, I heard about that."

"I'm not so eager to talk about that, if it's okay. Many people believe she just took off."

"So she didn't?"

Göran looked at her. "Like I said, I'd prefer not to talk about it."

Maya straightened up. "Okay, I understand. But if you're not at the university any more, how do you support yourself? Surely this can't be a very lucrative trade, the ghost business?"

He smiled. "You have no idea. There are tons of publica-

tions all over the world that deal with supernatural phenomena in various ways. I've probably written for half of them. In
different languages. Lucrative might not be the right word, but
I get by."

"So you're saying that you, how should I put it? ... *believe*
in ghosts?"

Göran laughed aloud and tossed his head. "Nathalie used
to ask the same thing. Back then I was extremely uninformed
in the subject and I never knew what to say."

"But you do now?"

"Oh, I've been doing this for almost three decades now,
and when you've studied something that intensely, with any
luck you eventually gain a certain amount of knowledge. And
what's more, I've more or less developed a relationship with
the spirits in this particular place. They're my neighbors. I've
gone long periods in which they're the only ones I meet."

Maya felt herself becoming a little tense. She found his
madness amusing, to be sure, but at the same time there was
something about his manner that made her ill at ease; something that made him seem not quite harmless.

The intelligent fools are also the most dangerous.

She couldn't remember where she'd heard that. Was it Leif?

"So what have you settled on?" she asked.

He cocked his head and gave her a long look. Then he
stood up, fetched the coffee pot, refilled their mugs, and sat
back down.

"If we humans are different from each other when we're alive, that's nothing compared to what happens to us when we die. What we call ghosts can be wildly varied phenomena. I think the place and its history guide the form its eventual spirits take on."

"How about this place?" Maya asked. "How would you describe the ghosts you believe haunt Mossmarken?"

"I've got to know them as . . . how can I explain it? Loosely connected human trash."

Maya leaned back. "Okay?"

"Imagine a person when their body and soul are gone. What's left over. The trash."

"What do you mean?" she asked.

"Thoughts drained of contents that can't find their way home. Eternal torment without pain. Erased memories that get stuck. That sort of thing."

"But," Maya said, "isn't what you're describing . . . nothing?"

Göran looked pleased. "Exactly. That's precisely why I say it's a contradiction to say that ghosts exist. Because a ghost is a negation, an emptiness. But this emptiness, this lacking thing, it can possess enormous power. A sort of . . . hunger. I believe that was what I felt when I moved here, what interested me from the start."

"And how do you claim that these undead spirits, which don't exist, are connected with the disappearances?" Maya asked.

He squinted. "What do *you* think?"

Neither of them spoke for a moment. Maya was feeling distinctly uncomfortable. She needed to get out of there.

"I don't quite understand, but you claim...they hunger for...living people?"

"Yes, for the body and soul they lack."

Göran leaned toward her and looked into her eyes. His pupils dilated as he blocked the light.

"The problem is, since these spirits also lack a brain, they have no idea that once their victim is dead they can't make use of the body or the soul. It's completely illogical. But when it comes to ghosts, you can't expect logic. That's about all I can say with certainty."

Maya closed her eyes and tried to bring his lines of reasoning together. "So you're saying that of everyone who might be buried out there, some are like the Lingonberry Girl and were sacrificed to appease the gods, and some have been more like swallowed by the ground, called there by those who are already dead?"

"Yes. Although in modern times I expect it's only the latter. It's not as if we sacrifice humans any more."

Maya stiffened. The muscles in her face pulled tight. She had forgotten that the general public didn't know all the details surrounding Johannes Ayeb and Stefan Wiik.

"Okay?" said Göran, who seemed to have noticed the change in her. He observed her for a moment and ran his thumb over his lips. "Human sacrifices?" he whispered. "You think Stefan Wiik was sacrificed?"

"I can't get into any..." She threw up her hands. "Sorry!"

"You don't have to say anything; I can see it on your face. What did you find in his grave? Tools? Jewelry? Other valuables? Money?"

She looked at him beseechingly, but it seemed he had come to his own conclusions.

"It's like I've always said, as long as they're being sacrificed you might as well send as much as you can along with them."

"Who have you talked to about this?" she asked.

"Who have I talked about this with? I've been working on this for almost thirty years; who *haven't* I talked to?"

He appeared to gather himself.

"May I ask one more thing?" he asked, his voice eager. "If you were at the museum in Karlstad maybe you know that people sometimes used poles to keep the bodies in place, and maybe also to keep them from rising as the undead. It's true that there's only anecdotal evidence that poling truly stops the undead, but I have to ask—this man you found, from Brålanda, is there any chance he was...you know, run through by a pole?"

Maya could tell that their roles were reversed. Now he wanted something from her.

"I'm sure it won't be long before that sort of information gets out to the newspapers, in that event," she said. "But until then, you'll have to be patient."

He shrugged.

"Listen," she went on, "these undead...how would you expect them to look? In a physical sense?"

"Well, not like you would picture a ghost, if that's what you're thinking. No transparent old folks—although I have heard that images of the dead can emerge in water. The only physical form I myself have potentially seen them take on is... smoke or mist. It sort of slithers up. Surrounds its victim."

"You've seen this?"

"It was a long time ago. I suppose it's what made me start taking this seriously. As a physicist, I had a hard time imagining how something without a body could materialize in the first place."

"What did you see?"

"A black grouse. It was early morning. I saw it before it saw me and I was trying to sneak up so I could keep watching it. It was puffing itself up, the way grouse do. Then it started flapping its wings in a panic. It was like it got sucked right down. And that was when I saw those coils of smoke. The whole grouse was gone in a matter of seconds. Literally swallowed by the ground. It was shocking."

"But couldn't it have been a very marshy area? Maybe it just got stuck," Maya tried.

"You would have thought so, but no. I couldn't help checking afterward. The ground was quite firm."

"This goes against your theory though, in a way—you say

the ghosts hunger for *people* with a body and soul because they don't have any."

"Sure, what do I know? Maybe it doesn't have to be a person. I suppose a grouse isn't so bad. Like I said, don't expect logic when it comes to ghosts."

He stood up. "Should we take a walk? There's something I'd like to show you."

Maya felt an internal wavering. "Out there? On the mire?" she asked.

He nodded.

There was a knock on the door. Two hard raps. Nathalie had just sat down at the table in the cottage and opened her laptop.

She opened the door cautiously and found Alex, the caretaker, with a toolbox in one hand.

"The door," he said, pointing. "The lock."

"Right," said Nathalie. "It sticks; sometimes it won't open, like I'm using the wrong key."

Alex didn't respond, just set the toolbox in the hall and got to work.

Nathalie watched him for a moment, then walked slowly back into the room and lay down on the bed. She listened to the buzzing of the drill, the rattle of the metal plate, muffled strikes against the sill and the door. There was something relaxing about the noise; it was almost hypnotic.

After a while, her phone rang. *The lab.* It had to be about the samples she'd sent in the other day.

"Yes, this is Nathalie Ström," she said, realizing immediately that something wasn't right. The woman on the other end fumbled for words as she tried to convey her message.

"We were a little . . . confused about the results of the analysis. So I wanted to let you know before I sent them back."

"Okay," Nathalie said in surprise. "What's going on?"

"There must be something wrong with the samples. We can't find any evidence of the components you're looking for: nitrogen, nitrous oxide or methane."

Nathalie nearly had a fit. "What do you mean? I took them just like I always do. That's impossible."

"I'm sorry, but it didn't register at all."

"Not a single one of them?" Nathalie asked.

"Not a single one."

She felt her mouth go bone dry. Dark thoughts rose to the surface.

They did it wrong, she thought. *The lab did something wrong. Or maybe it was Johannes, when he took the samples.* Then she remembered she'd done the most recent batch by herself.

No, it's the spirits. That's what they do. They crowd out everything else.

"I'm sorry?" said the woman.

"I didn't say anything," Nathalie rushed to say.

"Crowd out?" the woman said down the phone. "I don't understand."

"I said I'll take a look. I'll have to send new samples a little later. Or I'll just have to deal without them; it'll be fine. Good-bye."

She hung up before the woman could respond. Tears began to burn behind her eyelids and exhaustion overtook her. She leaned back and closed her eyes. She might have dozed off.

When she opened her eyes, a figure was standing right next to her, towering over her like a building.

"Oh my goodness," she said when she realized who it was. "Alex. You scared me...I forgot you were here."

"I'm finished now," he said.

She sat up. "Okay, great. Thanks for your help."

He didn't move. The light fell on him from behind, making him look like a big shadow with two white eyes.

"Thanks so much for your help," she tried again.

Then something happened. It was as if his whole being transformed. As if his absent gaze became perfectly clear for a brief moment.

She shuddered. Was he... *normal*?

But he just looked at her; he might have smiled a tiny bit. Then he turned around and left.

Maya and Göran were following a narrow path with sparse forest on either side. They ran across two other parties in their first half-hour: first a group of five teenagers and, later on, two women and a man in their thirties. They had to turn sideways to pass each other on the walkway.

"It's usually deserted out here," Göran muttered. "Funny what a corpse will do."

Maya wasn't entirely unfamiliar with the attraction of a crime scene. Many people wanted to experience the horror, see the site with their own eyes. She suspected that the old rumors and stories about the mire weren't helping.

They stopped now and again so Maya could take photographs.

The pictures were no good. She felt forced, tense. She also wasn't comfortable working in the company of Göran. She didn't know why; other people were seldom a hindrance, but there was something about the atmosphere around him. In addition, she was wearing the wrong kind of shoes and her feet were already soaked and cold.

"It's exciting to see how you work," he said. "I think I've become blinded to all this."

"Sure," Maya said. "That happens."

They walked in silence for a while.

"May I ask you something?" she inquired. "What do you know about what happened to the Larssons' older daughter?"

"Tracy? Not much. No one wants to talk about it. But I know that people half-*joke* that the spirits took her." He shook his head. "People are idiots. Joking about that kind of thing."

"But *you* actually believe that the spirits took her?"

"It's possible. Although I have no idea what the weather was like that day."

"The weather?" Maya asked, stopping short.

"There's a theory that ghosts identify their victims during sudden shifts in the weather," Göran said. "Or it's the other way around—the victim-choosing process influences the weather. Typically, a sudden storm blows in. Once the victim has been selected, it quickly calms down again."

"I don't get it—what does the weather have to do with anything?"

Göran sighed. "You're focusing on the wrong thing. Or rather, asking the wrong questions."

She shuddered. He was so convincing. As if he really, truly was 100 percent certain of his own ideas. So certain that he didn't even consider how it sounded to others' ears.

"What about you?" she said. "And the Larssons? And the people at the manor? Shouldn't those of you who live here be at greatest risk of being chosen some day?"

"Sure, and that's probably what happened to Tracy. Maybe the rest of us have just been lucky. Although you can see for yourself, all the abandoned houses out here. Who knows what happened to the people who lived in them? Not me. I have no idea. And I haven't got any good answers, either."

He stopped and gazed out at the quiet scenery.

"Didn't they just move and abandon their cottages? It shouldn't be that hard to find out," Maya said. "I think Yvonne Larsson said something about barely getting any money for their place."

"No, that's just it—who would want to move out here? This last incident isn't exactly a boon to our reputation. There are few things people find as tempting as an unsolved mystery, but they want to keep them at arm's length."

"Aren't you frightened sometimes?" she asked.

"Frightened? Not a bit. It would probably be the high point of my career to be swallowed up by ghosts."

"So you're a little disappointed that you haven't been?"

He laughed. "It's not too late. Everyone has to die somehow, and at least it would be interesting."

"But if I'm not mistaken," Maya said, "those who are drawn to the mire by the spirits don't get run through by a pole, do they?"

He laughed again, loudly, as if this were the funniest thing he'd heard in a long time. "No, I don't think they're capable of that much. Poling is a concrete action taken by humans who are very much alive." He stopped and gestured toward a part of the bog that was overgrown with trees. "This is the spot I wanted to show you."

Maya thought she could make something out between the branches. "A hut?" She followed Göran in.

"This is Nathalie's old hut, where she and her friend Julia used to play."

Maya looked at the wood, which looked new, and the metal roof, which couldn't be more than a few years old. She ducked in and opened a small cupboard. It contained comic books and packets of biscuits. They didn't look old in the least.

"But it must have been fourteen years since Nathalie was here. This hut has been used recently. It's in perfect condition."

"I know. It's a funny story—I helped them build it. It's beyond the statute of limitations by now, I hope. Their parents didn't know about it. I'm sure they wouldn't have allowed it. The girls weren't actually allowed to be out in the bog by themselves. But they wanted to so badly, and I figured it was better if they had a good place I knew about instead of just running around."

"But you've maintained it all these years?"

"No, that's just it. I thought you would want to know; someone...took over this hut once the girls were done with it."

"Do you know who it is?"

He lowered his head. "Yes."

"Who?"

"I don't want to get anyone in trouble. I want you to know, I have no problem with him, but..."

"Who is it?"

"His name is Alex. He's the caretaker at the manor."

"A grown man?"

"Alex is an adult physically, but mentally he's immature. He lives in a house near the manor and probably knows this bog better than anyone else."

"Why is that?"

"This is where he spends all his free time. He looks for birds and other animals; he keeps some sort of journal about them. This is his favorite place."

Maya looked around. From inside you could see a great distance, although the hut itself was well hidden.

"This Alex," she said, "how would you describe him?"

"What do you mean?"

"Well, what does he look like? His posture...how does he walk?"

"Why do you ask?"

"I saw someone in this area when I was taking pictures around the bog, someone who...seemed to move in a very particular way."

"Sure, that could be Alex, he sort of hunches over as he walks," Göran said, stooping to demonstrate. "As if he wants to be shorter than he is."

Maya took out her phone but found that she had no signal.

"I have to make a call," she said with an urgent glance at Göran.

"We can go over to the manor; it's closer to civilization," he said. "And maybe we can talk to Alex while we're at it."

~

"We just finished serving lunch here, but I'm sure there's some left if you're hungry," Agneta said as Maya and Göran stepped into the foyer of the manor house.

Agneta gave Göran a big hug and smiled at Maya.

"And the police are back again? Did the Create-your-dream-life course tempt you back, by any chance? Because I hope it's not bad news."

"No," Maya said. "We just wanted to talk to the caretaker here at the manor."

"Alex. I just saw him. Hold on a minute and I'll get him."

She disappeared, but soon returned.

"I don't see him anywhere at the moment. He must have gone over to his place. Do you know where he lives?"

"I do," Göran said.

A narrow gravel path led into the forest from the garden. Maya guessed the red-painted cottage she could glimpse down the path had once been a workman's home.

"This is his place," Göran said. "I've been to visit him a few times. Nice guy. Quiet, but sweet somehow."

They knocked and called out, but there was no Alex in sight.

"He uses that as a workshop and storage shed," Göran said, pointing at an outbuilding nearby.

The door was open. It smelled fresh inside; tools were hung on the wall so tidily it was almost creepy, and the floor was cleaner than in Maya's own home.

"Alex?" she called.

No response there either. Göran went back out as Maya continued to look around Alex's workshop. There was a map in a plastic tray on the workbench. She bent over it to get a better look.

It was a dog-eared map of the bog, full of notes and symbols. She realized that some markings showed where he had seen certain birds and other animals. There were others she couldn't make any sense of.

She took a picture of the map with her phone and headed for the door; on her way out she enlarged the picture and inspected some of the markings at closer range.

There were six marks with the same symbol. It was possible that one of them, if she hadn't misread the map and its directions, was the site where Stefan Wiik was found.

Tracy's death wasn't the only tragic event that summer," Nathalie said.

She was sitting in the hospital, staring at Johannes in his bed. The sound of traffic came through the open window; a laugh down on the street, someone starting a car.

"I thought I would tell you about the other part too. It's not easy, but I've got this far after all. I might as well keep going. I might as well tell you everything."

Then she didn't say anything for more than twenty minutes. She ran her index finger up and down Johannes's wrist, thinking about that night in August 2002, the end of everything. About twelve-year-old Nathalie, who had lost her best friend after watching Julia's older sister drown in the mire. About expanding silence and a pain that cut to the bone.

Why didn't anyone talk?

Why did everything get so quiet?

That last day began in her room in their house in Moss-marken. She remembered waking up to the radio and the sound of the coffee-maker. The sputtering sound she used to think was cozy and comforting now seemed like a persistent scraping, an angry hiss. Her soft bed, which had always felt so wonderful, now seemed slack and full of despair. The mouths in the wood grain on the ceiling were screaming for real, louder than ever before.

The box of cornflakes and the milk were out when she got up; an empty bowl and cold spoon awaited her.

"Good morning." Her mother's voice; how ghostlike it sounded in her memory now.

"Where's Dad?" Nathalie asked, even as she saw his red shirt bob past the kitchen window before he stepped through the door, his hands black with oil. A gust from the dry garden before the door closed behind him.

"Morning, Natti. Sleep well?"

The memory of words that no longer existed. The words from the last day. They floated around in her, drifting through the inside of her body, extinguishing hope and starting fires. How could words that no longer existed hurt so much?

Nathalie continued to stroke Johannes's wrist; she didn't notice how rough she was being. Her breathing grew shallow.

Everyone who lived around the bog was supposed to gather at the Nordströms' that evening; they were supposed to have some sort of meeting, and after dinner her parents started setting out bottles. They each mixed a drink before their guests began to arrive.

"We're going to have the other grown-ups round tonight," her mum said. "You can have some chips to take up to your room, if you want."

And then they arrived. Göran. Agneta and Gustav. Yvonne and Peder. A few more from other homes and farms. The memory was hazy.

Nathalie remembered falling asleep and waking up suddenly. She recalled loud, agitated voices. The silence that followed once all the guests had left the house. Her head was spinning. Then she heard more arguing. Her father's voice, furious.

And the shots.

She remembered the shots.

She was no longer stroking Johannes's wrist. She was holding it, squeezing it, as if to keep from falling. As if it were the only solid object there was to hold on to.

She remembered how she went to the kitchen, how she saw her mother lying bloody on the floor. The blue tunic Nathalie had picked out for her a few years earlier.

Blue? You think so, really? Sure, maybe.

Her dad, Jonas, right next to her mum.

He's broken. His head is broken. Call the police. Dad's head is broken and he's lying on the floor next to Mum. There's blood and it's just pouring out, their blood is leaving them. I can't stop it . . .

Wait outside.

I'm waiting outside.

How she went out to the car and waited inside it until the police and ambulance came.

After that there was a gap in time before everything inside her shut down and turned off; it felt like she was floating around among the stars with her parents; they were dancing around, laughing and holding each other.

Had she died and gone to heaven too?

She felt like there was no border between them and her; it was like they *were* the love they felt for each other, which sparkled at school ceremonies and on sunny autumn days and in the car on the way to the swimming hole, which hid in her mother's eyes and her father's voice.

At the same time, panic slowly drilled its way into her, like sharp, ice-cold steel. It was a promise on the way to being broken, a promise about her whole life, which lay bleeding in the kitchen. And the bright light, blue like Mum's tunic. All that blue, blue everywhere.

The song of sirens.

And the questions afterward, the answers.

"There's no good way to say this, Nathalie. We believe your dad shot your mum and then himself."

I want to get out of here. Now.

Can you take me away from here, now?

How do you get away from yourself?

Leif wasn't answering his phone so Maya left a message. But eventually she lost patience and hopped into her car to drive through the forest and on to the E45 highway toward Karlstad.

She was already pulling into the car park outside Leif's apartment building by the time he called her back.

"Are you home?" she asked.

"Yes," he said.

"I'm coming up. Straightaway."

He met her in the hall, a curious expression on his face.

"You came all the way here on your day off?" he said. "Must be something important."

"Coffee?" Maya asked, out of breath.

"Coffee," Leif replied, heading for the kitchen.

Maya impatiently took a seat at the kitchen table as Leif took out two mugs.

Then she told him what she'd found in the caretaker's cottage. Leif leaned back, listening with his arms crossed. Maya concluded by showing him the picture of the map on her phone.

"So you're saying..." He shifted in his seat. "You think..."

Maya lowered her head and looked at him. "I think the

spots he's marked could be other sacrificial sites. Anyway, he marked almost the exact place where we found Stefan Wiik."

"But why?" Leif asked. "Who is he?"

"He's been working at the manor as a caretaker for a few years. He's slightly developmentally delayed, they say."

"Who is 'they'?"

"I just heard..."

They didn't speak for a long time. The cuckoo clock on the wall ticked off the seconds with a reluctant, muted creak.

"First we'll go and investigate the places he's marked," Leif said at last. "We won't make a big deal of it. Just the two of us. To check it out."

They printed out the map and found a compass and shovel in Leif's storage room. Then they drove all the way there, one car following the other through the forest. Forest, forest, forest. Maya had almost forgotten how much forest there could be in this region.

When they arrived at the Mossmarken car park, she walked to Leif's car and got into the passenger seat. They examined the map and decided which mark they should try to find first.

Twilight was falling like a silk curtain. They walked briskly across the bog, following the map as best they could.

Fifteen minutes later they were approaching the spot where the pole ought to be. They split up and searched separately. They walked back and forth on the walkway, next to the walkway, out over the bog. This particular area was easy to walk on; there was no water lying in wait between every step. The problem was finding the mark. On the map it covered an area almost fifty meters in diameter.

"Oh hell," Leif called.

And then: "Here. Here it is, Maya! Something's sticking up over here!"

Leif dug carefully as Maya aimed the torch and tried to assist him by moving tussocks and piles of dirt out of the way. She spent long moments just crouching down and looking at the surface; every tussock was like its own world, with various colors of moss and delicate webs of tiny, bell-like flowers.

Just under an hour later, they saw something in the peat. Something that didn't appear to belong there.

Leif knelt. He pressed lightly with his fingertips, drawing his hand across the smooth surface, almost stroking away the dirt. At last he straightened his back and turned to Maya.

"Shit, Maya, I think it's...skin. Or leather." He hastily wiped his nose with his wrist. "I could be wrong, but...I think it could be a person down there."

An hour after that, they were met by technicians and a patrol car in the car park. They walked as a group to the discovery site in their white protective garb, like a procession of ghosts across the walkway. Once again, a tent was erected on the bog to protect any evidence.

And then hours passed. Morning broke into a new day. The only sound came from the camera and the protective gear when someone moved. And now and then, a brief comment or question.

"How will we handle that?"

"Brush, please."

"Here's something."

It really was a person, down there in the ground.

Maya allowed the lens of the camera to follow the progression as the body emerged bit by bit. An arm, a head, an ear. A woman, encapsulated in the turf, embraced by nature.

"Check the pockets," Leif said to the technician bent over the body. He paced back and forth as he watched her fingers search the clothing that remained.

A few minutes later, she held up a familiar cloth bag.

"Recognize this?"

Leif took the bag, opened it, and studied its contents. He met Maya's gaze and gave a short nod.

Maya put the camera aside and went to sit down nearby.

She turned away from the crime scene and gazed out at the bog. The dull sky, the silhouettes of trees. They were fortunate—there was no breeze, so the cold was tolerable even though she was dressed too lightly.

Dusk fell again and tiredness embraced Maya. For the

first time she heard someone ask Leif how they had found the body. He told them about the map and the marks.

"So there are more sites?" the person said.

And Leif squatted on his heels, took off his gloves, and ran his hands over his face. "Yes," he said at last. "There are more."

FIVE

Maya tied on her muddy boots, hung the camera bag over her shoulder, and headed out into the chilly morning. She was greeted by the sound of a woodpecker, a mechanical clatter across fields and pastures.

Her body was buzzing with lack of sleep.

Three hours in bed: that was all she had got the night before. The same went for the night before that. She had experienced a lot of things in her life, but what was happening now was beyond anything else: the proud barking of the dogs as they found one body after the next, the spotlights like sad stars shining above site after site, barricades going up.

There weren't enough staff, so Leif had to call in reinforcements and extra crews.

In just a week they had dug five human corpses out of the mire—and they weren't dealing with historical discoveries.

Tina Gabrielsson, forty-eight, from Trollhättan, who had disappeared after a business trip to Karlstad in March 2004.

Sergio Manchini, fifty-nine. Went missing while jogging at Hunneberg Park in Vänersborg, March 2008.

Eira Wallgren, seventy-seven. Disappeared after a visit to her husband's grave in Nygård Cemetery in Åmål, October 2010.

Karl Fahlén, sixty-two. Last seen outside his house in Mellerud, where he lived alone, in October 2014.

The last victim they found turned out to be twenty-one-year-old Sara Månsson, who vanished on her way home to Edsleskog in October 2006.

Her face was leathery but perfectly intact, and her parents were able to identify her in the usual way. As if she had died only very recently.

Yes. It's her.

After ten years.

Maya had met Sara's parents at the police station. They were waiting to talk to Leif as she walked by. She greeted them and asked if they wanted anything to drink.

"No, thank you," they replied.

They were so alike that she was taken aback: the same wavy, short hairstyle; the same plain colors and slight frames; the same dutiful gestures and friendly tones, devoid of happiness. As if they had supported each other until they grew together, as if they needed to be two of the same kind to keep from falling over.

"I never actually believed that she would be found," the mother said.

Maya sat down across from them.

"So in some ways, this is still like finding peace with a dreadful reality," she went on. "To have the opportunity to bury her, maybe find out what happened. And above all, the part I always thought was unattainable: to see her one last time. To get to touch her one last time."

She emphasized each and every one of the last three words. One. Last. Time.

"It was the other way around for me," said the father. "For all these years, I've been inclined to believe she was still alive, that I would get to see her again some day. I refused to believe she was dead. With every year that passes I imagine her one year older. And now..." His gaze fixed on a point beside Maya. "She was somehow still twenty-one years old. She didn't look a day older than when I said good-bye on the morning she disappeared. Everything I imagined, everything I built up and believed all those years just fell to pieces."

He pressed his fingers to his eyes. "I had given her a haircut the day before she disappeared; she always used to ask me to cut her hair. She still had that hairstyle. It was..." The father ran his hand along one temple. "It was sort of short here, and longer at the back. It wasn't very attractive," he said with a chuckle, "but Sara didn't care. 'It's fine, Dad,' she would say."

He collapsed in his seat and ran his hands back and forth over his head.

Nothing could compare to meeting a person whose last hope has just vanished, the hope of seeing a child or a relative alive again. The circumstances might vary; the details were always different, but the space the bereaved moved in always seemed to be the same. There was nothing to hold on to. Nothing at all.

"Are you a police officer?" the mother asked quietly.

Maya shook her head. "I'm a photographer. I've been taking pictures of the discovery sites, among other things."

"Do you know about the coins? I heard she had a bunch of coins in her pockets."

Maya looked the woman straight in the eye. "I'm the wrong person to answer that type of question."

"But what does it mean? Why did she have them? Where did she get them?"

Maya gestured toward Leif's office just as the door opened. "He's the one you should ask about that sort of thing."

~

"Counting Stefan Wiik, who disappeared in 2012, we now have six bodies," Leif Berggren said later as they sat in the conference room of the police station in Karlstad. He pointed at a map with the discovery sites marked. Next to it was the list of names and pictures of all the known victims. Maya noted that he had his clever spectacles under his chin. A red pair.

"All the victims ended up there in the last twelve years," he went on. "Tina Gabrielsson, who was in the bog the longest, vanished in 2004. All the bodies have similar head injuries, from blunt force trauma; they all had a pole through their bodies and a large number of coins in one or more bags in their pockets. Mostly ten-kronor coins. Almost exclusively. They all went missing in March or October, and as you can see here, there was one every other year. For a reason we aren't yet aware of."

"This also corroborates the theory that Johannes Ayeb was intended to be the next victim," Maya said. "It's been two years since the last victim vanished. Karl Fahlén."

"Yes; that's our assumption," Leif said.

Since the excavations had begun, Maya had been working more than the sixteen hours a week they had originally agreed on. She tried to attend as many briefings as possible and spent most of the rest of her time in the field. At the moment she was listening in the company of around a dozen others.

"Where are we with the caretaker?" wondered a member of the investigative team.

"I'm getting to that," said Leif. "We've searched Alex Hagman's home. We have seized tools, clothing, shoes and anything that might bear traces of links to the victims. Alex himself has chosen not to say a word, so at present we haven't got anything out of him."

Maya was tired. Her eyelids drooped and her thoughts were vaulting around inside her head. Distracted, she was sketching out Mossmarken on a piece of paper and marking three of the inhabited places she knew best: Göran's house, the manor house, and the Larssons' farm. She drew a line from one point to the next. All but two of the crime scenes were near the road. Practical, if you didn't want to carry a body very far.

She observed the triangle formed by the lines and noted that all the sites were within that area.

It's like the Bermuda Triangle, she thought.

"But as I was saying, to return to the victims," Leif said. "We know there's one every other year. The first was in 2004. But if we back up two years from there—where do we end up? Well, 2002. And who remembers what happened in 2002?" He paused briefly. "We had two tragic incidents in Mossmarken, but we also found…"

"The Lingonberry Girl," said one of the officers.

"Exactly," said Leif. "A human sacrifice from the Iron Age, run through with a pole. So it's not a bold guess to say that what we've just found in the mire has something to do with the Lingonberry Girl. An unusual sort of copycat, maybe; a madman with a bad sense of humor; or maybe it's something else entirely. It may well turn out that there's something all the victims have in common: maybe they were all members of a cult or God knows what; but it could also be that the purpose is most important and the victims were chosen at random, that it could have been anyone."

He bent forward and looked through his documents.

"What's more, as most of you already know, the medical examiner found traces of narcotics in Karl Fahlén's body. It's the kind that's injected intramuscularly, which is an advantage in an assault and might tell us something about the attacker's method."

"How does that relate to Alex Hagman?" asked one of the officers.

"That's just it—the motive and to some extent the method don't match Alex. He's got a mild mental handicap, which doesn't fit in with what we've learned so far."

Leif had spoken to the manager of the manor house, who was shaken and upset by the accusations. They were not good publicity for Quagmire Manor, and she vehemently asserted that she was absolutely convinced Alex was innocent.

"I can vouch for him; he's no killer," Agneta said. "There is no kinder man on earth; he is the very picture of goodness. He's trustworthy. And hardworking. He's been working for me for several years; I think I can say I know him."

Maya had been there when Leif spoke to Agneta. She had seen the shadow that passed over Agneta's face when she spoke of Alex. *The doubt.* That tiny, tiny drop of uncertainty in a sea of conviction.

Could he be the one, after all?

Alex certainly didn't fit the image of a calculating murderer. But to call him the *very picture of goodness* could hardly be a legitimate description.

He'd had to change schools several times during his youth

due to his violent behavior; he hadn't been able to sit quietly at his desk or follow instructions. His mental disability had never been fully investigated; he and his family had, in various ways, opposed any attempt at examination.

Only after his school years, when he landed a job as a lumberjack, did he settle down, once he was able to spend time in nature every day and do physical labor. His mother died young and his father passed away soon after he started working at the manor. He had no friends. Alex appeared to be alone in the world, with nature and animals as his only interests beyond his job.

His medical records said that he liked to seek out and create patterns, and Agneta could confirm this. Once he had discovered that the fence was broken in three different places. He destroyed it in two more spots, presumably so it would better match the image in his head.

"I had to shake him by the collar a little that time," Agneta said with a faint smile, "and explain that if he's going to work here he has to *fix* fences, not break them."

It had gotten too warm in the room at the police station, and one of the officers stood up to open a window.

"But Alex is the only lead we have?" one of the investigators asked.

Leif nodded and ran his hands over his tired face.

"The usual confessions from run-of-the-mill crazies have

been coming in, naturally, as well as lots of tips about people who were in the area or have acted strangely in one way or another in recent years. But for the moment our focus is on Alex Hagman; he has some explaining to do."

"How is Johannes Ayeb doing?" an officer asked.

"We're hoping, of course, that Johannes will regain consciousness soon, but unfortunately there's not much the doctors can tell us about when that might happen. We simply have to wait for him to recover."

At that instant, Leif's phone rang.

"Look at this," he said to the others before picking up. "This is what we've been waiting for—information on the samples we took from Alex Hagman's cottage."

The group fell silent and followed every shift in Leif's expression.

"Okay, thanks. Now we know," he said at last, ending the call.

He looked at the others with an expression that suggested he felt more baffled than satisfied.

"There we have it. The noose is tightening—we've got a match. They found Johannes's DNA on one of Alex's shovels."

Nathalie couldn't sleep. The night wind whined down the chimney, branches struck the window, darkness tiptoed around her. Everything that was happening—what was she supposed to do with it?

All the dead bodies.

Everything rising to the surface.

She had been in for questioning twice. Questioned for information, as they said, about her activities and observations in and around the manor and the bog.

They repeatedly asked her about what had happened when she found Johannes. How she had discovered the grave that suddenly wasn't there.

They asked about her relationship to the area, what she was doing there. She didn't want to hide anything, so she told them all about her parents, information they already knew, and how she had lived in Mossmarken as a child. She was starting to get used to it, talking about what she hadn't been able to talk about before.

And they asked about the caretaker, Alex. What she thought of him, whether there was anything she had noticed.

"Like what?" she asked.

"You know...whether he acted oddly."

"Well, I mean, he's kind of special. You knew that, didn't you?"

He had once brought down some wood for her, she said. Another time he had fixed a window latch. He was quiet but helpful. Did they consider that odd?

The officers looked at her with a mixture of pity and suspicion. She realized this made her feel unnecessarily ingratiating and she told them about the time Alex fixed the door lock, and how she had felt the situation was slightly threatening; it had occurred to her that he might in fact be perfectly right in the head. That it might all be an act.

"But for him to have anything to do with this...is that what you think?" she said.

"We don't think anything at the moment. We're investigating," said the police inspector.

Then, at last, she told them what she had seen and heard when she set off into the bog to look for Johannes. In the darkness and fog that settled after the storm, she had seen vague shadows, sure, maybe, now that she thought about it. But it was hard to say—they seemed to flicker before her eyes in the dark, so perhaps they were only illusions. Although there had also been the sounds. *The sounds?* Yes, agitated whispers and retreating steps.

The officers fell silent, but she could tell what they were thinking. *And you're telling us this now?*

It started with Johannes. The words buzzed through her head now, in bed. *If she hadn't gone after him, if she'd let him sink.* The thoughts cut like knives, paralyzing her.

It would all have remained hidden.

How could she think that way?

She gathered her strength and got up. She pulled on her dressing gown and rubber boots, grabbed her torch, and stepped into the night to pee.

Veils of clouds cut across the sky.

Everything appeared to be dark up at the manor, in the witching hour.

She hurried back inside and locked the door behind her. Just as she was crawling back into bed, she caught sight of a figure in the dark, over at the edge of the forest.

She turned out her lamp and cautiously approached the window. Just ten meters from the cottage was a man in a dark coat, staring straight at the house.

She couldn't tell who it was.

Gustav?

But why would he be out there at that time of night? Or was it a guest at the manor, out on a night walk?

Trembling, she carefully fastened the blanket and sheets over the three windows. She stood in the center of the room and examined them, looking for gaps, but didn't find any. Then she picked up her phone and crawled into bed. She wondered if there was any friend she could call, someone in another time zone who could still help her feel less ill at ease.

But she had a poor signal and decided not to try. Instead she laid her head on her pillow and closed her eyes.

All she could hear was her own breathing, shallow and shivery. It took a long time for her to relax and drift into deep, dreamless sleep.

Maya had arrived at the police station early to get some evidence photography out of the way.

Alex Hagman's shovel, the one with Johannes Ayeb's DNA on it, was the top priority, and several fingerprints had been secured and colored with fluorescing dye. Alex Hagman himself had been taken into custody and his cottage cordoned off for further investigation.

Maya placed the shovel on her studio table and inserted a filter that would make the fluorescing agent clearly visible on film.

The shovel looked almost new; the metal of its handle and blade were bright red. She adjusted its position, propping it up where needed and reducing glare so that the prints would be as clear as possible.

It took her about an hour to get good pictures of three unique fingerprints. She entered the photos into the digital archive where the leader of the investigation could reach them.

She liked being back at her old workplace. Naturally, many things had changed in the years she'd been gone—all the rooms had been renovated and all the technology updated—but, for the most part, it felt the same.

"Something's missing, though," Leif said that night while visiting Maya's house. "Beyond the stories of Alex's violence at school, the most conspicuous thing we've found is one *mildly*—by today's standards—pornographic image on his computer. It's a naked woman on a beach drinking out of a goddamn coconut."

Maya had insisted he leave work early for once so he could come and have dinner at her place. At first he protested, saying that if he was going to take time off he wanted to spend it with his wife, whom he'd hardly seen since this all started, so Maya simply called to invite Birgitta too. They could stay over in the guest room if it got too late.

They were sitting in Maya's living room, drinking coffee and cognac. But they couldn't seem to avoid shop talk.

"There's nothing in what we found on Alex that can answer the *why*," Leif went on as his wife leafed through one of Maya's photography books.

"Agneta says he seeks patterns in what he sees and does," Maya said. "Birds appearing in different spots at different times; the way other animals move around..."

"Yes, I know," said Leif. "But what does that have to do with the victims in the bog?"

"Well, all the victims were sunk and poled in an identical manner," Maya said. "I'm just saying that might be the answer for why: Alex is creating patterns."

"That seems far-fetched," Leif said grimly, reaching for his snifter of cognac.

"I know," Maya sighed. "But is there anything to suggest

that Alex is...superstitious or particularly interested in history?" she asked, watching the fire reflected in Leif's eyes.

"No," he said, "that's just it—we haven't turned up anything like that. And Alex himself is still refusing to talk."

"But it's no coincidence that all the victims were killed after the Lingonberry Girl was discovered, and that there are almost exactly two years between each disappearance. It has to be connected somehow."

"Of course, but the question is how it's connected to Alex. I mean—was it his interest in patterns and order? He didn't even live here when it all started, did he?" Leif asked skeptically.

"No, I don't believe it either," Maya said. "Whoever committed these murders isn't trying to copy the Lingonberry Girl for the fun of it, or to create any patterns. But it's clearly a ritual of some sort. After all, sacrifice is a rather particular action."

"Pretty old-fashioned, if you ask me," Leif said.

"Sure, but often it's about maintaining a relationship, about communicating with invisible forces. Maybe that's exactly what our killer is doing—or thinks he's doing. To get what he wants or be spared what he doesn't want. And I'm absolutely with you, it doesn't mesh at all with what we know about Alex Hagman. I can't picture him carrying out any of this."

"No," said Leif, "but he sure as hell did point out exactly where these people were on his map."

"Yes," Maya said. "But maybe he only discovered the poles

and marked them for that reason, just as he did with the species of birds. Maybe they were landmarks for him."

They fell silent for a while.

Birgitta looked up from her book. "You should hear yourselves."

"Why's that?" Leif asked.

"Communicating with *invisible forces*," she parroted.

Maya laughed.

Leif shook his head in resignation. "You know," he said, staring straight ahead.

"What?"

"I feel like…I could go along with just about anything at the moment; I don't have much more to give. I thought I did, but in this type of situation I feel like I don't have what it takes. I'm just too tired. I don't have the energy to think. I want to potter around in the garden, or some damn thing. Play golf."

"You've never golfed," Birgitta said. "And the garden is dead now. It's autumn."

"Play with the grandchildren, then, or *something*."

"We don't have any grandchildren, Leif."

He swirled his snifter and brought it to his lips. "Anyway, soon I'll leave for good," he said, turning to Maya.

"So you keep saying. But okay, we have two years until your retirement, so two years to solve this, then?" she said, leaning across the armrest and clinking his glass with hers. "Two more years, that *is* a pretty long time."

Man Ray jumped up and curled himself in Maya's lap. His whole cat body expressed pleasure, rising and falling with his purring breaths.

"Everything but the motive points to Alex Hagman. But it feels like we're about to put the wrong person away," Leif said in resignation.

"Why don't we ignore Alex for the moment," Maya said, "and concentrate on what happened around the mire before all these murders. The Lingonberry Girl was discovered exactly two years before. The same summer that Tracy Larsson died and the Nordström family's tragedy occurred."

Maya stroked the cat and turned to gaze into the fire.

"There are so many question marks. Why did Tracy walk into the bog? And Nathalie's parents, why did Jonas kill his wife and then take his own life? And spare his daughter? I'm thinking..." she began as she followed the moving flames. "I'm thinking *that's* where we should look for our answer."

The muted October light rested over the cemetery. An older woman sat on a stool she'd brought along next to a large family grave, and two children were bounding down the gravel path nearby. Otherwise the cemetery was deserted.

Nathalie looked at the sketch she'd received from a helpful man at the parish office.

Over there. It was supposed to be over there, her parents' grave. Her legs felt heavy and she broke into a cold sweat.

Now she could see the grave.

Nordström, carved into stone.

She hadn't borne that name for such a long time; she had changed it immediately afterward, taking Harriet and Lars's shorter one, Ström. As if to draw a line, to get some distance. Instead it turned into a different sort of symbol, a symbol of how part of her had been erased, hidden. How she had fled, in silent panic, from a shame that was never her own.

The gravestone was small, simple and unassuming. Names and year, nothing more. Someone had decorated it with a lantern and a vase of a few maple twigs. She wondered who that could be—maybe one of her father's brothers. All her grandparents were dead and the aunt who'd tried to keep in touch had moved to Västerbotten.

Her Aunt Eva had been single and wanted Nathalie to

come and live with her in Åmål, but she had refused. There had been only one way. She wanted to get away from her former life, away from school, away from Åmål, as far away from Mossmarken as possible. Today she felt a pang of regret that she had been so firm and decisive on that front.

She crouched down and tried to work out how you were supposed to act at a graveside. What to think; how to think. What the point even was.

"Hi," she began in a whisper.

She looked around anxiously, but there was no one nearby.

"It's me."

The effect of those short words was shocking: her feelings welled up, blowing through her body like a storm and forcing it into a minor convulsion.

Out came a tear. One single tear. She caught it on her fingertip and looked at it as if it were a valuable discovery.

She turned back to the gravestone.

"It's been...a very long time. Since I saw you."

Silence.

"Mum. Dad. What the hell happened?"

Silence again.

"I miss you."

Then came the rest. Her body relaxed and the tears fell from her like a cleansing rain. She spread out her jacket and sat down.

*   *   *

Half an hour later, she was still there. The wind had dried her face. Her gaze wandered and fell upon another stone in the memorial park nearby.

The name "Tracy Larsson" and the year. It was hands down the most decorated site within view. She stood up, stretched, and moved to a bench by the gravel path. From there she could look at both graves, and she thought about how long she had been trying to protect herself from it, from this reality. How much it had scared her all these years. And how nice it was to stop fighting. To finally see reality, dressed in cut and carved stone. It wasn't so bad.

Nothing was as bad as running away.

Then a man came walking down the gravel path. She recognized him. He was the same, strangely enough, with his neat beard and sturdy build. Many years of hard work, mostly to his benefit, it seemed.

He approached Tracy's grave and stood there for a while. He tidied up the decorations and planted something. Then he turned around cautiously and looked at her.

"Hi, Peder," she said. "It's been a long time. Do you remember me?"

Her voice felt strong. Clear.

He stood up and walked over to her, leaning forward as if to get a better look.

"Is that you, Nathalie?"

"Yes."

"Well isn't that . . . I heard you were in the neighborhood. Otherwise I never would have recognized you."

"I know. It's been years."

It was surprisingly easy to chat to Peder. It seemed almost as if he had the need to talk to someone, and she just happened to be on hand.

They discussed the recent events, all the bodies that had been found, and how surreal and horrible it was. Then they started talking about Julia, how she was doing.

"I'm sure she'd be happy to hear from you," he said.

His smile caught her off guard. She remembered thinking, as a child, that he seldom laughed. Now it transformed his whole being, breaking up his aged face and rearranging all the lines.

"I'm sure she'd be very happy," he repeated. "You were such good friends."

"I've been meaning to," she said. "Soon."

Then she steeled herself and asked the question straight out. It was on a whim, but she couldn't help herself now that he was right there.

"Peder," she said, her voice thin, "can you tell me a little about my parents? I need to understand how Dad could have done what he did."

He sat down and gazed at her; a sympathetic look came across his face.

"I know there's no way you can know for sure," she went on, "but it would mean a lot to me if I could just find some clue. I can hardly remember them any more..."

"We didn't know each other that well," Peder began. "I thought it seemed like they were pretty happy together, your parents, I mean; of course they fought now and then, but who doesn't?" He ran his hand over his beard. "We've talked a lot about it, Yvonne and me."

"You saw them the night it happened?" Nathalie said.

"We had a meeting at your house," he said, nodding.

"But they weren't fighting at the time?"

"It was so long ago, Nathalie. And there was so much unpleasantness that summer." He stood up. "Well, I have to be getting back. But promise me you'll visit Julia. And please do drop by our place too. You live in Gothenburg now?"

"Yes, but for the time being I'm staying at the manor."

"Good, maybe we'll see each other tomorrow. Agneta has invited everyone to a new neighborhood meeting. It will be the first one in fourteen years."

When Nathalie came back to her cottage, at first she wasn't able to unlock the door. It took a while for her to realize it was because her hand was shaking. Finally inside, she went into the room, leaned against the wall and sank down on the floor.

Everything was spinning. Everyone was watching her. She got up, covered the windows in a frenzy and sat back down, but she still felt like she was being watched. The walls. The bed. The air.

She didn't understand. The unexpected encounter with Peder seemed so gentle and undramatic when it happened, but it must have set something off, or else she was going crazy. Or both. She could sense it, how the dams were buckling, how the past was rushing toward her like cold water, in under her skin.

She could hear her parents' voices clearly now, upset as they were arguing about some mundane thing—it was always about the small things, whether to have the windows open at night, or if Nathalie could go by herself to this or that place.

But what did she not remember? What darkness did she not recall? It must have been there all along, in her father's eyes. How else could he have done what he did?

I want to know!

She wasn't sure if she screamed out loud or not.

All she could hear was a thundering in her ears, as though from something inside her that was about to burst.

W elcome!" Göran was wearing an apron and hold- ing oven gloves when he opened the door. "Come in. Great to see you again!"

"Nice to be back," Maya said.

She hung up her coat and followed him into the kitchen. It smelled of garlic and herbs.

This had been his idea. He'd called that afternoon to ask if he could invite her to dinner. She was well aware that he might have a hidden motive or agenda: to get some inside informa- tion on what was going on in the investigation. But after their last meeting she had grown more interested in him, and not only because he had directed her right to Alex Hagman but just as much for his knowledge and ideas about the mire. She had accepted without a moment's hesitation, even though she had Oskar visiting.

So Oskar drove her to Mossmarken and dropped her off at Göran's door.

Call when you want me to pick you up.

Sure.

Now she was standing in Göran's kitchen, watching him pour two glasses of wine.

"Oh...you want some, right?"

"I'd love some. I'm getting a lift later."

"Was that your husband in the car?"

She laughed. "Sure, who else?"

She took a sip of wine and leaned against the doorjamb. "What about you, you live alone here?"

"Yes. I've been on my own since my wife vanished," he said. "So, you're married?"

Maya chuckled. "No, he's not my husband, I was only joking. It's just me. And the cat, these days."

"Then who drove you over?" he asked.

"Well…" she said, walking into the living room and having a look around. "He's this guy named Oskar. An assistant."

Her gaze moved across the walls, trying to absorb everything she hadn't had time to see on her last visit. She liked this room, with its walls covered in books about ghosts. The atmosphere of his quiet, intellectual madness.

She sipped her wine. She spotted two enormous glass jars on a shelf by the fireplace. She approached them and looked at their labels. They said "June 22, 2015" and "Feb. 2, 2016."

"What are those?" she asked.

"That's…" Göran leaned into the room to find out what she was talking about. "They're just samples from the bog. I like to try to bring some material home when I run into something noteworthy out there."

"Noteworthy?"

"It might be that I feel some sort of presence, or I see those veils of mist I told you about. Then I scoop up some air in a special sampling pouch, and I try to transfer it to these jars." He was speaking loudly to be heard from the kitchen.

"So it's...air?"

He came out with a large earthenware casserole, which he set on the table. "Yes. It's probably just air. So it seems. They've been there for a long time now, and...well. Nothing has happened."

I just have to let go, Maya thought. There was nothing to hold on to in what Göran said, so there was no point in even trying. She just had to go along with it. And in some ways, it was liberating. The exact opposite of how it sometimes felt when people had very firm conceptions of so-called true phenomena. Opinions they sometimes defended as if they were a matter of life and death.

She had often been privy to such discussions. Sometimes she had to excuse herself and leave the room. And it wasn't to make a point, it was a purely physical reaction. She couldn't breathe.

"Dinner is served! Chicken casserole," Göran said. "I hope you like it."

"If it tastes half as good as it smells, you're a genius."

She sat down and took a helping. Tasted it. Closed her eyes. "You *are* a genius."

"Let's not exaggerate. But it's true you aren't the first to praise my cooking."

He served himself and leaned back. "How is your photography project going?"

"Well. There'll be an exhibition. Nothing big, mostly for fun. Even if the theme is a serious one."

"Oh, that big? A solo exhibition? You're established on that level...as an artist?"

He didn't know who she was. Heat flared in her chest. All the interviews in the local paper she'd agreed to; all the pictures they'd published of her—a man like Göran should have an inkling who she was.

He smiled at her. "I'm just kidding. I've read about you. Didn't I tell you that last time? You've been in the paper every other week. Since even before you moved here."

"I know. It was mostly while I was working on that exhibition with the portraits of naked children. There was a lot of debate over it."

"But you live in Fengerskog now?"

"I just bought a house there."

"That art school has done a lot for this area."

"It really has."

"Or *those* art schools, I should say. Since there are two now."

"Exactly. This wine is good, by the way," Maya said, taking the bottle to look at the label. "Is it Italian?"

Göran nodded.

"Well, my God," he said, taking a deep breath.

And they began to talk about everything that had happened.

Four hours later they had moved to the sofa and chairs and nearly emptied a second bottle of Italian wine. Maya realized she hadn't called Oskar.

"It's almost midnight. Someone was going to pick me up."

She went to check her phone, which was in her handbag in the hall.

"Someone was trying to reach me," she said with a mildly guilty look. "Someone wants to go to bed."

"Can't you just get a taxi? Or sleep over. That's fine too."

"Are you sure? It wouldn't be too weird?"

"It feels perfectly natural at the moment." Göran laughed. "So we can keep talking for a while. I don't think we're done yet."

She sent a text to Oskar to explain. They drank more. Laughed and buzzed and eventually started talking about a volume of essays Göran had read called *Visiting with Ghosts*. It was about the ghosts that moved in linguistic, literary, scientific and political worlds. Amusingly enough, it had been written by a man with the same name. Göran Dahlberg.

"It's not your book?"

"It *is* my book," he said with a laugh, "but I didn't write it."

"Really?"

"Definitely. It contains over one hundred micro-essays, and it's really something. To be honest, that's probably where I got most of the knowledge I consider relevant, nowadays, on the nature of ghosts."

"Does it say how to keep from being affected by them, on a physical level?"

"Well, other books are probably better for that, but in general it's quite comprehensive."

Maya countered by telling him about one of her favorite photographers, Francesca Woodman, whose esthetic she considered ghostly, to say the least.

"I suppose that's what I like most about her," she said, Googling some pictures on her phone. They were largely black and white staged photographs from the seventies, often with the young artist's own nude body erased and dissolving, or vanishing into the wallpaper.

"Look at this," Maya said. "It's not just that she takes control, flipping the traditional perspective and making herself the subject. It's also the way she does it. By exposing her own body in such a straightforward and uncompromising way, she makes herself invisible. Her body becomes transparent, sort of. A neutral channel for what she wants to convey."

They bent over the screen and studied the photographs.

"Lots of people read self-destruction and desperation into the way she portrays the dissolution of her own form, her own identity," Maya went on. "And I suppose that's understandable, since she took her own life when she was twenty-two. Although not even the portrayal of a death wish is necessarily destructive, in my opinion."

"No?" Göran asked, straightening his back.

Maya leaned back and thought for a moment.

"No, I see it more as...a secret longing for home. For what we are. In my eyes, her pictures are playful examinations of the relationship between body and being, between form and formlessness."

"A longing for home?" Göran asked. "How so?"

She picked up one of the tealights on the table and blew it out. "Like that, I mean. See the smoke dissipating?"

"Yes..." he said hesitantly, after a moment. "Or, no. It's gone now."

"Exactly. Don't you see yourself in that?"

Göran looked at her, smiling dejectedly. "Sounds kooky to me."

Maya let out a peal of loud laughter.

"What?" Göran asked.

"Nothing," she said. "That just sounded so funny, coming from you."

The leather chair squeaked as she shifted and leaned forward.

"Göran, can I ask you something?"

"Sure."

"After Tracy died—is there anything particular you remember from that time?"

He appeared to be racking his memory, then shook his head. "I know I'm heading for dementia, but . . . no. It depends what you mean."

"What about that neighborhood meeting at Nathalie's parents' place?" Maya asked, afraid she wouldn't remember his response. The wine was really starting to make her fuzzy.

"Right, it was the last one," Göran sighed. "We ran out of steam, and then everyone just wanted to move away from here."

He told her that they'd once held meetings at least once a year, in each other's homes, to discuss common concerns. More people lived around the mire back then, but not everyone attended each time.

He thought he remembered representatives from two other households there, beyond Nathalie's family and those who still lived there today. Texas and Laila had been in their thirties at the time and hadn't taken over their respective farms yet, but their parents usually attended the meetings.

One year it had all been about a new culvert over in the creek; another it was winter upkeep for the road. This last time, they had been planning to discuss the potential construction of a new hunting stand. But as their alcohol intake increased—and there was sometimes quite a bit of the stuff at those meetings—the conversation turned to everything that had happened that summer.

"We started talking about the bog body, and what happened to Tracy, of course. It was all so painful," Göran said.

"I guess I've probably repressed most of it. Plus I was pretty drunk."

"But an argument broke out, didn't it?"

Maya had read the police report from the night in question, and the description sounded more like a drunken brawl than an orderly neighborhood meeting.

Göran was quiet. She sensed calm resignation somewhere deep inside him.

"We talked about all sorts of things, but I remember the others tried to push me on my knowledge of the undead; the trouble they could cause. Whether it could have been the undead that caused Tracy's death. If anyone should know, it was me, they said, since my wife had disappeared too."

"Who said that? Everyone?"

"No. Some of them didn't believe my theories at all, and they got angry. Yes, we started arguing, that's true. I remember arguing. But then we broke up the meeting."

"But what did you say, exactly?"

"I don't remember. Why do you want to know?"

"It might be important."

"Sorry. You'll have to ask the others."

"But you told them that the undead exist; don't you have any recollection of who agreed with you, and what you decided should be done?"

"No, I don't remember. You have to keep in mind that this was many years ago. All I recall was saying that there wasn't much you could do, except be careful. I suppose I told them how to protect themselves."

"And then you didn't have any more meetings?"

"No, but it's funny you should mention it. Because Agneta invited us all to one tomorrow; I think she wants to get some sort of sense of community in the middle of all this misery."

"I'm going to that meeting too."

"You are?" Göran asked, looking at her in surprise.

"Yes, just for a little bit. Agneta promised I could take some photographs inside the manor house, and a group shot of all of you. It might turn into something for my project," she said. "But what was I going to say...? Yes, what do you think actually happened to Nathalie's parents?"

"What do I think happened to them?" He raised his eyebrows. "What do you mean?"

"You know...why did her dad shoot her mum and then himself? The same night as your meeting. You must have wondered, didn't you?"

Göran shook his head. "All I can say is that the family had problems that must have led to what happened. Nathalie came over sometimes when the screaming and shouting were at their worst. I think they were usually kind to her, but they certainly could fight. And Jonas got aggressive sometimes when he drank. So...I don't know. Sometimes everything just goes to hell."

He gave a huge yawn. "Well, it's getting to be bedtime for this old man. I'll make up the bed in the guest room."

~

Just as Maya was crawling into bed in Göran's guest room, her phone rang. She looked at the screen. It was one thirty, and the number was one she didn't recognize.

"Is that Maya Linde? Hi, it's me, Nathalie Ström. The biologist. Sorry to call so late, but I had to. There's something I'm worried about."

"What is it? Tell me."

"I . . . I just have to ask, is it true that you found a shovel with Johannes's DNA in Alex's shed? That it's the strongest evidence you have against him?"

"Where did you hear that?"

"I read it online."

Maya sighed to herself. "Why do you ask?"

"Is it red? I mean, really red? And basically brand new?"

"Tell me what you're thinking, if it is. If the shovel is red," Maya said.

"The thing is, I borrowed a shovel from Alex when I went out in the bog to take samples. And Johannes was with me; I even think he was carrying the shovel!"

"Okay, Nathalie," said Maya. "That's no problem. No

problem at all, but I'm glad you told me. Try to get some sleep, and Leif will give you a call tomorrow. Okay?"

"Okay. Goodnight."

"Goodnight."

Maya texted Leif the new information.

Well, hell, she thought afterward, almost relieved. *There goes that evidence. Alex might be eccentric, and he might be able to see patterns and order and variances in nature, but there's no way he's the guy we're after.*

All at once, her exhaustion was gone. She lay awake in the guest room, thinking about Alex, thinking about the conversation she'd had with Göran about the neighborhood meeting. Then she looked at the artwork on the walls. Surprisingly meaningless landscape paintings. They didn't match Göran's personality.

She grew thirsty and got up for a drink.

A beautiful old secretary desk stood in a corner of the room outside the bathroom. Göran had placed the folder containing his own investigation into the disappearances on top of a stack of documents.

She picked it up, and just as she was about to open it she noticed a photograph underneath. It was of a woman she recognized.

Tina Gabrielsson from Trollhättan. The woman who had gone missing in Karlstad in 2004, during a business trip.

Göran had photos of everyone he suspected had vanished

in the mire, so it wasn't strange that she should find this one. But he hadn't shown her this particular photo. It was also different from the others, which were all Photostat copies or newspaper clippings. The photo of Tina Gabrielsson was an original from a photo studio in Gothenburg. Maya turned it over and read the back.

Thanks for a wonderful weekend.
Tina

She stood stock-still, paralyzed. As if every movement, starting now, involved risk. As if she were in a gaping maw, in a cage.

Göran knew Tina Gabrielsson.

Had she been naïve? Was Göran actually insane?

Maya rapidly and silently gathered her belongings and hurried downstairs. Too fast. She tripped over the sleeve of a sweater she was carrying and fell headlong down the stairs.

She landed with a thud, raised her head and listened.

"Hello?" came a sleepy voice from Göran's bedroom. "Maya, is that you?"

She stood up, pulled on her shoes and jacket, and rushed out of the house. When she got into the garden, all the energy inside her died away. *The car.* She didn't have a car here.

At that instant, the hall light came on behind her.

She staggered around the corner as fast as she could; she came to the road and hid behind a hedge.

She watched as the front door opened: the fog of Göran's breath.

"Maya," he called into the night.

His voice blended with the sounds from the mire, a vague wail from a bird in the distance and a shattering wind that cut through the trees.

She heard him again, or was it him? It was as if the words suddenly sprang from the landscape, as if they rose from the fen.

"Where are you, Maya?"

She kept running, afraid that a car would come, that she would see the glare of headlights. As she ran, she called Oskar.

He didn't pick up. She called again. And again. At last she heard his sleepy voice.

"Hello?"

"You have to come and get me," she said. "Now."

Nathalie could not fall asleep. The knockings seemed to come from every angle, from inside her head, outside on the door, from the mire. She curled up under the duvet to hide from the echo but it only grew stronger. So she rose and dressed.

I give up. The words rang through her. *I don't care any more. I don't care about anything.*

She went out of the cabin and into the chilly darkness, faltering between late night and early morning. She didn't close the door properly, or button her coat. Her feet steered her aimlessly forward. Along the footbridges, slippery from the night dew, over the vigilant landscape, open as the invitation to an embrace.

Somehow, she just wanted in there. Into the darkness and the damp void, as if it were the womb from whence she came.

Walking further into the mist, her borders felt blurred, the perception of who she was, where she was. What everything was about.

Then, a shout cut through the air.

The sound rattled her awake, brought her back to full consciousness. Fear prickled her arms.

Natalie stood still for some time, but heard nothing more. Maybe she had imagined it? She began to move her feet again, slowly. Suddenly, another sound. Much closer this time. A branch cracking, followed by sinister silence.

Hello? she said, voice thin.

And then she saw it. A shadowy figure in the distance, body crouched over the mire as if ready to spring. At first she thought the darkness was playing tricks on her, or that her own mind was, but it seemed too real: someone was standing there, not responding to her call. And then the figure began moving toward her. It looked like a man, and he was holding something in his hand, a stick or a pole.

As the panic exploded through her body, she turned around and ran. In the back of her mind she knew how dangerous it was to run over the mire in the dark, but the instinct to get away drove her forward. Her feet flew over the moss, finding stable ground with remarkable agility, as if it were her second nature; a skill planted early. When the footbridges split, she veered left, and soon thereafter she noticed the trees were getting taller, so she dared to step beyond the path and ran into the woods, hoping that the ground would carry her.

She ran without looking back for several minutes, then she came across a hut of some sort and jumped in behind it for cover. She couldn't see anyone, so she caught her breath for a moment, still not sure what the darkness was hiding. When she looked around she realized where she had actually ended up.

It was *her* hut. She'd run into the place where she'd spent endless hours as a child. She gazed around in astonishment, as if she could not believe her eyes, reached out and let her fingertips trace the rough planks, and then quickly crouched to crawl inside. She sat down where she'd sat down a hundred times before, peering out through the glassless window. The wind outside picked up, fierce, sudden. Nathalie stared out into the darkness, on the lookout for her pursuer, but no one came. She waited in silence, heart racing. Minutes went by, an hour passed.

And then, slowly, something stepped forward.

But not from the darkness outside.

It came from the darkness within.

If she had not been so exhausted in every part of her being, maybe she would have resisted. But now, instead, she surrendered to the force of memory that overtook her as she crouched in her childhood hideout.

It was the last day. The last summer. She was at home. Twelve years old.

Late summer had seeped the last color from the tired plants in the garden; her dad stretched out on the sofa after dinner while her mum cleared up. Nathalie was mostly just wondering why Julia never called any more. After all, Julia was her best friend.

She wandered over to Göran's house and peered through the kitchen window. Someone was sitting inside, as usual. The curtains were drawn, so only a silhouette was visible. The figure seemed to be listening attentively, nodding now and then, and asking the occasional question. Someone was taking notes.

She decided to make the rounds of the gravel path outside the house and look for cigarette butts. Her parents gave her one krona per butt instead of an allowance.

Once she'd gathered a small pile she switched to practicing handball jump shots on the lawn. They had a tournament the next weekend: the Summer Cup in Åmål. She wanted to get in some good goals. Maybe she could impress someone in the stands.

She picked up a rock, ran, jumped and threw. She really had the technique down.

After she went back inside the house, it didn't take long for the guests to start appearing. Agneta and Gustav, Yvonne and Peder. Göran arrived soon after, and someone else. Everyone was in high spirits at first: cheese, cookies and wine were served. Nathalie was given a bag of chips to take to her room.

She sat on her bed and opened the latest issue of *Buster*. She made believe that she was a goalie, saving every last shot. That she was a hero.

She grew tired and dozed off. She might have slept for a couple of hours or more.

"Come on, for Christ's sake, get your head out of your ass. How fucking stupid can you get?"

Someone was shouting; they sounded drunk. A commotion ensued.

"But this is serious!" someone else cried. "You have to listen!"

She heard her father trying to calm the quarrellers down. "Okay, it's time for you all to go home. We'll talk about this another time."

A short time later, Nathalie went to the kitchen for a glass of water. Bottles and glasses scattered the table. She saw a few guests crowding in the hall among jackets and shoes; she met Göran's gaze and cautiously nodded hello.

Then she sneaked back up to her room and crawled into bed. She heard the guests leaving and the footsteps on the stairs as her parents went up to their bedroom.

"I fell asleep again," she whispered as if she were sitting next to Johannes, talking to him again. "I slept for a while. Then I heard..." She put her hand to her mouth and realized that she was shaking. "A sound woke me up. It wasn't the shots that woke me up... I always thought they did, but I woke up before that. I woke up because of a... different sound. Someone came over."

It felt like the sounds in her head were being tapped out by a hammer.

Knock, knock, knock.

Knock, knock, knock.

Someone came over. Someone knocked at the door before the shots rang out.

I heard the knocking. I heard the voice.

Nathalie stepped out of the hut. The morning had broken, a soft light spreading across the mire. She needed to get back. She needed to remember everything.

~

The wild grapes had sent long fingers through the cracked pane to squeeze the back door from every direction; years of patience had broken it open.

It was like the house had been waiting for her. As if it took a breath as she arrived, drawing her through the door. She remembered how frequently she'd come in this way when she wanted to avoid attracting attention. It led straight to the narrow staircase to the first floor, where the den and the big bathroom were. Plus she could get to her room without passing the kitchen.

Now it was dark and smelled of moisture and decay. Her past was literally disintegrating. Fading away. Hazy contours wherever she turned. The large sideboard in the hall; its drawers were closed but she knew: the old phone books in the bottom drawer. Then mittens, hats, bottles of hairspray and tubes of hair gel.

She looked into the mirror, past all the moisture and all the spider webs, through all the cracks. She saw the picture of herself as a twelve-year-old. She was back in the house.

She was home again.

She wanted to remember. She had always wanted to forget, but now she wanted to remember. There was a truth in what had happened that summer, and it hadn't come out. But she knew; somehow, she knew. And now the images needed to surface.

The sound of the coffee-maker that came on automatically at seven; the smell of food cooking in the afternoon. The fan, always broken.

It all flowed together. Drifted apart.

Nathalie moved through by the glow of her mobile phone.

She went down the hall that led to the kitchen and her bedroom.

The bottles and glasses were still on the kitchen counter, from that last night. Deserted, abandoned, enveloped in years of moisture.

She went to her room and sat on the bed. The hardwood floor, stained dark; the wallpaper she'd chosen, with little red cherries. The bed with its beige velvet bedspread, a Christmas present. Next to that, the desk. Posters on the wall: the Ark and Kajsa Bergqvist.

Now the animals lived here. A veil over everything.

But she couldn't see the decay any more. She was twelve

years old; she was there again. It was dark outside her windows. And the knocking woke her up.

Knock, knock, knock.

Knock, knock, knock.

She heard the quick steps down the stairs. She got up, opened the door a crack, and sat down on the floor. Her gaze aimed straight into the hall, past chairs and table legs.

She heard her dad: *It's them again. They're back.*

Silence, for a moment. And then her mum's voice: *Jonas! What are you doing?*

I'm only going to scare him. I'm going to give that bastard a scare.

The front door opened.

At first she couldn't tell who it was; she could only hear muffled voices, forced whispers.

"You two are sensible folks; you two, at least. We can't lose more of our own. You understand that, don't you?"

"What do you mean, lose?" she heard her father say.

"We all know what happened to Tracy. The mire is hungry; we have to feed it. And save what we have left."

The silence that followed.

Then, her father's voice: "You've totally lost it. You can't seriously be saying that we should—"

"Listen to me," the other voice interrupted. "You know the mire; you know what it's capable of. If we're going to keep living here, we have to do something!"

"What happened happened," her dad said. "It was a terrible tragedy. But it won't happen again."

"Oh yes it will, the mire wants its gifts, and from now on it won't be any of our own, it won't be any of us, anyone living in Mossmarken!"

"You're out of your mind! Get out of here. I need to close the door," said her dad.

"You can't ignore it; you know what happened to Tracy. Are you prepared to sacrifice your Nathalie?"

"Get out of here at once. I'm calling the police. Go away. Get out! Out!"

A commotion in the hallway.

"What the hell?" said the voice. "You have a...*you're* the one who's cra—"

And then the shot.

Then total silence.

Then bodies moving swiftly.

"*What have you done?*" She heard her mother's broken voice.

Another shot. A quick maneuver with the bodies. The rifle, down into her dad's hand.

No one noticed her; no one even considered that Nathalie might be in the house, that she was sitting on the floor in her room, that she was a witness. That she saw.

The only thing that lingered as she was left alone was the sound of the car with its motor running outside, eventually driving off. And the words of the man who had killed her parents. His voice. She remembered it now. In fact, she had never forgotten it.

The mire wants its gifts, and from now on it won't be any of our own.

SIX

The air in the room carried a scent of jasmine. The flocked wallpaper and heavy curtains wrapped the attendees in earth tones and softness.

Gustav was on a chair near the door; Laila and Texas had each chosen an easy chair next to a small table. Peder and Yvonne were sharing a Victorian sofa along one wall.

Göran was alone in a corner. He had avoided looking in Maya's direction when she came in, and she wondered what he was thinking, why he hadn't answered her texts, why he hadn't even reacted to her sudden exit.

She'd tried to tone down the incident in front of Oskar; she didn't want the whole school to start talking. But he certainly had looked worried when he picked her up out there in the middle of the night.

"What did he do?" he asked, furious.

"He got an idea into his head; it was best for me to leave," she lied vaguely. "Thanks for picking me up."

She had sent a text to Göran to tell him she'd seen the photo of Tina Gabrielsson. That she now knew he'd known her. If he was as innocent as he pretended to be, he should at least make an effort to explain, she thought, to explain why he'd tried to conceal their acquaintance.

She had also called Leif to say they should bring Göran in right away, because now Göran knew that she knew.

But Leif wanted to wait and see.

"It's not the right time, Maya. And it's not a crime to know the victim of a crime. We have to remain calm and avoid getting ahead of ourselves."

"But it's odd that he hasn't said anything," she persisted. "We've seen each other quite a bit in the last few days, and talked about what happened in the area, and he hasn't said a word about it. I'm going to see him at the manor; what am I supposed to say?"

"Easy, Maya. We'll bring him in when the time is right."

She had put on the wide-angle lens, rigged up the camera on a tall tripod, and unfolded her stepladder to raise herself up higher. That way, she could capture all of them.

Agneta came in and stood where everyone could see her.

"As you can see, we have Maya with us today," she said, gesturing her way, "and she's going to take our picture. I think all of you have met her already. It will be fun to see what she comes up with." Agneta straightened her back and smiled ceremoniously. "But while Maya is fiddling with her photography things, we can start with the reason I wanted us to meet today. We're here to talk about a few items and maybe that's a good thing, to do this sometimes, to discuss common . . . concerns, so to speak."

Then the door opened cautiously and Nathalie stepped into the room. She had a peculiar look on her face. There was something liberated about her. Something sorrowful, yet strong and steady.

The others registered her arrival but soon went back to listening to Agneta.

Only one person continued to observe Nathalie. Nathalie locked eyes with him, and it was as if he couldn't look away. His gaze twisted and turned and tried to escape, until at last it seemed to resign itself. At that instant, Maya clicked the shutter release.

At the same time, the double doors opened and Leif Berggren appeared.

"Hello," Agneta said, a question in her voice. "We're a little busy just now, if you'll excuse us."

"Oh?" Leif said. "What are you busy with?"

"We're...going to discuss recent events. We have all been deeply affected by what's happened. And it's not the first time we've dealt with difficult things out here, as you may know," she said, turning to the others for support.

"I can wait."

Leif walked in and sat down in an empty easy chair, looking around for Maya and finding her standing on a stepladder with her camera in one corner. "Go on."

The others exchanged uncertain looks.

"Perhaps I can inquire what this is in regard to," Agneta

said with forced courtesy. "We're holding a private meeting. What were you planning to wait for?"

"For some colleagues who are on their way. We'll need to interrupt this meeting soon."

"What?" Agneta said. "What is this all about?"

"What is this all about?" Leif repeated. "It's about a number of people who were found in the bog out there. People someone killed and buried during the last twelve years. It's about a young man who was knocked out but has now regained consciousness and had some interesting information to share."

"He regained consciousness?" Agneta said. "Well, that's good news."

"*Good news?*" Leif said.

Maya could tell that Leif was irritated, that he was about to lose control. He was crossing a line. But he probably hadn't had a good night's sleep for a long time.

"There are certain people in this room," he went on, "who will hardly think that's good news."

Leif let his eyes wander from Agneta to her husband, and then to Peder, Yvonne, Texas, Leila and, finally, Göran.

Leif lowered his head.

Eyes darted this way and that; those in attendance looked at each other with rising unease.

"Are you saying one of us..." Agneta said. "That's absolutely insane. Those of us who live here by the mire suffer almost as much from all this as the families of the victims."

"Of course it's insane. The question is, how could it have happened?" Leif said. "And that's what I hope to learn soon. We're dealing with a total of six murders and one attempted murder—and that's just what we know so far."

"*Eight* murders," said a voice behind him.

At that moment, two uniformed officers stepped into the room.

"What?" Leif asked, turning to Nathalie.

"It was *eight* murders and one attempted murder," she said.

"Who is it?" Laila shrieked.

The police crossed the room and approached Peder and Yvonne.

"I can explain..." Peder said, standing up. Yvonne followed his lead and held her arm up in front of him as if to protect him.

A brief scuffle broke out; handcuffs and keys rattled. "Wait...what are you doing?" Yvonne was shaken. "Is this necessary?"

It seemed like time slowed down, like the moment became encapsulated in an eerie, silent spell. Peder and Yvonne's eyes darted around the room, as if defying the stunned faces of the others.

"What is it now?" Texas finally asked. "What did you do?"

Agneta scratched the corner of her mouth with a fingernail. She seemed to want to speak, but the sounds that fell from her mouth didn't form whole words. Then a darkness passed over her face as the truth of what had happened came crashing over her.

"There's just one thing I want to say before we go," Peder said, shaking the officer's hand from his shoulder in irritation. "There was *no other way*. No other way. We didn't do it for fun. We did it for all of you, too, for the sake of the neighborhood. Don't forget that." He threw up his arms. "I wish I didn't have to do it. Göran can tell you. He knows all about how the mire works. You're not free now, if that's what you're thinking."

"What have you *done*?" Texas asked, his eyes roving around the room.

Göran was sitting with his back perfectly straight, his face white.

"I don't understand," he whispered.

Yes, that's what happened," Yvonne Larsson said during interrogation at the police station in Karlstad. Maya was in the next room, following the conversation between Yvonne, Leif and one other interrogator.

Yvonne sat with her hands in her lap, pulling them further and further up into her sleeves as if she were trying to sneak off unnoticed, out of her clothes, out of her own skin. She blinked.

"We realized that we were...obliged to do something. We knew what went on out in the mire; we had experienced it ourselves, of course. Göran Dahlberg talks about the bog's hunger too, about all the people who have vanished throughout the years. We were just as frightened as everyone else and we knew it could be our turn again at any time. The mire is never satisfied. No one can judge us if they haven't been through what we have. We had lost our darling, darling child. We couldn't lose another one, could we? You wouldn't want that either, would you? If you had children. Do you have children? Well, then you understand."

She was pleasant and forthcoming and entreated Leif and the other interrogator as if she thought she could get them on her side, as if they would have no trouble understanding her point of view, her actions.

"So I stand by it. What we did. It wasn't always pleasant; it certainly wasn't. But not everything in life is meant to be pleasant. Sometimes you just have to do what you have to do. That's just the way of it."

She took a deep breath. "What worries me most is that the mire will be waiting for a gift, and no one...no one will do anything."

After a few days, Peder turned inward more and more. His large body looked out of place on the small chair in the interrogation room, as if it didn't know how to simply sit. As if it were used to constant work, moving, doing. Keeping up. Making decisions.

"I actually wanted to stop for a while," he admitted. "I did. I thought we could settle for keeping the children under close watch in bad weather. But then there was the little boy who disappeared. The mire was...threatening us. We wanted to protect Julia above all, and later her children. It's easy to be careless one time, and then it's too late, forever. It felt safest for us to keep that hunger satisfied, so to speak. Often we used animals and so on, but sometimes...sometimes it was people. We knew it was necessary. We filled their pockets with money to show our respect, to show that we understood the importance. I didn't want to have to go out looking for another child. We did it for the sake of the children. Do you understand? We had no choice."

We did it for the sake of the children.

SEVEN

Nathalie was wrapped in a big down coat and sitting in the outdoor seating at the manor café when Maya arrived. Agneta had left some of the patio furniture outside—a gift on a day like today.

"What fantastic weather," Maya said, looking up at the sky.

"I know. It's wonderful. Have a seat." Nathalie gestured at one of the chairs.

"Thanks for your call," Maya said. "I'm really glad to see you."

"I'm planning to head back to Gothenburg soon; I only have a few samples left to take. But it seemed like it might be nice to talk before I left."

Maya nodded. "Sure."

At first they chatted about Nathalie's dissertation and Maya's upcoming exhibition, and they ordered two large cups of tea. Then they came to Peder and Yvonne.

"I'm having such a hard time taking it all in," Nathalie said. "That my childhood friend's parents are guilty of all this. That Peder shot Dad and then Mum. *Accidentally* shot Dad, but still, he shot Mum…"

Maya looked at her for a long time, taking a deep breath as she searched for words.

"But can't you…don't you still feel a little relieved? It

turns out your dad was never guilty; he never killed anyone. He didn't kill your mum *or* himself."

Nathalie turned her face to the sun again and closed her eyes.

"I do, actually," she said quietly. "In the midst of all this craziness I do sometimes feel relieved; it's like I've got them back, my dad, my parents. All the crap is gone. The pressure is gone. Yes, I feel...empty." She laughed and turned to Maya. "In a good way, I mean."

"I understand. That's good to hear."

"At the same time...I've also been feeling this sadness I never felt before. Because it happened. Because I lost so much of my childhood. It's new to me, not burying those feelings. It...aches somehow."

Maya let her gaze rest on Nathalie. "Let it ache. I believe you can handle it, that there's a relief there. In letting go of that resistance. Allowing that sadness to be, letting it travel around and run riot and change you and then letting it wither. That's when you'll feel that you are in fact greater than your sorrow. That you're greater than *everything* you think and experience."

As the hot tea cooled in the October air, the conversation turned to Nathalie's upcoming journey home.

"By the way, who did you end up with?" Maya asked. "When you moved to Gothenburg. Relatives?"

"No, I didn't know them. Which suited me just fine, for

what it's worth—I wanted a fresh start. But it wasn't great. Apparently someone thought that the more God-fearing the family, the better off I would be. So I ended up with what must have been the most religious people in the city."

"Aha," Maya said.

"Or...I'm sorry. Do you believe in God?"

Maya chuckled and waved off the apology. "That's a hard question to answer if you don't know what the person asking means by the concept of God. God means different things to different people. So maybe we shouldn't get into—"

"Well, what does it mean to you?" Nathalie interrupted.

"For me, God is..." she began, "a sort of timeless reality that can't be described or explained...or even approached by thought—it can only be unveiled inside yourself and experienced directly."

Nathalie could tell this wasn't the first time Maya had talked about God.

"And when it happens," Maya went on, "you know with your whole being that all separation in the world is imaginary; that all is fundamentally united."

"And what does this...this *all* consist of, in your view?" Nathalie asked.

"One word that at least points in the right direction is *emptiness*."

Nathalie furrowed her brow and then burst into laughter. "Really, emptiness?"

"Yes…" Maya said. "But it's not *empty* emptiness. It's just empty of shape, borders, thoughts, concepts."

"Okay," Nathalie said hesitantly. "Which means what?"

"Oh, how should I put it…?" Maya said, leaning back and apparently choosing each word with great care. "It's a type of… space made of pure consciousness out of which the world is created in every moment. It's a wakefulness beyond intellect, an unchangeable existence, and not only are people able to find it within themselves—it is our very source and our deepest true nature. And that's what…" She laughed, as if recalling a feeling. "That's what's so funny about the search for spirituality, that in the end you are struck by the knowledge that you *are* what you're looking for. It's not something you can touch; no one can see it." She paused. "*It is the thing that sees.*"

They soon parted ways, but the words continued to sound in Nathalie's mind; they rang through her body with a bright tone from another world, a world where she saw herself by a lake, through the eyes of a deer.

It is the thing that sees.

∽

Later that afternoon, Nathalie packed up her equipment, folders, papers and books. Her computer, with her dissertation and all her research results.

It was time to go home to a future she couldn't imagine. A future without a safety net was what it felt like.

Or maybe it was the opposite. Maybe, for the first time, she had solid ground to stand on. Something had changed within her, something had been redirected and her perspective had altered. She was almost looking forward to seeing her foster parents again.

After the night in the hut and before the meeting at the manor, only a few hours before Johannes woke up, Nathalie had been back once more to sit at his bedside. His mother was there when she came in, singing something to him; it sounded like an Arabic song.

"Keep going," Nathalie said when she stopped.

But Maria shook her head and smiled. "I'm done. I used to sing him that song when he was little."

"It's nice," Nathalie said as she sat down. "How're things here?"

"There's good news from the doctors," Maria went on. "They say he might be close to waking up."

"Really?" Nathalie felt a wave of emotions strike her. She looked at Johannes and was about to touch his leg, but stopped herself.

"So he'll wake up soon," she said.

Maria smiled. "There are indications that he might, anyway. We'll see. I'm not taking anything for granted. But thanks for spending so much time here; I truly appreciate everything you do," she said, putting her hand to her heart.

Now, standing in the cottage folding clothes and placing them in her suitcase, Nathalie heard the knock on the door and right away she knew it was him. She recognized the light touch of his hand on the wood, the gentle melody of his knock.

She opened the door and there he was, thin and fragile, but his smile contained all the energy in the world. Not far off, behind him, she could see the taxi that had brought him here. He was supporting himself on a rolling walker, and he looked at her without saying anything.

She didn't know how to react; she was so used to being the one who looked, the one who watched.

"Johannes," was all she could muster.

She couldn't even bring herself to hug him.

"Nathalie," he said, and smiled.

He took a step forward, reached for her hand, and brought it to his cheek.

"I heard what you did," he said. "Thank you. Thank you so very much."

She gave a quick shake of her head and smiled. "It was... nothing."

She realized that she felt perfectly at ease. Something inside her felt new. And quite simple.

"How's your unfortunate joy?" she wisecracked. Then she was afraid she might have crossed a line.

Until she saw his reaction.

"Presumably it's going to be even more unfortunate now," he said. "Where are we going to live? In Gothenburg?"

"I don't know where *you're* going to live," she said with a smile. "But Gothenburg is pretty overrated, isn't it?"

Hung on the walls were black and white square images, one meter by one meter, mounted under simple mats in narrow, black-glazed wooden frames.

First there were four landscapes. Then four images of deserted, decaying houses and gardens. And finally, disjointed body parts. A foot, a hand, a turned cheek. A closed eye, the back of a neck and some hair. In the end, she had chosen to leave out the portraits of the residents of the bog.

Maya gazed out of the large window and found that soft snowflakes had started falling. Indoors, out of the cold, red wine and crackers were on offer.

But this was no typical opening, no typical exhibition. She had elected to minimize the mingling, or preferably do away with it completely—it didn't seem of interest. She just wanted to display her photographs, her experience of the mire.

There was great interest, naturally, when the newspapers found out that the area's biggest artist was going to have a show at the art school gallery. Then, when they learned that she was going to show landscapes from Mossmarken, with a clear reference to what had just happened out there, the interest grew to enormous proportions, even from the national media. Social media were flooded with posts, even though no one had seen the pictures yet. And opinions were divided. Many people were upset, extremely upset that she was exploiting—as they saw it—the tragedies in Mossmarken.

Maya had come to an agreement with the gallery that she would first have a personal, unannounced opening and allow the press and the general public to come the next day, when she would be far away from Fengerskog.

So now it was just her and twenty or so friends, including Nathalie and Johannes. Göran was there too; he looked worn out. Broken.

"It's probably the wrong time to explain the Tina thing," he said nervously, almost before he had come in.

"Okay," she said. "It's up to you."

"We'll talk about it some other time."

"Sure, another time."

Instead of insisting, she filled his glass at regular intervals. Until at last the words came anyway. His words. He was leaning against the wall, his glass in one hand, waving her over.

"I want to tell you," he said, "straight out. Yes, Tina and I had an affair. She would come and visit whenever she was in Karlstad on business. The time she disappeared, we had agreed to meet out here, but she never showed up. I was shocked. I never said anything, partly out of consideration for her and her family, but I also knew I would be a suspect if I told anyone about our relationship."

Guilt appeared to be weighing heavy on him.

"But what did you think? That the spirits took her?"

He shrugged. "We know now that wasn't the case—with her, anyway—but..."

They were silent for a moment. Göran raised his head and looked straight into her eyes.

"But there are still lots of people missing. You've probably only found Peder and Yvonne's victims." He averted his eyes. "I'm starting to think it isn't *possible* to find the others who vanish. That the people the spirits lure in just...dematerialize. They haven't found that little boy, or Tracy, or my wife..."

Maya placed her hand on his arm and squeezed it kindly. "You know, I'm so glad you're here, Göran. I really am."

When the last guest had left, Oskar came home with her. Maya lit some tealights, ran a bath with lavender oil, and poured two glasses of cava. Then she undressed and got in. Oskar stood in the doorway, watching her.

"Aren't you coming in?" she asked.

He slowly took off his clothes, approached the bathtub, and sank into the hot water.

Nathalie walked slowly up the stairs in the apartment building in Åmål and rang the bell. Her heart felt like an overworked muscle that wanted nothing more than to rest after everything that had happened. But she had to do this. This one thing. It was the last thing she would do before leaving Dalsland for Gothenburg.

The woman who opened the door was a stranger. There was nothing immediately familiar about the obese person standing before her.

They stood there looking at each other, but after a moment Nathalie could somehow see, deep down, the Julia who had once been her best friend. It was something about her eyes, how her high cheekbones arched up toward their corners.

"Nathalie?" Julia said.

"Julia," said Nathalie.

She took a step forward, put her arms around her childhood friend, and hugged her hard. At first Julia stiffened, but then she seemed to relax, and soon the tears came, rising as if out of a newly discovered underground spring. Increasing gasps and sobs that drilled into Nathalie's shoulder. Shudders that created shock waves throughout her body.

After several minutes, she wiped her face on the sleeve of her sweater and tried to calm down.

"What is there to say?" she said.

"Yes, what is there to say?" Nathalie said with a sigh.

They sat down on the living room sofa. Nathalie was still holding Julia's hand.

"What if I knew?" Julia said. "All along. What Mum and Dad were up to. And what happened to your parents—what if I somehow knew the whole time, but I was just too close to really see?"

Nathalie shook her head. "Could you even have imagined what they were doing?"

"I don't know. But maybe I should have . . . suspected something."

"It's still difficult to imagine something like this, Julia. They must have become really ill after Tracy died."

Julia sighed. "Yes, our family was broken too. And I have such a guilty conscience over it, that I never realized they changed. But I was so absorbed in my own problems."

She looked at Nathalie.

"You're the only one I've talked to so far, about this. I haven't even told the kids yet; I don't know what to say. And I'm afraid to show myself out in the world. I'm afraid to turn on the computer. I know people are writing about Mum and Dad all over, about us. It's horrible."

"I know. But just hold on, and everything will calm down soon. People will find other things to write and talk about."

"I hope you're right. But I don't know if I can believe it," she said. "And what's more, it feels like everyone's going to judge me too. I'll never get away from this." Julia looked down at the table.

"What will happen with the kids?" Nathalie asked. "And will you keep living here?"

"Yes, probably." A smile formed a tiny crack in her tense face. "The kids will live with me from now on; I should have brought them here ages ago."

They drank coffee and ate half-frozen chocolate marshmallows straight from the plastic package. Talked. Reminisced. Then Nathalie said she should get going.

"I want to get home to Gothenburg before tonight."

Julia drew a breath, placed a hand on her shoulder as if to stop her, and hurried off to the bedroom. She soon returned with a journal.

"There's one more thing I want to say. I think I need... to tell someone about this."

She held out the book. "This is Tracy's diary. I used to go in her room and read it in secret; we used to do that, do you remember? We read her poems too. But the diary—I read what she wrote right before she disappeared. I never told anyone about it. That's something else I have to learn to live with. What it says in here."

"Why? What does it say?" Nathalie asked.

"Tracy was seeing an older guy, remember him? They had a relationship. But he... he, like, didn't want her. Or, not all the

way. Only sometimes. Then he met someone else. And then…
when you read what she wrote here it's pretty clear that she
didn't want to go on living. It's like she had truly made up her
mind."

Nathalie looked at Julia. "Was it that serious?"

"She was so different at the end. Sad. But I didn't tell anyone."

"You told me."

"I did?"

"Yes."

Julia leafed through the book. "Here. In the last week of
her life she wrote a lot. Mostly dark thoughts. She wrote this
final entry the night before she died. Look here. Listen to what
she writes."

Julia read aloud, carefully and slowly, with a pregnant pause
between each sentence.

It's as if I don't exist any more. As if you left nothing
behind when you went. I'm not eating. Not drinking. I just
want to dissolve and disappear. Let go and fall until it's all
over. Until I'm over. Until this hell is fucking over.

Nathalie felt the memories of that night, fourteen years earlier, enter her. She remembered Tracy's striped nightdress; she
remembered muddy bodies and silent windows. The sense of
reality cracking, of something bursting, a wound that would
never heal.

"So it wasn't ghosts," Nathalie said. "She took her own life."

"But the worst part is," Julia said, "that none of this would have happened if I had just shown Mum and Dad this diary, if we had talked, if we had... So in that sense, it's my fault."

Nathalie swallowed. "In that case, it's just as much my fault. I saw Tracy in Åmål right before it happened, while she was fighting with that guy. I knew how sad she was too, how desperate she was, but I didn't know what to do, if there was anything I *could* do."

She fell silent for a moment before going on.

"We were kids, Julia. You don't deserve to bear the weight of all this."

Julia nodded, her eyes full of tears. "We were kids," she repeated.

EPILOGUE

The temperature had been rising for a while. The past weekend had spoiled the area with warm spring days, and Maya had discovered that buds were starting to appear on the birches by her house.

She hadn't been to Mossmarken since late last year. Now she was ready. They had buried her dad the day before, and she needed a long, fortifying walk. Maybe she could stop by Göran's place. They had seen each other a few times during the winter, tried to come to terms with all the misunderstandings, and she felt like their relationship was getting back on an even keel again.

Now she was walking briskly along the walkways that criss-crossed the bog. This was the first time she had experienced this place in spring light, which was completely different from the drabness of autumn—the decay that ruled then, the thriving mushrooms.

The fragile things were waking now. The bushes were starting to come into leaf in a tender shade of green. The grass tussocks were changing color. She could hear birds everywhere.

She followed a few thrushes with her eyes. They hopped from branch to branch, then flew off.

The wind had blown up a little bit, but now it seemed to have died down once more.

She continued over the bog, but didn't notice that one of the thrushes had lagged behind the others. It fell to the ground behind her; it seemed almost lame and cried out in pain. At the same time, there was a flash across the dark mirror of the water and an image seemed to appear under the surface. If Maya had seen that image, she likely would have described it as a glimmering mosaic of a young woman with a gray and white striped nightdress and brilliant blue eyes.

The bird on the ground flapped its wings.

An instant later, it was gone.

ACKNOWLEDGMENTS

Helene, Jacob and everyone else at the publishing house, as well as Astri, Christine and Kaisa at Ahlander Agency for kind guidance in a new world.

Everyone who has read and shared opinions in various phases: Carina, Pelle, Kerstin, Elin, Cissi B, Jenny, Camilla, Cissi F, Göran, Daniel, Lisa, Annika, Andreas, Pia.

Ingrid, Gullmar and Susanne for childcare and lovely writing time in the chaise longue by the fire out in Romelanda. Thanks too to Ingrid for answers to bird questions.

Maria, for all the good lunches. My turn soon?

Viol och David, for letting me use your cabin to write in.

Cultural journalist Erik Schüldt and science historian Per Johansson for incredibly engaging, inspiring radio programs and podcasts—perhaps, above all, the pioneering podcast *Myter och Mysterier*—which have been invaluable companions during the creation of this book. Thanks also go to Per Johansson for his readthrough.

Mukti, Adyashanti and Open Gate Sangha, for the clarity you uncover.

For clever answers to dumb questions and for patient fact-checking, thank you to the following eminent experts:

Martin Cederwall, professor of theoretical physics at the University of Gothenburg and Chalmers

Mats P. Björkman, biogeochemist at the Department of Earth Sciences, University of Gothenburg

Christian Fischer, archeologist and former director of Museum Silkeborg, Denmark

Elisabeth Nordbladh, professor of archeology at the University of Gothenburg

Per Möller, medical doctor

Anne Majakari, forensic photographer with the Örebro Police

Louise Larsson, forensic photographer with the Karlstad Police

Carl-Erik Steen, detective inspector with the Karlstad Police

(Any remaining errors are completely and fully my own.)

Finally,

Edvard and Alma—for all the times you asked me to write while I was putting you to bed, "It's so cozy." And Anders—for everything. We share this story. Too.

ABOUT THE AUTHOR

SUSANNE JANSSON was born in 1972 in Åmål, Sweden. She later moved to Gothenburg to work in advertising and then to New York to study photography. After returning to Sweden, she worked as a freelance photographer while studying journalism, and for the past twenty years she has been combining her work as a photographer with being a freelance journalist focusing on reportage and profile stories in areas such as arts and culture. She has also written crime short stories for weekly magazines.

The Forbidden Place is her debut novel.

Susanne Jansson lives with her family in Lerum outside Gothenburg.